Dr. Grant

CATHARINA MAURA

For those that fight to escape the clutches of the past every single day.
For the ones that defy the odds.

Contents

Chapter One

Noah

"I'm sorry, Noah," Dr. Johnson says, barely able to look me in the eye. "The money they offered me was far more than I was expecting to retire with."

He looks out the window, his shoulders hunched in defeat, and I follow his gaze. I expected to be in his seat one day. I imagined myself looking out this very window the way he's doing right now, watching patients drive in and out of the clinic's parking lot.

My gaze roams over the doctor's office that was supposed to become mine one day, my heart sinking. I spent months interviewing in search of the perfect practice to join. In the end, I decided to work for Mr. Johnson because he promised he'd let me take over the clinic within a few years. Had I known that he'd sell it just months after I started, I'd never have accepted his offer.

"And you're certain that they don't need another general practitioner?"

Dr. Johnson shakes his head. "They want the clinic, but not the staff. I've tried to reason with them, but they won't budge on it." He inhales deeply, a hint of concern in his eyes. "I know this puts you in a bad position, Noah. I'm sorry to do this to you, and with such late notice too."

I nod in understanding, even as worry gnaws at me. I can't blame the old man. He's only doing what's best for him and his family. Had I been in his position, I probably would have done the same.

I rise from my seat and offer Dr. Johnson my hand. He shakes it, his grip tight and an apologetic look in his eyes. I was looking forward to learning from him for at least a few more years, but I should've known better. I never should've expected as much as I did. Life has a way of letting me down every time I get my hopes up.

I'm overcome with worry as I make my way home. I'm drowning in student debt, and my career isn't starting the way I planned. I thought med school would be my ticket to financial security, but so far all it has landed me with is crippling debt.

Dr. Johnson is letting me go with one month's notice, but that might not be enough time to find something new.

The house is quiet when I walk in, and today the silence feels suffocating. I pause in the hallway, my eyes drifting over the family photos my sister and I hung on the walls. I spent years studying in an attempt to follow in my father's footsteps, and part of me feels like I'm not living up to the dreams he had for me.

My sister and I tried so hard to turn this into a home, to leave behind the memories of our parents' blood staining the floor in our old house. Without a job, I'll lose the home Aria and I built.

I stare at one of the photos that usually brings a smile to my face. It's one of me with Aria and my best friend, Grayson. I'm standing in the middle, between them, but despite that, Grayson's eyes are on Aria. They always have been — he just doesn't quite realize it yet.

I wonder if today would be any easier if they were here and not a six-hour plane journey away. I'm not sure. Besides, I might very well be seeing them soon if I can't find a job. I would hate to have to ask Grayson for help, but I might not have a choice.

Gray has offered to pay off my student debt multiple times now, but I don't ever want to take advantage of him that way. Not unless the situation is truly dire and I'm truly out of options. Which I soon might be.

Three full hours fly by as I call every single person I interviewed with in the last year, everyone that has even remotely indicated that they would be inclined to hire me, only to find that every single position has already been filled. At this rate, I won't even be working as a doctor for the next couple of months. Finding a good job and getting through the required interviews will take time. Time that I don't have.

I lean back on the sofa and look around the house, my heart aching. While this isn't the house that we grew up in, it is the house we turned into a home. How would Aria feel if we lost it? If I'm unable to pay the mortgage, they'll repossess the house. I've failed my sister in many ways, but this? This would break her heart. This home is her safe haven. Despite her moving away to work with Grayson, I want Aria to have a home of her own, even if it's just to come visit every once in a while.

In the few years before I was old enough to gain custody over Aria, she and I were forced to live with aunt Dorothy, our mother's cousin, a woman we barely knew. While Aria never complained, I knew she was uncomfortable. I don't ever again want to be in a position where I'm unable to provide for my sister, no matter how old we get.

I stare at the phone in my hands, desperation drowning out my pride. I know Gray wouldn't miss the money if I asked for help. If anything, he'd be happy I reached out. That doesn't make it any easier to ask, though. Making this call feels like failure to me.

Just as I've convinced myself to push aside my pride and do what I must... my phone rings. I frown at the unfamiliar number and pick up hesitantly.

"Hi. Is this Dr. Grant?"

I clutch my phone and sit up. "Yes, that would be me."

The woman on the phone sighs as though in relief. "I'm calling from the human resources department of Astor College."

I frown, confused why a prestigious private college would call me.

"We have a vacant position at our campus clinic, and Dr. Johnson highly recommended you."

My mind is buzzing as she walks me through the role. It's perfect for me. The pay is even better than what I make working with Dr. Johnson, and since the college is close by, I won't even have to move.

"Would this be something you're interested in?"

I smile to myself, only barely able to keep from laughing out loud. Would I be interested?

"Yes, that sounds great," I say, forcing myself to stay calm.

"Perfect," she says, going straight into scheduling an interview.

I sit back in disbelief as she ends the call and stare at my phone. I scroll through my contacts yet again, but this time I'm smiling as I pause on Grayson's name.

Chapter Two

AMARA

My heart is racing as I study my latest invention. It took me weeks to build this little device, and if it does what I'm hoping it will, I'll be able to secure funding for my company.

All that's left to do now is test it. If I fabricated it without any design flaws, then this little toy will make me orgasm harder than I ever have before — without making a sound.

I have sky-high expectations for a toy this small. To me, it's far more than a sex toy. It's a ticket to the fulfillment of my every hope and dream. It's my road to independence.

My hands are trembling as I put it down and reach for the stupidly big bottle of lube I bought. A nervous giggle escapes my lips, the sound breaking the silence in my bedroom. Thank God for online shopping. I'm able to design and create sex toys without an ounce of shame, but the idea of buying lube has my cheeks heating in embarrassment.

I suppose that's part of the reason I decided to create products like these, though. I wanted something obscure yet powerful, something you could use privately without worrying about the sound it might make.

My heart is pounding in my chest as I grab my little invention, totally unoriginally named *Secret O*. Yeah, I may need to rethink that.

I smile to myself as I carry the ridiculously large bottle of lube to my bed. I didn't think the largest size they had would be this... huge. It looks like it's a family-sized bottle of water. It's weird, and it just increases my nerves.

Will I even be able to come when I'm this nervous? I'm not sure, but I'll have to try. I've been putting the testing phase off, and the longer I wait, the longer I deny myself funding.

I inhale deeply as I open the bottle of lube. I can't put too much on because my toy relies on suction to stay in. When I created it, I wanted to make something you can walk around with without worrying that it might slip out. Obscurity is what I'm going for with this one.

I'm trembling as I lie back and fiddle with the lube, taking my time and delaying the inevitable. I'm scared my toy won't do what I expect it to do. I'm scared my hopes will all come crashing down on me.

I inhale shakily as I turn it on and push it in, taking note of the ease it slips in with. My eyes fall closed as my lips tip up into a smile. It feels good. Thank God.

I can't help but giggle, relief rushing through me. It feels *really good*. There's a small part on the edges that stimulates my G-spot, and it feels better than the touch of most men I've been with. It's working perfectly, and I can't hear a thing. No sound, no hint of the electronic device inside me.

I swallow hard as my thoughts fade away and desire overcomes me. This toy is good. The way it feels... there's nothing like it. A soft moan escapes my lips, and I bite down on my lip. Yeah, I can't resist that feeling for too long. I already want to come.

My muscles contract involuntarily, an orgasm catching me by

surprise. I was not ready for that... and it didn't feel as good as expected.

Damn it. I should've timed it. It felt rushed, like I didn't come as well as I wanted to. I'll need to look into that. Maybe different settings? A buildup in speed? I'll have to try a couple of options and see how they affect my experience before we move onto further testing.

I throw my arm over my face and sigh happily. This is good. I didn't expect it to be perfect, but it's already far better than I thought it'd be.

Now for the real test, though... what will it feel like when I walk around with it? I'm nervous as I sit up in bed, moving carefully. This entire product's appeal is in its obscurity and its staying power. If it slips out when I walk around, it'll be a failure, no matter how good it feels. It won't have a unique selling point other competitors haven't already perfected.

My feet hit the floor, and I'm nervous all over again. Okay, so far, so good. I nod to myself as I walk over to my bedroom door, thanking my lucky stars I'm home alone.

Considering that I'm twenty-seven, it is perhaps a little strange that I still live at home, and right about now I'd much prefer not to. Testing my toy while walking around the house and worrying about someone coming home just makes my nerves skyrocket.

I rest my hand against the wall in the hallway, my eyes falling closed as yet another orgasm threatens to overwhelm me. Oh shit. This invention of mine is brilliant. Even now that I'm worried and overthinking, it's still keeping me turned on. It isn't slipping out — it's not moving at all. It's still perfectly positioned against my G-spot, and I giggle to myself. Amazing.

I jump up and down in the hallway, my giddiness increasing by the second. This is perfect. I'm grinning as I skip through the long hallway in my grandfather's mansion, noting every sensation, every feeling.

It's not perfect yet, but the key elements are all there, and they're all working perfectly. I walk back to my room in a daze, turned on, proud, and relieved all at the same time. It makes for some powerful emotions, and my relaxedness almost brings me close to another orgasm. This time I smile and let my eyes fall closed as it washes over me.

It's stronger this time, and the way my muscles clench around the toy only increases my pleasure. It's almost painful, in the very best way, but I'm not sure how much more of this I can take.

I walk over to my bed and lie back, reaching for my toy. I freeze when I realize I didn't 3D print the small handle I had in mind for it.

Fuck.

I swallow down my panic as I try to get it out, hurting myself with my nails and only managing to push it in further.

This is a prototype. I can't be too rough with it, because if I break this, I'll be back at zero — I won't have enough time to build a new one in time for my investor meeting.

I tug at it, trying to grasp the edges and failing. It's engineered to stay in using suction, and without something to pull it out with, it's going to be almost impossible to remove.

What do I do?

My cheeks heat at the mere thought of having to ask for help. Who do I ask? My mom? She already isn't happy with the way I'm choosing to put my engineering degree to use, and she keeps reminding me not to use the university's facilities for my own research purposes. I've managed to get around that by explaining to her that it's part of my PhD project, but asking her for help with this would lead to a breaking point for sure.

I hesitate before picking up my phone and calling my best friend, Leia. She picks up almost immediately, much to my relief.

"Hey babe," she says, her voice as cheery as ever. The background noise tells me she's outside, so with a bit of luck, she can come over.

"Leia, I need help." Leia and I met at the start of our PhD program four years ago, and in that time we've been through

8

enough craziness together for her not to bat an eye at my current predicament.

"What happened?"

I groan and pull a hand through my hair. "I tested the toy. It got stuck in me. I was stupid enough not to 3D print the handle." She bursts out laughing, and I shake my head. "It's not funny!"

"It is. Girl, I have a class to teach in five minutes. The soonest I can get to you is in two hours."

I sigh and shake my head. "I have dinner with my mother tonight. You know what she's like. I need to be ready in time."

Leia pauses, both of us trying to think of a solution. "You need a stranger," she says. "Someone that'll just forget about this. Better yet if they can't speak at all. A lawyer?"

I think of the ancient Astor family lawyer and burst out laughing despite the fear that claws at me. I can just imagine the look on his wrinkly face, and I'm tempted to call him just to find out how scandalized he'd be.

My smile melts away when I realize exactly what I need. "I need a doctor. Doctor-patient confidentiality and all that shit. I can't go to our family doctor, though. I don't trust him."

"The college clinic," Leia says. "That's your best bet, and it's close by."

I nod, gathering my courage. "Okay. Yes, okay."

Leia giggles, and I roll my eyes. At least one of us thinks this is funny. "Good luck, babe. I can't wait to hear how that goes."

Luck. Yeah, I'll be needing a ton of that if I'm going to see this through.

Chapter Three

NOAH

"This will be your office," Maddie tells me. She's a nurse at the Astor clinic, and she's taken it upon herself to show me around, practically shooing away the lady from Human Resources.

I follow her in and can't help but smile. It's a fully equipped office, but it's far more luxurious than what I had at Dr. Johnson's clinic. There's even a fully leather patient check-up bed. It's insane.

Taking this job is the best decision I ever could've made. The college is only a twenty-minute drive from home, the pay and benefits are great, and the resources they provide me with are top notch. I'm lucky they called when they did. Even the interview was surprisingly pleasant.

Maddie rests against my desk and smiles at me. "We're so lucky to have gotten such a handsome doctor," she says, smirking. "You're definitely going to brighten up my days."

I smile, but not for the reasons she's thinking. I can hear Aria's voice in my head, and I just know my little sister would've sicced Human Resources on Maddie real quick. She's all for equal treatment, and she'd never stand for this type of behavior. I miss her. I'll have to hop on a video call with her and Gray soon, even if it's just to fill her in on the new job. She's probably heard about it from Grayson already, but I know what she's like. She'll want to hear all about it from me directly.

"So," Maddie says, drawing out the word. "There are a couple of things you need to know, though I'm sure HR has already filled you in."

I turn to her and nod. Since the entire university and everything on its grounds is owned by one family, there are bound to be some unwritten rules. I don't want to fuck this up. This job opportunity is far too good.

"One: don't fuck any of the students. Like, really don't. It's an instant dismissal. Don't even go anywhere near them, because if Mr. Astor finds out he'll lose his shit. Apparently, his daughter fell in love with one of the staff and threw away everything for him, only to have to come back home, all alone. No one knows the full story, but ever since then, Mr. Astor has been crazy about boundaries for staff members."

I nod. I have no intention of fucking some preppy student. Fuck that shit. I can't stand the drama — and the lack of experience. Maddie grins and runs her hand through her hair. "That doesn't include me, of course. I'm not a student."

I shake my head at her bravado. She's trouble. I can already see it. I definitely can't ever fuck her, because she'll never leave me alone if I show her the tiniest bit of attention.

"Two: sleep with a patient, and your career is ruined. Doesn't matter if they aren't a student. Faculty staff is off-limits too. Mr. Astor will legit report you wherever he can. He's done it to the doctor you're replacing. Last I heard, the poor guy still hasn't found a job, and it's been a few months. Doubt he'll find anything. If the Astors want something, they get it."

I nod, a chill running down my spine. I'd better be extremely careful. It's been a while since I was at college, but I remember what it was like. I doubt I'd be tempted, but it won't hurt to be a little extra mindful of my interactions with patients.

"That's it, really," she says, before turning to show me how the systems work. I've barely spoken a word, but thankfully I don't have to. Maddie speaks enough for the both of us.

I smile as I think of the horror I'd see on Grayson's face if he were in my situation right now. A chatterbox is his worst nightmare. Me? I don't mind it so much. I prefer being around people that fill the silence that always seems to surround me.

"That's all, Dr. Grant," she says, smiling up at me. She's leaning in, showcasing her breasts. I smirk, and that only seems to embolden her. "Don't hesitate to let me know if you need something," she says. "Like... anything."

"Sure thing, Maddie," I tell her. "Thank you for the warm welcome."

She giggles as she hops off my desk and walks to the door, looking back over her shoulder. "Anytime, Dr. Grant."

I breathe a sigh of relief when the door closes behind her. She's a whirlwind, that girl. I shake my head and reach for the white doctor's coat hanging on the hook behind my desk.

This is everything I've always dreamed of. An office of my own, being referred to as *Doctor*, and helping patients on a daily basis. This is a dream come true, and I need to make sure I don't fuck it up.

I sit down in the far too posh seat behind my desk and shake my head. How could I have gotten this lucky? I smile bittersweetly as I reach for my bag and take out two photos: one of my parents, and one of just Aria and me. I place both photo frames on my desk, already feeling much more at home in this office.

Would Mom and Dad be proud of me today? I'd like to think they would be. Neither Aria nor I are very religious. We stopped believing the day our parents were brutally taken from us. Yet somehow, I still want to believe they're watching over us.

I'm startled out of my thoughts when my desk phone's loud-speaker crackles, the receptionist's voice resounding through the room.

"Dr. Grant, I have a patient here to see you. I'm sending her file over now."

I nod, my heart pounding. "Send her in," I say, just as I click on the patient file. My eyes widen when I read the patient's name. Amara Astor.

Astor? Fuck me. Just my luck. It's not a common enough surname for her not to be one of *the* Astors.

I'm nervous as the door opens and try my hardest to hide it, but all my composure is lost the second I lay eyes on her.

Bright blue eyes. Long wavy red hair. She's breathtaking. Fuck. I tear my gaze away and tug at my tie, suddenly feeling suffocated.

I offer her my hand in introduction and she nods at me, her cheeks flushed and her breathing uneven.

Does she have a fever? Fucking hell. I'm a doctor. She's obviously here because she needs medical help, yet here I am, acting like a goddamn pig. No wonder Mr. Astor has his rules in place.

"I'm Dr. Grant," I tell her, taking her hand in mine. I could've sworn her touch fucking zapped me, but she doesn't seem to notice a thing as she shakes my hand. "Amara Astor," she tells me, and her voice... fuck. It's rare for a woman's voice to turn me on, but she does it for me.

And she really shouldn't. She's my patient, after all.

"Doctor," she says, her voice soft. "Let me preface this by telling you that I'm a mechanical engineer. A PhD student, actually. This sounds like the lamest excuse, but I swear I'm not lying." I frown, intrigued. Amara shakes her head and looks away. "Maybe this is a bad idea. I shouldn't... I can get help elsewhere. I didn't expect you to... Why are you so young?"

I put on my most reassuring smile and shake my head. "Don't you worry, Ms Astor. There isn't much I haven't seen yet."

She laughs, the sound betraying her nerves. "Oh boy. You have no idea how wrong you are." She looks into my eyes, seemingly gathering her courage. "Dr. Grant. I need your help. I... I have a sex toy stuck inside me."

She has... what? What the fuck?

Chapter Four

NOAH

A sex toy? Is that what she said?

I try my best to school my features, praying my face doesn't betray my shock. I will my face to remain blank and nod at the stunning redhead standing in front of me.

"I can explain," she tells me, her cheeks blazing. She can barely look me in the eye, and something about her stirs my heart. I bite back a smile and shake my head, holding a hand up.

"That's all right, Ms. Astor," I say, gesturing toward the patient bed in my office. The damn thing is nicer than anything I own, and it's perfectly suited for a woman like the one standing in front of me.

She smiles at me, and fuck me. My heart skips a damn beat. I didn't think she could get any more beautiful, but fucking hell...

I swallow hard as I follow her to the bed, pulling on my gloves. Her lips fall open when she sits down and I bite down on my lip. Whatever it is she's got stuck in her must feel pretty damn good if that look in her eyes is any indication.

"Please be careful, doctor," she says, her voice soft. I nod oddly nervous. I spent years doing medical rotations. This is far from the craziest thing I've experienced, yet somehow, I'm as nervous as when I was an intern.

She hangs her head as she slowly exposes more of her skin. My eyes follow her fingers as she pulls up her red dress, exposing her thighs first, until I can just about catch a glimpse of her bare pussy. No underwear.

Amara presses her legs together and looks up at me hesitantly. Beautiful. The way that blush stains her cheeks crimson, the way those blue eyes of her betray her nerves. She's without a doubt the most beautiful woman I've ever seen.

"Don't laugh, okay?" she whispers.

I shake my head reassuringly and smile at her. "I won't. I promise."

She pulls her dress up to her hips and spreads her legs, squeezing her eyes closed. I bite back another smile as I kneel in front of her, taking in the faint strawberry smell. Lube?

"Okay, let's take a look," I murmur, placing my gloved hands on her thighs to spread them just a little further. Amara gasps and places her hands on my shoulder. "Are you okay?" I ask, worried.

I didn't think her face could get any redder, but it does. "Um... yes," she says, her voice husky. She's so fucking sexy, and I doubt she even realizes it.

"I won't hurt you, okay?"

She nods, and I lean in to take a look. I can't see anything. Whatever she's put inside her is in deep.

"Can I touch you? Please let me know if at any point you don't feel comfortable."

She nods, and I carefully push my index finger into her to feel where her toy got stuck. Whatever she's got in there is vibrating ever so slightly, but it certainly isn't budging. Interesting.

"Oh," she gasps, her grip on my shoulders tightening. "Oh my god."

I freeze when her muscles tighten around my finger, her entire body shaking. She comes on my finger, and my cock hardens instantly. Fuck.

"I'm so sorry," she whispers.

"It's okay," I tell her, trying my best to avoid eye contact. I don't want to make this any more awkward than it already must be for her. "I'll need something to grip it with," I tell her, and she nods, facing the window.

"Please be careful, Dr. Grant. The toy... it's my own invention. I'm an engineer. This is my only prototype, so please don't break it."

I nod as I walk back to her, a set of tools in hand. I hold up medical pliers and she looks at me, her expression a mixture of worry and lust. Damn. She looks so beautiful sitting there, her legs spread, her long hair covering her body.

"No," she says. "That might damage it, and since this is a prototype, it's not quite safe enough for us to break it while it's inside me. There'd likely be some electric shock."

I nod. "Something soft then."

"It relies on suction. That's why it won't budge."

I kneel in front of her again. "All right. I'll have to break the seal somehow."

She tenses when I carefully push two fingers back into her, feeling around for the edges of her toy. Amara pushes her legs closed just as I manage to wrangle a finger in-between her skin and the toy. Her grip is fucking tight, and I tense as a moan escapes her lips. She pushes her hips up against my hand as her eyes fall closed, another orgasm washing over her.

"Oh God," she moans. "I'm so sorry, Dr. Grant. I... I can't help it. I'm so sorry. Your fingers... I can't."

I smile and bite down on the edge of my lip, my fingers still buried deep inside her. "Don't you worry. It's only natural. You're going to have to keep your legs open for me, Ms. Astor."

Her eyes widen and she opens her legs back up for me. "Call me Amara," she whispers, looking away. "I came on your hand twice... it's strange hearing you call me by my mother's name."

"Amara," I whisper, and her pussy spasms again. Fucking hell. She's sensitive, and my filthy mind can't help but wonder what it'd feel like to have her squeeze my dick. She's so sensitive I reckon she'd come all over my cock, multiple times.

"I think I've got it," I tell her. "Bear with me, okay?"

I manage to pull it just slightly lower, and that's all it takes. The weird-shaped tool slips out of her, and I breathe a sigh of relief. I doubt my sanity or my cock could take another second of this.

Amara moans loudly as it slips out of her, revealing how insanely wet she is. I grab her toy, my sick mind wishing I wasn't wearing gloves. I wish I'd gotten a feel of her, of her wetness.

I lift it up and rise to my feet with a smile on my face. Amara looks at me with wide eyes as I place it down next to her. She hops off the bed, only to tumble straight into my arms as though her legs can't carry her.

I catch her, my arms wrapping around her instinctively, and she gasps. It takes me a moment to realize that my erection is pressing up against her stomach, and I take a step away hastily, my hands on her shoulders.

"I do apologize, Ms. Astor," I tell her, unsure what else to say. I'm as in control of my body's response to her as she was of her orgasms just moments ago, but that doesn't excuse my lack of professionalism. I shouldn't be getting turned on by a patient. Not just a patient. Amara Astor. While I don't know for sure who she is, I know she must be related to Mr. Astor. To Astor College. A moment of unprofessionalism with her could cost me my future.

"To be honest, this really just makes this whole experience far more bearable," she says, grinning. "At least I wasn't the only one turned on."

I smile involuntarily and look away, shaking my head. "That shouldn't have happened," I tell her, letting go of her. "And you needn't be embarrassed. I'm merely doing my job. However, I strongly advise against inserting unsafe prototypes. If nothing else, refrain from doing so without medical supervision. This could have gone quite wrong."

"I'm an engineer, Dr. Grant. I'm not going to stop testing my own inventions. Medical supervision is a good idea, though... are you volunteering?"

My eyes widen, and Amara bursts out laughing as she grabs her toy and throws it in her handbag. "You're cute when you're flustered," she tells me as she walks past me, seemingly unaffected by the ordeal we just went through. "Thank you for your help, Dr. Grant," she says, and then she's gone.

The door closes behind her, and I stare at it, fully fucking mesmerized. This girl. Who the fuck is she?

Chapter Five

A M A R A

"Sorry I'm late, Mom." I sit down opposite my mother in a restaurant that will probably bill us a crazy amount of money. Money that I wish I could invest in my company instead. I glance around at the widely spaced tables, the servers in tuxedos, the dim lighting. It's beautiful, but it's excessive.

"I was wondering where you were," Mom says, crossing her arms. I smile nervously, hoping she won't actually ask me where I went. I'm an adult, but I still haven't mastered the art of lying to her face.

My little accident and subsequent visit to Dr. Grant's office completely derailed my plans. I was going to dress up and do my hair for my standing dinner date with Mom. I know how much she looks forward to our dinners, and every week I try my best to look the way she wants me to, even if it's just for one evening. Mom hates it when I look *unkempt*.

"I was working and lost track of time," I tell her. Technically, that isn't a lie. I have no idea how much time I spent in Dr.

Grant's office. All I remember is his golden-brown eyes, that chiseled jaw, and those hands of his... oh, those hands.

Mom shakes her head at me, and I sigh, hoping she won't go into preacher mode, telling me that I should join the family business instead. My eyes roam over her, and the tiredness she exudes pains me. When was the last time I saw my mother laugh? I can't even remember. Not since Dad left. That's for sure.

I can't ever end up like her. I need to make sure of it. If I can't get my company to take off before I finish my PhD, I'll have to find a job. There's no way I'll remain dependent on Grandpa, like Mom is. Or worse. Become dependent on another man.

I can't allow myself to be in a situation where I'll have to come running home. I love Grandpa, but I want to stand on my own two feet and be beholden to no one. I don't want to end up like my mother, with no career of her own and a child in tow, knocking on her father's door after she swore she'd never return.

"You work too much, sweetheart. I barely see you these days."

"I'm sorry, Mom," I murmur, feeling bad instantly. "I just really want to get this right, you know? This company... it's my every dream come true."

Mom nods, but I doubt she gets it. Even though there are so many businesses Grandpa would happily let her run, she has no desire to have a job of any kind. She wasn't always like that, though. I still remember the woman she was before Dad wrecked our lives.

"I know, sweetheart. I get it, I do. But don't forget to enjoy life, okay? All you do is work. When is the last time you went on a date? You're going to end up alone at this rate. You don't need a job. We have enough money, Amara. If you really want to do this whole running a business thing, just ask Grandpa to invest. Why are you making things so difficult for yourself?"

I freeze, trying my best to stay calm. "And what happens when Grandpa decides that he's done entertaining me? What if he uses my company as leverage? You know as well as I do that Grandpa wants me to work for him. Do you really think he'd fully support me? The only way he'd provide me with funding is if I agree to work for him after a couple of years. I'm not willing to do that, Mom."

Mom grits her teeth and looks away in anger. "Why not, Amara? Why do you insist on making life so difficult for yourself? Your grandfather is one of the richest men in this state, and look at you, going around begging for money for your little company. When will you stop making a fool of yourself? You're not a child anymore, Amara."

I swallow hard, my heart twisting painfully. "Is that all you think it is, Mom? Do you believe in me at all? Don't you want me to chase my dreams? Don't you want me to at least aim for independence? Do you truly want me to rely on Grandpa for the rest of my life?"

Mom sighs and runs a hand through her hair. "What's wrong with that, Amara? Have you learned nothing from me? I'm a prime example of what happens when you follow foolish dreams, Amara. Be realistic. You have a good life — a better life than most. Be thankful and do your part. Gregory wants you back, doesn't he? He's young, but he's got a bright future ahead of him. Give him another chance, Amara. Go on a date with him. Take the easy road. Both he and your grandfather are offering you so many opportunities, yet here you are, playing foolish games."

I hate the helplessness I feel, the way my throat tightens up. "You want me to get back together with the guy Grandpa picked for me? The guy that approached me because I'm the means to a *merger* for him? What about my happiness? What about what I want? You followed your dreams, didn't you? Why won't you let me do the same? Surely you understand what it's like to want independence? To lead a normal and happy life? You know what it's like to rely on Grandpa and then have the rug pulled from under your feet the second you tell him you want to deviate from the path he's set for you. He took away your inheritance and put you out on the street with a baby in your belly, and you still want me to just fall in line?"

Mom grits her teeth and stares me down. "And he took me back in with open arms, didn't he? He knew I'd come back home, eventually. Besides, he was right. I was foolish to fall for your father. I missed out on the life I could've had because I chose to be with your father, and I can see you making the same mistake. Except in your case, it's not a man you're following. It's a foolish dream. Grow up already, Amara. Count your blessings."

I swallow down the anger that's clawing its way up my throat. "Has no one ever told you that a gilded cage is still a cage, Mom?"

I hate that so many of our conversations end like this. I always have so much to say, so much to tell her, but as soon as we start talking, I end up swallowing down my words. She's a hypocrite. She knows exactly what Grandpa is like. She couldn't stand it herself, and she didn't return until she was out of options. Had she gone back home sooner, our lives might not be as destroyed as they are.

She followed her dreams, but she's undermining mine.

Chapter Six

NOAH

My desk phone buzzes in a way it's never done before and I frown at it, confused. I didn't even realize it could make that sound.

I'm still staring at it when my door opens and a man I've only ever seen in photos walks in. I jump out of my seat, shocked.

"Mr. Astor," I say, extending my hand. What is he doing here? And why is he here unannounced? My mind immediately drifts back to last week, and I silently pray he hasn't found out how I touched his granddaughter, because that's who Amara is. She's his only granddaughter, and if Maddie is to be believed, she's the apple of his eye.

His grip is tight as he shakes my hand, and I silently take him in. Looks like Amara has her grandfather's blue eyes. He's as tall as I am, and the suit he's wearing probably equals a month's salary for me.

Mr. Astor looks around my office as though he's seeing it for the very first time, and I wouldn't be surprised if that is the case. He strikes me as the type of man that has a medical team on call, which makes it all the more strange to have him standing in my office so unexpectedly. Even throughout my interviews, no one ever mentioned him. I didn't think I'd ever meet him. This college and the campus clinic it houses are but one of his many assets.

"How is the new job?" he asks. "Everything to your liking?"

I'm quick to nod, surprised he realizes I'm new. "Everything is great," I tell him. "This office is well-equipped, and the nurses are friendly and helpful."

He nods and walks around, touching things absentmindedly, and I silently note everything I'll have to disinfect all over again. "That's good. And how is the work?"

"It's great," I tell him honestly. It's pretty much the same job I used to do at Dr. Johnson's clinic, except there are no old people. It's mostly middle-aged professors and students coming in with routine issues. I enjoy it. I enjoy actually being able to help. During my hospital rotations we usually had cases that left me feeling like my all would never be good enough, but here I make a difference every day.

"I'm glad to hear it," he says, pausing in front of my desk. "I'm happy to have you here, Noah. You seem to be doing well. You seem happy here. The opportunities I can give you are endless. This clinic," he says, gesturing around at my office, "can be yours if you want it."

I freeze. I never even thought that would be an option. My expression must be transparent, because Mr. Astor smiles. "Do a good job, and I'll let you buy in." I nod, in shock, and he smirks. "I consider my employees family, Noah. I want you to do well, and I'll help you grow so long as you work hard. So far, everything I've heard about you has impressed me. You put yourself through medical school while taking care of your little sister and putting her through school too. You've done extremely well for yourself, and I'm always on the lookout for exceptional men. Men that can help me build my empire."

I just stare at him dazedly, unsure what to say. When I started working here, I assumed it'd never be more than a salaried job. I assumed I'd do this for a while and then attempt to buy into a clinic elsewhere. Owning anything with the Astor name on it? I didn't think that'd be possible.

"I'm grateful for the opportunity to work for you, Mr. Astor. I assure you I won't let you down."

He nods, but his gaze is calculative. "I don't think you will." He straightens his suit jacket, and just as I think this weird little visit is over, he looks at me, his gaze sharp. "I understand my granddaughter visited your clinic not too long ago. What was she here for? We have an in-house doctor on call, so there shouldn't have been any need for her to come here."

I tense and keep my face carefully blank. "I'm afraid I cannot breach doctor-patient confidentiality," I tell him, my tone unwavering. I think back to the notes I took about her visit and wonder if he somehow has access to those. It might be a good idea to edit them and make them a little more vague, just in case.

He looks at me, and his expression sends a chill running down my spine. I straighten defensively and hold his gaze. I may want to climb up the ladder, but I'm a doctor first and foremost. I won't compromise my ethics.

He nods, and my shoulders sag in relief. "I love my granddaughter, Noah. There is nothing I won't do to ensure her happiness. I will help you achieve your goals, and I'll check in with you often to ensure you're on the path you wish to be on. However, you *must* stay away from my granddaughter. Amara is not for you."

I push aside the sudden resentment I feel and nod. "I can promise you I won't seek her out, but I will not deny a patient my care," I tell him, making my limits clear.

Mr. Astor smiles. "Very well. I suppose that's as much as I can ask for."

I nod and shake his hand. He tightens his grip and holds onto my hand. "There's a charity function next month. Why don't you attend? I'll introduce you to some people that you should get to know."

My heart constricts at the mere thought of what he's insinuating. I thought he was making empty promises when he said he'd support my career, but it looks like I was mistaken. Attending this event might very well land me connections I could otherwise never have access to.

"I would love to," I say, tightening my grip on his hand before letting go. He smiles and turns to walk away.

I stare after him as he walks out of my office and collapse into my seat the second the door closes behind him.

I've only just about caught my breath when the door opens again. I shoot back out of my seat and then relax when I realize it's Maddie and Georgia.

Maddie rushes up to me with wide eyes while Georgia closes the door behind her. "What did he say?"

I shake my head and glare at Georgia, the receptionist. "Why the hell didn't you warn me?"

She looks at me apologetically and shrugs. "No time. He walked in and demanded to see you. All I managed to do was sound the alarm seconds before he walked in."

I stare at my desk phone. "That screeching noise was meant to be a warning? How the fuck was I supposed to know that?"

Maddie shrugs. "Tell us what he told you. Why did he come here? He hasn't been here in years."

I sit down and lean back as I fill them in, hoping they might have an explanation for his erratic behavior, but they don't. They're just as clueless as I am.

I'm guessing that it's Amara's visit that led him here. As my patient, she was already off-limits. But now, with her grandfather's warning fresh on my mind? Now she's forever out of reach.

Chapter Seven

Amara

"It was so awkward. I'm still not over it. Couldn't you have warned me that he's really hot?" I say, clutching my phone tightly between my shoulder and my ear as I try to maneuver my way through the crowds on campus with a stack of heavy books in my arms. Leia has been trying to get me to talk about my visit at the doctor's office all week now, and she's finally worn me down.

"Hot? He's middle-aged and balding. To each their own, of course... but I didn't think he was hot at all."

I frown, confused. "Dr. Grant can't be middle-aged. He's in his thirties, I guess? Definitely not bald. He's got thick dark hair," I tell her, remembering the way I imagined myself running my hands through it.

Leia falls silent. "Grant? I don't think that was his name. The campus doc had some basic name. Something like Williams? Interesting... I guess the doctor you saw was new then."

"Must have been," I murmur, my thoughts on Dr. Grant. He's gotta be the most handsome man I've ever met. I'd definitely have noticed him on campus at some point in the last couple of years.

"You should go back to his office. He said you shouldn't test things without medical supervision, right? Just take one of your toys back to his office and see how he reacts."

I roll my eyes. "Hell no. I can't ever face him again. Leia, it was so humiliating. I came on the man's hand, while he was trying to do his *job*."

"Was he wearing a wedding ring?"

I chuckle and shake my head, even though she can't see me. "No. He wasn't."

"Good. Then I don't see the problem. This could be the start of an amazing love story, Amara."

I burst out laughing and almost lose grip of one of my books. "More like a bad porno. I can't even imagine how awkward it must've been for him. I don't even want to know what he thinks of me now. He must think I'm some sort of freak. I'm so embarrassed, Leia."

I hoist my books up, trying to balance them as I make my way to my car. "Fuck," I whisper-shout as my gaze lands on the entrance of the campus convenience store.

"What?" Leia responds.

"Ley, it's him. I swear, it's him. Walking out of the convenience store right now. What do I do? I have to hide."

"Oh shit. Seriously? Okay, act natural. Don't be weird."

Dr. Grant's eyes meet mine, and I turn straight around, turning my back to him. "Why did I do that?" I say more to myself than to Leia.

"Damn it. *What* did you do?" Leia asks, her tone apprehensive.

"I should've just said hi or nodded. Shit. I just turned around. Literally just u-turned the second my eyes met his. Why am I like this?"

Leia bursts out laughing, and I clutch my phone tightly as my cheeks heat. I can't face Dr. Grant now. I bet I look like a ripe tomato with my red hair and my blazing cheeks.

"Why *are* you like this? For someone so beautiful you really are awkward as fuck."

I try to glance back as subtly as I can, only to find Dr. Grant still staring at me, a wide grin on his face. He takes a step toward me and I almost drop my phone.

"Shit. He's heading this way. I need to go. Love you, bye!" I whisper-shout into my phone as I end the call.

I'm about to lock my phone and throw it in my bag when it buzzes again. I click the message open without thinking, assuming it's Leia sending me some terrible advice... but it's not. The message is from a number I don't recognize, yet I instantly know who it is.

I stop in my tracks, my books falling to the floor as the world around me fades away. My heart beats so loudly that I'm certain I can hear it. I grip my phone tightly, trying my best to push aside the nausea and panic that's slowly overtaking me.

How dare he? How dare he text me now? After all these years, he messages me as though he didn't destroy our family, leaving tattered lives in his wake.

Hi, Ami. I've typed this text and deleted it over a hundred times, because I don't know what to say. I don't even know if you want to hear from me at all, but I miss you. I miss my little girl. Not a single day has gone by without me thinking of you, and I would really love to see you, even if it's only once. Love, Dad.

See me? He wants to see me? After what he did? The mere thought of him sickens me. That man... he's a monster.

I inhale shakily, trying my hardest to ground myself, to keep the panic at bay. Despite my best efforts, my throat closes up and my breathing gets shallower by the second. It becomes difficult to inhale fully, and fear grips me. I clutch at my throat and try to blink the tears away, but that doesn't help silence the need to run, to escape the memories that assail me. I take a step forward and stumble over the books at my feet, my knees hitting the floor before I can brace myself.

Tears start to run down my cheeks in earnest, and through them I can see the redness of my bloodied scraped knees as I reposition myself on the cold street. I don't feel the pain, though. No, it's just an excuse to let go of the heartache keeping me captive.

A sob tears through my throat and I pull my knees up to my chest, welcoming the sharp pain that comes with the movement. I can't tell whether it helps dull the pain in my chest or adds to it, but I lose myself in it nonetheless.

I haven't seen my father in over fifteen years. I haven't heard from him, and the mere mention of him brings my mother intense agony. How could he? How could he reappear now after all the damage he's done?

I try my best to inhale, to calm myself, but I'm lost in a downward spiral of memories and heartache, and all I manage to do is choke on another sob. Helplessness overcomes me, and I hate myself for it. I hate how weak I am. I hate that I can't even control my own body.

"Step aside! I'm a doctor."

His voice cuts through the overwhelming noise, and it isn't until then that I realize that I'm surrounded by people, some of them asking me if I'm okay while two girls kneel beside me.

"Amara," he says, and my eyes meet his. His gold-specked brown eyes hold a reassuring gaze, and I know right there and then that I'm going to be fine.

Dr. Grant kneels on the ground in front of me and pushes my hair out of my face before cupping my cheeks. "Look at me," he orders, his tone brooking no argument. "I've got you, okay? Don't look at the blood. Your scrapes are superficial. You're okay, but you're having a panic attack. Breathe with me, Amara."

I nod and follow his instructions, my eyes never leaving his. It only takes him a few minutes to calm me down, to hand me back control over my body. The second I'm able to take a full deep breath, I almost burst into tears all over again, from relief this time.

"See," he says, "you're fine."

I nod, and he smiles at me as he places one arm underneath my knees while his other arm wraps around me. Before I realize what he's doing, he lifts me off the floor as though I weigh nothing.

"Grab her stuff," he barks out, and a wide-eyed woman in a nurse's uniform jumps into action, bending down to gather my things. Dr. Grant doesn't wait for her. Instead, he walks toward his clinic, keeping me in his embrace.

"I can walk," I whisper.

"I know you can," he says, glancing down at me. "But you're injured, and I'd like to examine you before I let you get on your feet."

I stare at him as he carries me to his office, holding me securely. I take in his chiseled jaw, the small amount of stubble, and his messy hair. He isn't wearing his white doctor's coat today, and somehow, he looks even more handsome in the white dress shirt he's wearing. Something about him puts me at ease, yet has my heart racing at the same time. It's a jarring feeling. I can't remember the last time I felt this safe, this taken care of... yet I'm also nervous.

"Thank you," I whisper.

He looks down at me and smiles. "Don't thank me just yet. I'm going to disinfect your wounds, and when I do, I doubt you'll be very happy with me."

Happy, huh... I don't know what happiness feels like, but I suspect it's a little bit like the way he's making me feel right now, and that feeling is dangerous.

Chapter Eight

Noah

My heart is racing as I carry Amara into my clinic, Maddie hot on my heels. I'm usually calm when dealing with accidents and emergencies, but not today. Something about Amara tugs at my heartstrings. Watching her succumb to panic, seeing the color drain from her face... I can't remember the last time I felt so helpless. Over the years I've come to excel at detaching myself from my patients, but something about Amara is different. I felt her pain as if it were my own.

Maddie rushes around me to open my office door, and I carry Amara in gently. She's quiet in my arms, her breathing even, and her cheeks a beautiful rosy color. She looks fine now, yet my heart is still in disarray. I'm worried. I know she's not truly hurt. Her wounds are superficial, yet I can't take it. I guess it was the look in her eyes, the devastation that momentarily consumed her.

She's still trembling ever so slightly as I place her on the patient bed in my office, her feet dangling off the edge. She looks up at me, our eyes locking. Those blue eyes of hers... I could lose

"I can disinfect her wounds, Dr. Grant."

I blink, tearing my gaze away from Amara. I forgot Maddie was even here, and the look on her face tells me she knows it. The silent warning look she sends me has me hesitating, but I shake my head against better judgement.

"That's quite all right," I tell her. "I'll do it myself."

She nods and walks over to the cabinet in my office, clearly insistent on not leaving me alone with Amara. I bite down on my lip as I take the glass bottle from her.

"I won't require assistance," I say, knowing full well that I'm making a mistake asking to be alone with Amara. There's something about her I can't resist. I'm a rational guy, and her grandfather's warning is still ringing through my ears loud and clear, but it isn't enough to make me resist temptation, to make me walk away from a chance to have a moment alone with her.

Maddie looks into my eyes, and I force a polite professional smile onto my face. She stares at me for a second, and then she nods.

"I didn't think she'd leave," Amara says the second the door closes behind Maddie. She sounds amused, but there's an edge to her tone. One that fills me with curiosity.

"Me neither," I murmur as I open the bottle of disinfectant.

"She's pretty," Amara says, her tone oddly aggravated.

I smile to myself and look at her. "Is that so?"

She purses her lips, a hint of impatience in her eyes. "You don't think so?"

I kneel in front of her and look into her eyes as my hand hovers over her scraped knee. "Not as pretty as you are," I say, right before pressing the damp cloth on her skin, distracting her. She hisses, but her eyes never leave mine. I almost wish I didn't have to focus on her wounds, because I don't want to break this moment between us, and I should.

She smiles at me, and I smirk as I clean up the rest of her wounds. "That's the second time I've got you on your knees in front of me."

I grin and drag my attention away from her bloodied knees. "So it is. Are you turning this into a habit, Ms. Astor?"

"Amara," she corrects me. "I told you to call me Amara... and what if I am?"

I place my hands on either side of her, my eyes on hers. "I guess I'll just be at your mercy, falling to my knees at your beck and call."

She laughs, and my heart skips a fucking beat. She's beautiful. The way her cheeks dimple, the way her eyes narrow when she laughs, yeah... she's the most beautiful woman I've ever seen.

Tearing my gaze away from her is a battle, and it's a losing one. I can't stop smiling as I stick bandaids on her knees, my eyes trailing upward every few seconds.

"Do you flirt with all your patients?"

I smirk unapologetically. "Only the ones that come on my fingers."

Her lips fall open, and then she bursts out laughing. "You, Dr. Grant, are just the worst."

I know I'm taking it too far, but I can't resist her. I can't resist that smile of hers. I want to tease her, make her laugh. I shouldn't, though. She's a patient. A student. Harold Astor's *granddaughter.*

I rise to my feet, my smile falling. Amara isn't someone I can flirt with. I've never once been unprofessional or inappropriate with a patient, not even when they were blatantly into me. Why is it different with her? Why her, when she's someone I can *never* get involved with.

I force my polite physician smile onto my face and take a step back. "You had a panic attack today, Amara. Is that something that occurs often?"

She looks away, the mood instantly changed. "No. I haven't had one in years. It surprised me, too. I... there was a trigger. I just, I got a text message from someone I hadn't heard from in years, and my thoughts just started to spiral. I couldn't understand why he'd contact me now, and I lost control over my emotions."

He? I involuntarily grit my teeth. Whoever contacted her must have caused her enough pain for her to respond the way she did today, and it has my every protective instinct jumping into action.

"I can refer you to a psychologist," I tell her, wanting to help in any way I can.

Amara grimaces. "I'm still seeing one," she says, her voice soft. She looks up at me, her fingers brushing over my arm briefly. "It's not what you think. There's nothing crazy or overly concerning going on, Dr. Grant. The message... it was my father."

I relax involuntarily. I didn't even realize I'd been so tense. Amara looks away, her arms wrapping around herself. Her father, huh? I gathered from Maddie's endless gossiping that Amara's father left them years ago, forcing her mother to go back home to Harold Astor after he disowned her, but that's as much as I know.

"I haven't heard from him in years, and I couldn't understand why he'd contact me now. I started to overthink things and worry about my mother. About having to tell her he contacted me. She's not going to respond well. I might have overreacted, but my mother would easily put me to shame."

I move closer to her involuntarily and shake my head. "I didn't think you overreacted, Amara. Not even for a second. There's clearly pain there, and you're only human," I murmur, brushing her hair out of her face gently. "It must have been overwhelming and surprising. I can't even imagine how you must have felt."

She nods, a hint of surprise in her eyes. "Thank you," she whispers. "Thank you for being there, for helping me. I'm not sure I could've pulled out of that suffocating feeling if you hadn't been there."

I shake my head. "You would have."

She looks away, a haunted look in her eyes. My heart tightens when she reaches for her handbag beside her. I don't want her to go.

"I've taken up so much of your time today, Dr. Grant. I'll pay your consultation fee, of course, but I wanted to apologize."

I shake my head. "There's no need. I dragged you in here, after all. This one's on me."

She rises to her feet and walks to the door, turning back to look at me with a playful look in her eyes. I'm glad she managed to shake off the sadness that surrounded her just moments ago, but I can't help but feel that it's all just bravado. I excel at putting up a front. She isn't fooling me.

"I've had you on your knees twice now. I should really return the favor sometime soon," she says, her eyes dropping down to my trousers, and then she walks away, leaving me feeling out of it. This woman is an enigma, and with every interaction she cements herself further into my thoughts.

I shake my head as I walk to my desk, my eyes dropping to the photo of my parents. I'd give the world to speak to them one more time. I know not all parents are the same and that Amara must have her reasons... but from where I'm standing having parents that want to be part of your life is better than having none at all.

I lift the photo frame with trembling hands, my heart aching. Would I remember them without the photos? Every day, the memory of them fades a little more. The pain never dulls, but it's starting to get harder to remember the feel of my mother's arms, the smile on my dad's face.

I'd give anything to have one more moment with my father, and I hope Amara won't come to regret staying away from hers.

Chapter Nine

NOAH

"The cleaners found this in your office," Maddie says, holding up a gold earring. I take it from her and inspect it, recognizing it as Amara's.

I close my fist around it and nod at her. "I happen to know whose that is. I'll make sure it's returned to her."

Maddie stares at me and shakes her head. "Whose is it? I'll contact the patient to let them know they can retrieve their item at the front desk."

I bite down on my lip and look away. She hasn't explicitly said anything, but I know she disapproved of the way I carried Amara into my office the other day. The last thing I want to do is cause more friction at work by admitting it's hers.

"Let me guess," she mutters. "Amara Astor."

I shrug. "I'll return it to her."

Maddie crosses her arms, her stance defensive even though there's clear worry in her eyes. "Dr. Grant, I wasn't joking when I said that the Astors aren't to be messed with. You might get away with messing with a patient, *maybe*... but you'll never get away with messing with Harold Astor's granddaughter. I see the way you look at her, and it's a bad idea. It's a really bad idea to get involved with her in any shape or form. Mr. Astor is incredibly protective of his granddaughter, and for some reason, you're already on his radar. Make sure you stay on his good side. Getting with Amara Astor is career suicide."

I grit my teeth, instantly annoyed. "I'm well aware and don't appreciate your insinuations, Maddie."

She looks away, stricken, and I instantly feel awful because she's right. I *have* been flirting with Amara, and I do treat her different. I just can't help myself.

"Just be careful, okay? A single rumor could destroy you. She'll walk away unscathed, but you won't."

I nod and watch her walk away, a tinge of worry settling in my chest. I overstepped when I had Amara in my office a few days ago. The way I flirted with her was unacceptable, and it was unprofessional. It was unlike me, yet I did it without thinking.

I stare at the earring as I walk back into my office, dropping it onto my desk. It taunts me as it lays there, the sunlight making it sparkle, drawing my eye to it over and over again. What is it about Amara? I barely know her. Is it the unconventional way we met? Perhaps it's just that she both intrigued and aroused me straight from the start. I haven't stopped thinking about her since she first walked into my office.

I'm startled out of my thoughts when my office door opens. Not even Maddie walks in without knocking, and my surprise makes way for shock when a woman walks in.

She doesn't even have to tell me who she is. It's obvious. The same hair. The same eyes. I have no doubt that the woman in front of me is related to Amara. I'm guessing this is her mother, but I have no idea what brings her here.

"I'm sorry," she says. "I should've knocked, shouldn't I? I wasn't thinking. I'm so sorry," she adds, looking flustered.

I smile and shake my head. She looks nervous, the way many

patients do when they walk in. "Don't be. I wasn't seeing a patient. Please, take a seat. How can I help you?"

She pauses, her tense shoulders relaxing slowly as she sits down in front of me. She offers me her hand, and I shake it. "Charlotte Astor."

I nod. "Noah Grant."

She leans back and smiles at me. "I apologize for dropping by unannounced. I was in the area and I've been wanting to meet you ever since my father first mentioned you. Walking in uninvited is more my father's trademark move than it is mine, I assure you. We're not all as insufferable as my dad is."

She laughs, and in that moment, the resemblance to Amara is obvious. So that's where she gets her smile. I look away, trying my hardest to recall my own mother's smile and failing. What did her laughter sound like? I can't remember, and the realization makes my heart tighten painfully.

"My father speaks highly of you, Noah. I understand you put yourself through medical school while providing for your younger sister? Your accomplishments are astonishing. It takes a lot to impress my father, and he seems intent on capitalizing on your talents. Rightfully so. With my family behind you, you'll go further than you can even imagine, and I'm excited to see it happen. I recognize the potential my father sees in you."

Her words leave me speechless, and it takes me a second to pull myself together. I clear my throat awkwardly and pull on my tie. "I only met your father briefly," I tell her, and she smiles in understanding.

"I know." She pulls an envelope out of her handbag and slides it toward me. "Yet somehow you managed to impress him enough to warrant a personal invitation to one of the most exclusive events of the year."

I pick up the embossed envelope and stare at it in surprise. Is that actual gold leaf on there? I've never seen anything like it before.

"You'll need to present this at the entrance. You'll need a tux, too. Do you have one?"

I shake my head. "I'll rent one."

Charlotte smiles at me and shakes her head. "That won't do. I don't mean to put any pressure on you, but I know my father has plans for you. He'll be introducing you to people that can transform your career, and I want you to fit right in." She pulls a tape measure out of her bag and holds it up. "I'll get one made for you."

She rises to her feet and walks around my desk, her attitude as bold as Amara's. Yet somehow, she reminds me of my own mother. Mom was also like that, commanding in a motherly and caring way.

"It really isn't necessary," I tell her, but she ignores me as she pulls me out of my seat. She's as much of a whirlwind as Amara is.

"It is," she says, her expression stern. "You don't realize it yet, but my father sees something in you, something extraordinary, something you can't even see yourself. You, my boy, are one of us now."

I spread my arms, mindlessly obeying her as she takes my measurements. "Why me?"

She pauses and smiles. "My father is never wrong. He set his sights on you joining the Astor business, and for him to do so can only mean one thing: he believes you can further grow his empire. It's rare for him to mentor someone, but he's been speaking about you enough for me to know that is what he intends to do."

Having Harold Astor as my mentor wouldn't just transform my career. It would change my life. Doors I can't even see would be wide open to me.

"I don't understand," I tell her honestly. "I've only ever spoken to your father once, and it was a brief exchange."

I don't want to get my hopes up. I've done it too often, only to crash and burn. I'd love to believe Charlotte, but life has taught me over and over again that everything has a cost — and more often than not, the price is too high to bear. Life has taken every-thing from me. I have nothing left to give.

Charlotte smiles at me and nods, almost as though she under-stands when I doubt she could. "My father has been wanting to get into biotechnology, and he's been talking about expanding his medical investment assets for the past year. Then you walked in, with a stellar academic record and the ambition required to succeed. I can only assume that your CV flagged in my father's system. He's always looking for potential, and he seems to have found it in you."

I stare at her in disbelief, a small seed of hope trying to take root deep within my cold, barren heart. I don't let it.

"You don't believe me," she says, a knowing look in her eyes, "but you will."

She takes a step back and glances at her phone, a smile on her face. "You'll look great in a jet-black tux."

I smile awkwardly, completely thrown by her sudden visit. She's nothing like I expected. She seems kind and friendly. If not for her clothes, I'd never have guessed that she's insanely rich. Amara is the same, and it's one of those things that further intrigues me.

"I'll get out of your hair," she says, grinning. "I'll have the suit delivered to your office."

Her eyes fall to the photographs on my desk as she reaches for her bag, and she pauses. The expression in her eyes can only be described as haunting. Her fingertips trail over the edge of the silver frame, and when she looks back at me, devastation mars her face.

"The way you lost your parents... I'm sorry, Noah. No one will ever replace them, but now that you're here I want you to know that you're no longer alone."

I nod, my heart constricting painfully. I didn't even realize that those were words I was longing to hear, even if they're only being said out of politeness.

Charlotte smiles at me, but it doesn't reach her eyes. Instead, sadness engulfs her. She nods politely as she walks toward my door, and I inhale shakily as it closes behind her, memories of my parents fluttering through my minds — bits and pieces, fragments that I thought were lost forever.

For just a single moment, I could swear I smelled my mother's perfume, and then it's gone, fresh grief overwhelming me once more.

Chapter Ten

Amara

I scroll through the search results for Noah Grant, frowning when I find next to nothing. He doesn't have social media profiles, and the only things I can find about him relate to his work or research he's done. In the few photos I can find of him, he looks blurry. Recognizable, but blurry.

How weird. These days it's almost impossible for anyone to be this anonymous. I've certainly never struggled much with finding out more about someone. If anything, I can usually give the FBI a run for their money. Leia praises my stalker abilities endlessly, yet now that I need them, they're letting me down.

I groan and drop my head to my desk. I want to know more about him. Specifically, I want to know if he's got a girlfriend. A man like him... I can't imagine him being single. But then again, would he flirt with me the way he did if he wasn't single? He doesn't seem like the type to do something like that.

"What are you doing?"

I sit up at the sound of my mother's voice and slam my laptop closed. How long has she been standing there? I didn't even hear the door open, that's how immersed I was in my stalking of Dr. Grant. How embarrassing. I hope she didn't see what I was up to.

Mom raises her brows and walks into my bedroom, her expression tense. I'm not sure what's going on, but the way she looks at me instantly has me on edge. For years now Mom has been distant, even with me. She doesn't let her emotions show. She rarely gets angry, and similarly, I haven't seen her be happy either. I'm not even sure what that looks like anymore.

This I remember, though. The worry on her face hits me right in the chest. It's an expression I haven't seen in years, and it brings back memories I thought were lost. Falling off the swing on the porch and scraping my knee when I was ten. Cutting my fingers when I was trying to make a solar powered fan at age twelve. There weren't many occasions, but every once in a while Mom's frost would melt away, revealing the woman I used to know. The woman that's staring at me right now.

"What's wrong?" I ask, my voice soft.

Mom pauses in front of me, holding a fist up. Her hand trembles as she uncurls her fingers, revealing a golden earring that I instantly recognize. I reach for it, but she snatches her hand away, keeping my earring trapped in her fist.

"Where did you get that?" I ask, my heart pounding. I lost it on the day Dad contacted me. The same day Dr. Grant carried me into his office. I haven't told her about Dad texting me, and I've been struggling with the decision. She won't respond well, and truthfully, I doubt there's any benefit to telling her.

I haven't responded to his text either, and I'm not sure I will. If just receiving a text from him brings me this much sorrow, then all I stand to gain by letting him back into my life is heartache. Besides, how dare he? How dare he show up now as though nothing happened, telling me he missed me?

"Why was this on Noah Grant's desk?" Mom asks, snapping me out of my thoughts.

I swallow hard, trying my best to control my facial expression. I'm not good at lying to her, but I can't have her finding out about Dad. "I went to the clinic the other day. I fell on campus and scraped my knees. Dr. Grant saw it happen and offered to help me dress my wounds." My voice is calm and controlled. I'm not exactly lying to her about the events of that day, yet I feel like I am. Something about this entire exchange feels off, and it isn't just Dad texting me that I want to hide from her. I instinctively want to hide that it wasn't the first time I met Dr. Grant, but I can't quite figure out why. It isn't just because of the nature of my first visit. It's the way she's looking at me.

Mom stares at me, silent for a few seconds before she nods, her shoulders relaxing. She hands me my earring and I take it from her, a forced smile on my face.

"Why didn't you tell me you got hurt? We have a private clinic you should've gone to."

I nod nervously. "Yeah, I know," I murmur. "But Dr. Grant saw me fall and helped me straight away. Why would I go to our family clinic when he was right there?"

I study Mom carefully, trying to figure out what she's thinking. Why is she asking me about Dr. Grant? I bite down on my lip, worried that she somehow found out about my first visit to his office. She'd hate the idea of me testing sex toys, and she'd be too worried about rumors of my little incident. It isn't me she cares about. It's my reputation.

"Have you seen or spoken to him since then?"

I frown and shake my head. "No. Why?"

Mom shakes her head. "It's nothing. You need to stay away from him. Don't go see him again."

I lean back in my seat and look at her through narrowed eyes. "Why?"

Mom sighs impatiently. "Why must you challenge me on everything? I'd never ask you to do anything that isn't in your best interests, Amara."

I shake my head. "That's not an answer, Mother. Why do you want me to stay away from Dr. Grant? He's been nothing but nice to me."

Mom purses her lips and looks away. "Your grandfather has decided to mentor him. He wants to train Noah so he can take over our current medical holdings and expand them further. Noah has potential far greater than any of the men that currently work for us. He's overcome challenges most people can't even fathom. That man needs a break, and Grandpa is going to give it to him. Don't stand in the way of that, Amara. Don't get involved with him in any way."

I frown and cross my arms. "I don't understand," I tell her. "That makes no sense, Mom. If Grandpa sees potential in him, then why is there a problem with me being friends with him? Not that we are, but still."

Mom looks down at the floor, her expression crestfallen. She takes a moment to pull herself together, and the pain she tries to hide just intrigues me further.

"Will you please trust me on this, Amara? Nothing good will come from you getting involved with Noah. I won't stop you from being friends with him, but it can never go further than that. Promise me, Amara."

She looks at me with such desperation that I nod without thinking. "Of course, Mom. I promise."

She exhales in relief and smiles shakily. "Thank you, sweetheart."

I nod even as my thoughts are whirling. I know my mom. I'm not going to get more information out of her, but something doesn't add up. Why would she want me to stay away from Dr. Grant if he's someone Grandpa trusts with his business? Grandpa doesn't approve of many people, and he rarely lets outsiders into his inner circle. Our entire board consists of only Astors. I don't doubt for a second that Grandpa loves his empire more than he loves me. If he's trusting Noah enough to mentor him himself and let him manage close to a billion dollars in assets, then there's no way he wouldn't trust Noah with me.

"How are things with your company?" Mom asks, raising my suspicions even further. She hates talking about my company, but she's standing here with a smile on her face, pretending to be interested.

"It's good, Mom. I have a meeting with Wilson tomorrow."

"Wilson?" she asks, and I grimace. I've told her about him multiple times now. "Oh, right. Your friend!"

"Yeah, but he's also my investor," I remind her.

Mom nods. "Oh okay, I hope it goes well."

Something is definitely up, and it's got something to do with Dr. Grant. I bite down on my lip as I stare at my mother. I haven't stopped thinking about Dr. Grant since I first met him. Mom might want me to stay away, but her words ensured I won't. She's hiding something, and I want to know what it is.

Chapter Eleven

Amara

"I'm sorry, Amara. I think it's a great idea, but there are other investments that would be more profitable. I thought this might have potential, but I don't see how it's any different from what's already on the market. I'm looking for something groundbreaking... and this isn't it."

My heart races as I look at Wilson, my investor. "What are you saying, Will?" I murmur. He's one of my oldest friends and he's been on board with my plans from the very start. What changed? He never said anything any of the times I told him about the progress with my prototypes. If he thought the product wasn't good enough, then why didn't he speak up sooner?

"I can't invest in your company. There are just too many other projects that are more profitable. I was trying to do you a favor, but in the end, this is business, Amara. I'm sorry."

Desperation claws at me as my hands start to tremble. I clasp them together tightly. "I can improve the prototypes, Will. There isn't much I can't build."

Wilson shakes his head, and his expression tells me there's no hope. He won't invest. "Why now? You had months to pull out. Months that I could've spent finding someone else. Why would you do it now?"

I see guilt flash through his eyes and look away. It isn't my intention to make him feel bad. I just want to understand. I shake my head and take a step away. "It's okay. Thank you for your time."

I turn and walk away, pausing when I hear Wilson call my name. "Amara," he says, his voice soft. "I'm sorry."

I smile tightly and nod as I walk out of his office, my heart breaking. I'm back at square one. Without an investor, there's no way I'll ever be able to get my company off the ground, and I don't trust Grandpa. I don't trust that he'd fully support me without an agenda. I can't ask him for help.

The sky lights up with lightning as I step out of Wilson's office building and I look up at the clouds as rain comes pouring down, matching my mood perfectly. A humorless laugh escapes my lips, the sound tinged with desperation. I'm trying so hard... I'm working as hard as I can, but it's never enough.

I grab my phone to text Leia to meet me at a bar not too far away from here, needing a pick-me-up. Or maybe just getting wasted will do tonight. I'm tired. I'm tired of feeling like everything I do is in vain.

My phone buzzes straight after I send the text, and I click open the app assuming that it's Leia replying. I freeze when I find another text from the number I've come to recognize as my father's.

I'm not sure you're receiving my messages, but if you are: I hope you're having a great day today, sweetheart.

I swipe the message away, ignoring it. Does he realize that hearing from him just makes an already shitty day even worse? I don't know how he even got my number, but every time he texts me, my heart breaks a little further. It's the last thing I needed today. I swallow hard and try my best to inhale deeply, not wanting to lose control over my emotions again. Lately it feels like I'm barely in control of my life, and I'm tired of feeling this way. I'm tired of all the roadblocks in my carefully mapped out plan. I'm tired of pain that I thought had healed bringing me to my knees once again. I'm tired of all of it.

The world passes me by as I walk through the streets, my steps slow, rain drenching me entirely. My clothes stick to my skin and a chill runs down my spine as sorrow overcomes me.

I stand still in the middle of an empty sidewalk, my eyes falling closed. At least I've got that going for me. The hot tears that stream down my face are drowned out by the rain to the point that I can't even tell if I'm crying or not. It's a strange feeling to be choking on sobs yet not feel tears fall from your eyes.

I'm startled when the rain stops pouring down on me and open my eyes, my gaze lifting to find golden brown eyes filled with concern. "Dr. Grant," I whisper, my voice barely audible over the sound of the rain.

"Amara," he says, grabbing my hand. He lifts it up and wraps my fingers around his umbrella before letting go and shrugging out of his jacket. "You're soaking wet. Are you okay?" he asks, wrapping his jacket around my shoulders. It smells like him, and it's still filled with his warmth. Somehow, the gesture just makes my tears fall even harder, and I start to sob all over again.

Before I know it, Dr. Grant has his arms wrapped around me, and my face presses against his strong chest. His umbrella falls to the floor, the rain drenching us both.

"Amara," he murmurs, his grip around me tightening. He buries one hand in my hair and wraps the other around my waist. The way he's holding me... when is the last time someone hugged me like this? "Did something happen?"

I shake my head and throw my arms around his neck, hugging him back tightly, selfishly pressing my cold wet body against his, stealing his warmth. Dr. Grant just holds me like that, his hand moving over my back, never complaining about the rain.

When I pull away, he lifts his hands to my face and cups my cheeks, his thumbs swiping at the wetness on my face. He looks into my eyes, and we stand there together. The way he's looking at me... it makes me feel like I'm not alone. Like he understands, even though he couldn't possibly.

"I'm sorry, Dr. Grant. That's the third time you've caught me in a less than desirable position."

He smirks at me and brushes my wet hair out of my face. "Not at all," he murmurs. "Far from it. Besides, isn't there some saying about meeting trice being fate?"

His words bring a smile to my face, distracting me from the pain I'd been lost in. How does he do this to me? No one has ever had this power over me, making me smile just seconds after I cried my heart out, and he doesn't even know it. I take him in, my eyes roaming over the white t-shirt he's wearing. The rain has made it entirely see-through, and my eyes linger on his well-defined muscles.

"Feel better?"

I nod and drag my eyes back up to his. "Yes, thanks to you. You seem to be my knight in shining armor, Dr. Grant."

He chuckles, and the sound washes over me, awakening a spark deep within. "Oh, I'm no Prince Charming."

I grin at him. "I called you a knight. You upgraded yourself to a prince all by yourself."

He laughs again, and this time my heart skips a beat. "I'm glad you seem better now. Do you want to talk about it?"

He genuinely seems interested, and it confuses me that someone might actually care. For years now I've only ever been known as Harold Astor's granddaughter, and almost everyone that approaches me has an agenda of some sort. Yet somehow, Dr. Grant seems different.

"My investor informed me he's withdrawing his support," I tell him honestly, my eyes filling with fresh tears. I let my eyes fall closed, trying my best to compose myself. "The toy... it was a prototype that I truly believed was going to be the start of an amazing company, but it all seems to have been for nothing."

"I'm sorry to hear that, Amara. Don't give up hope, though. These things have a way of working themselves out. Besides... you strike me as the type of woman that'll find a way."

I look into his eyes, surprised by the faith I see in them. So far, almost every single person around me has acted like my company is just a hobby, something cute that they entertain. This is the first time that someone other than Leia is taking me seriously. "Thank you," I tell him, and the way he smiles makes my heart skip a beat.

I take a step back and straighten, suddenly feeling embarrassed. I probably look like a mess, and Dr. Grant... well, he looks like *him*. Gorgeous. Dangerous.

"What brings you here anyway?" I ask, unable to suppress my curiosity. He's dressed casually in jeans and a t-shirt. It's a stark difference from the suits he wore the last two times I saw him.

He tips his head toward the building behind me and smiles. "The gym. My gym is in that building. I've been fighting some demons of my own, and a good workout session always makes me feel better."

I follow his gaze and nod, flustered. I'm always so composed, courtesy of years and years of mind-numbing socializing with boring socialites, but in front of Dr. Grant I turn into someone I barely even recognize: myself.

"Come on," he says, bending down to grab his umbrella. "Let me walk you home."

I shake my head and smile. "Actually, I'm meeting a friend of mine at a bar nearby."

Dr. Grant nods. "All right, lead the way. I'll take you anywhere you need to go."

Chapter Twelve

Amara

I'm quiet as Dr. Grant walks me to the bar I told Leia I'd meet her at. He's holding up his umbrella, covering me entirely, but more than half of him is getting wet. He barely seems to notice, though. Or maybe he does. Maybe chivalry isn't dead.

I take a step closer to him, and he looks down at me, his gaze unreadable. "You'll get wet," I murmur, my voice barely audible in the rain. "We both fit underneath the umbrella."

He nods and wraps his arm around me, placing his hand on my waist. The warmth of his palm seeps through my soaking clothes, and I melt into him. We walk in silence, his embrace keeping me warm, and our proximity keeping both of us relatively dry.

I don't remember the last time I felt this way. Walking through the rain with him, his arm wrapped around me... it feels peaceful.

"Here we are," he says, pausing in front of the bar.

I hesitate, not wanting him to go. I'm not sure what it is

about Dr. Grant, but his presence is soothing. "Would you like to have a drink with me?" I ask before I can change my mind. "Leia won't be here for a few more minutes. She's always late."

He looks away, and my heart sinks. He's going to say no, and that shouldn't affect me, yet I'm already disappointed.

"I'd love to," he says, surprising me. Dr. Grant laughs at my expression, and my heart does this weird little thing. Almost as though it flutters.

He collapses his umbrella, and I grab the jacket I've still got wrapped over my shoulders. Before I can take it off to return it to him, his hands close over mine, keeping them in place. Dr. Grant's gaze drops to my chest and he bites down on his lip, his eyes darkening. "Keep that on, Amara."

I look down, my face slowly turning scarlet when I realize that my top is partially see-through. My black bra is showing through my pale pink top, and my nipples are clearly outlined through it. I clutch Dr. Grant's jacket and cover myself up as best as I can, eliciting a chuckle from him.

I lower my head as I walk into the bar, and the sound of his laughter follows me. Why is it that every time I've been with this man, I've thoroughly embarrassed myself? Usually I'm so composed, but not in his presence.

My cheeks are blazing as he slips into the barstool next to mine, an amused grin on his face. "Have you ever had a hot chocolate with Baileys in it?" he asks, thankfully changing the subject.

I shake my head as I suppress a shiver. My wet clothes are starting to make me feel cold now, and I suspect Dr. Grant is chilly too. He smiles as he orders us drinks, and I take that moment to study him. He's handsome in a rugged way, and he carries a hint of danger. He's different from the rich men that usually surround me. Their power is in their money. They're nothing without it. But Dr. Grant? I have a feeling he could easily rip someone apart with his bare hands. He doesn't need to hide behind the illusion of power and influence.

"What will you do?" he asks, his tone betraying his concern. My smile melts off my face and I stare at the two mugs the bartender pushes my way. I hand one to Dr. Grant silently.

"I'm not sure. Wilson, my investor... he's a childhood friend, and he's the only one that was willing to invest in me. I only have a couple of months left until I finish my PhD, and if I haven't acquired funding by then, it'll be over. Right now, I'm making use of the college's research facilities, but soon I'll need my own."

He nods, his attention entirely on me. I don't remember the last time someone looked at me with this much intensity, and it makes me feel vulnerable.

"My grandfather... I guess my surname kind of gave away who I am. My grandpa is throwing this huge charity ball next week, and I might be able to find a new investor there. I'm not sure."

Dr. Grant nods, and just as he's about to reply, his phone rings. I watch him as he takes it out of his jeans pocket, his muscles flexing through his soaking wet t-shirt. I swallow hard and force myself to drag my eyes away.

"Excuse me for a minute. I have to take this," he murmurs, glancing up from his phone. I nod at him, and he smiles as he picks up, a twinkle brightening up his eyes.

"Hey," he says, his voice soft. The way he smiles, the tone of his voice... he's speaking to a woman, and a tinge of something I can't quite name settles in my tummy. "I miss you. I was hoping you'd call." That little tinge in my tummy? It transforms into full-blown jealousy and I look away, trying my best not to focus on his conversation, and failing. I'm not sure why I assumed that Dr. Grant was single. I should've known better. He's insanely hot, and he's a doctor. Of course he's taken. We hardly know each other, yet somehow my heart feels a little broken.

"I can't wait to see you this weekend and hear all about it. I booked a late-night flight so I get to see you Friday night, rather than waiting until Saturday morning."

I grit my teeth and wrap my arms around myself. Why does

this hurt? Is it because I thought he was flirting with me? I'm not sure, but finding out he's got a girlfriend hurts.

I sip my drink in dismay as he finishes up his call, and all the while, I wish it were me on the receiving end of his words.

"Sorry about that," he says, reaching for his drink. "That ball you mentioned... your grandfather invited me too. He came to see me at the clinic the other day. Caught me by surprise."

I look at him with raised brows. The ball is incredibly exclusive. Grandpa must really like Dr. Grant for him to have personally invited him.

"Your mother actually came to see me too. She delivered the invite and offered to get me a tuxedo made." He leans in and pushes my hair behind my ear. "I guess that is how you got your earring back? Shortly before your mother entered my office, it was on my desk."

I look into his eyes, my heart racing. Not just from his proximity, but also because of the instant worry I feel. "She came to see you and hand-delivered the invite?" That's unlike my mother. She has staff for almost everything she does. At most, she would have had one of her secretaries deliver the invite. Why did she go herself? Why is she going out of her way for Dr. Grant, to the point of having him a custom tux made?

Dr. Grant nods. "You'll have to save me a dance," he adds, smirking at me, and I tense, wanting to retort that his girlfriend probably won't like that, but not wanting to act jealous either.

Today has just been an endless myriad of bad news and confusion. I can't figure out why Wilson suddenly won't invest anymore, and I can't figure out the connection between Dr. Grant and my mother either. It feels like I'm missing something, and I hate that. On top of that, I don't know how to feel about my dad texting me again. Part of me expected him to give up after I didn't reply to his last text, but it doesn't look like he will, and I'm not sure how I feel about it.

"Amara!"

I turn to find Leia walking up to me, and I breathe a sigh of relief. She's exactly who I need right now. Leia looks at Dr. Grant wide-eyed, her eyes dropping to his soaking wet t-shirt as he rises from his seat to offer it to her.

"I see your friend is here," he tells me. He reaches for my phone on the bar and gives himself a missed call. "I'll head home now. Keep the umbrella and the jacket, okay? You've got my number now. Return the jacket whenever you want. Don't lose faith, Amara. You're amazing, and you will find a new investor."

Before I can tell him to take the umbrella at least, he's gone, and Leia is taking his place.

"Wow, who's the hottie?"

I grimace, suppressing the possessiveness I feel. I've never felt this way about any man, let alone one I've just met... but somehow, I don't like the idea of Leia checking him out.

"Dr. Grant. He works at the college clinic."

Her eyes widen. "No way. That's Dr. Grant? Guess I'm going to be faking some ailments then."

I tense, a rush of jealousy overcoming me. Leia is beautiful, with her long dark hair and those curves of hers. If anyone could steal Dr. Grant's attention away from his girlfriend, it'd be her, and I don't like the idea of that at all.

"I thought you were all obsessed with that one-night stand dude," I say, my tone harsh.

Leia frowns at me, and then she smiles. "You like him. Well, shit. Come to think of it, it took me days to get details about your doctor's appointment out of you. Now I see why. Ugh. I love this! It's the perfect meet cute."

I shake my head and sigh. Only Leia would think something like that would be cute. "He's got a girlfriend, Leia," I tell her, wanting her to knock it off. The last thing I want is for her to get my hopes up.

Leia's smile drops, and she sighs. "Oh. That sucks."

I nod and look away, sadness washing over me. "Today has been such a shit day," I murmur.

Leia wraps her arm around me, and I drop my head to her shoulder. "Tell me all about it, babe."

And I do. I tell her everything. I tell her about everything she missed out on, and with every word that tumbles out of my mouth, I feel just a little better.

Chapter Thirteen

Noah

I stare up at the hotel the ball is being held at, feeling out of place and intimidated. Grayson has taken me to some really nice hotel bars before, but this is different.

I tug on my bowtie nervously, hoping I don't look stupid. The suit fits perfectly, yet I still feel silly wearing it. It feels weird to wear an expensive tux that a stranger bought me. The Astors seem nice and I'm trying not to overthink things, but somehow I feel like there must be an ulterior motive of some sort. Could it really be that they see potential in me? I find that hard to believe, but for once, I want to have some faith. Not just in my own abilities, but in *people* in general.

I feel out of place as I approach the entrance. This is going to be awkward as fuck. I won't know anyone here. I probably should've brought a date, even if it's so I'm not alone.

My mind drifts to Amara as I hand the guards by the door my fancy invitation. She'll be here tonight. I haven't been able to stop thinking about her since she first walked into my office. She's probably the one woman in town that's most out of reach, yet I can't control my thoughts.

Even when I was visiting my sister last weekend, Amara was all I could think about. Amara kept me so distracted that it took me a while to realize what was going on between my sister and my best friend.

I walk into the ballroom, instantly feeling intimidated. This whole place reeks of money. Money that I don't have. I don't belong here, but someday I will. I have every intention of becoming successful, of making a name for myself the way my father did.

I nod politely when I notice Mr. Astor standing in the middle of the room, surrounded by men I've only ever seen on television. This is the world Amara lives in. She and I... we couldn't be more different.

I tense when Mr. Astor waves me over, and I'm oddly anxious as I walk up to him. I didn't expect him to speak to me at all tonight, and something about him unnerves me. A man this powerful... why is he paying any attention to me at all?

"Noah, my boy," he says, clapping me on the back. "Come, there are some men I need to introduce you to."

He excuses himself and pulls me along before I even realize what's happening, and before long I'm standing in front of the owner of one of the biggest pharmaceutical companies in the country. "Lucas," Mr. Astor says, "meet Dr. Noah Grant. He recently started working for me, and I have great plans for him. If I have it my way, he'll help me build a medical empire that'll rival yours."

His words have my heart racing. An opportunity like that would change my entire life. Hell, I could accomplish far more working for Mr. Astor than I ever could by myself, if he means what he says.

I shake Lucas's hand, and just minutes later I have his business card in hand, and an appointment to grab coffee with him next week. The next thirty minutes proceed in the same way. Mr. Astor personally introduces me to every single person in the room that could further my career, and every one of them pays attention.

I'm left reeling by the time Mr. Astor walks away. Any doubts I had about him just being nice for the hell of it are gone. He truly does have plans for me. Plans that could transform life as I know it. Plans that could get derailed if I get involved with the one person he told me to stay away from — the woman that captured my eye the second she walked in.

I lean back against the wall with a champagne glass in hand and watch Amara flit through the room, clearly in her element. In this world where I'm entirely out of my depth, she's a fucking queen. The black dress she's wearing shimmers with her every move, highlighting her amazing body, and around her neck she's wearing diamonds that sparkle underneath the chandeliers. I bet just her jewelry equals a year's salary for me.

She's beautiful... and Mr. Astor was right. She's not for me. I know she isn't, yet my heart tightens when she smiles at another man. He offers her his hand, and she takes it, letting him lead her to the dance floor.

I take him in, the expensive tux, the shiny shoes. He's handsome, and he's clearly rich. I can't compete with that. Not that I would.

I watch as he twirls her around on the dance floor, making her laugh. The way his hands move over her body betrays the intimacy between them. Boyfriend? Ex-boyfriend? Maybe he's just a lover. Either way, he's something to her, and it doesn't sit well with me.

She and I are nothing more than acquaintances, yet I can't help the possessiveness I feel. I want her eyes on me. I want my hands on her body, the way they were when she and I stood in the rain.

Amara pauses on the dance floor, her eyes wide. I have no idea what he just told her, but she looks shocked. I tense when her dance partner grabs her hand and pulls her toward the large balconies. The two of them disappear through the flowing curtains, and I grit my teeth.

I will myself to stay put, to push what I just saw out of my mind... but I can't. There's something about Amara Astor that I cannot ignore. That single second of distress in her eyes was enough to have every alarm bell in my head ringing, and I'm barely thinking straight as I walk towards the doors she disappeared through.

"You know I want you back."

I tense, pausing just out of sight. Amara is leaning back against the balcony, and the guy she's with has her trapped between his arms. She doesn't look uncomfortable, though. Angry, maybe... but she doesn't look like she needs help.

"We're over, Gregory," she tells him, crossing her arms over her chest, her beautiful eyes narrowed.

"Maybe," he murmurs. "But maybe not. You won't find another investor, Amara. Your grandfather warned every one of us not to invest in you. I'm the only one that'll be willing to go against him and risk his wrath. Just tell me you'll let me take you on a date, and the money is yours."

Her eyes widen, and the flash of pain I see in them makes my heart tighten. Mr. Astor... why would he do that? It makes no sense.

"Just one date, Amara. Do you really want to see your dreams fade to dust?"

I straighten and walk around the corner, my footsteps loud on the otherwise empty balcony. Amara's eyes find mine, and something flickers through them, but I can't quite place what it is.

"Amara," I say, forcing a smile onto my face. "Didn't you promise to save me a dance?"

Chapter Fourteen

Amara

Dr. Grant smiles at me and holds out his hand, waiting patiently. He's ignoring Gregory entirely, and somehow that just makes him even more sexy. No one ignores Greg. He's the heir to an oil empire, and not one person I know ever stands in his way.

Except for Dr. Grant.

"She's preoccupied," Gregory says, and Dr. Grant finally looks at him, his brow raised as though he isn't impressed in the slightest. I can't help but laugh as I slip my hand into his. He pulls me towards him with more force than I expected, and I tumble into his arms.

The way his arms wrap around me makes my heart race, and I instinctively push my body against his, wanting to be even closer to him. Dr. Grant's eyes meet mine, and my heart skips a beat. That chiseled jaw, those honey brown eyes... and those lips. I swallow hard and drag my eyes away before they have a chance to betray the desire I feel.

"Where does that lead to?" Dr. Grant asks, tipping his head to the staircase behind us.

I grin and turn around, grabbing his hand as I pull him along. "You'll see."

My eyes meet Gregory's as we walk past him, and for a second I worry that I've just put Dr. Grant at risk. Gregory doesn't like to lose, and he doesn't like having anything taken from him. I'm certain the only reason he wants me back is because I dumped him before he could leave me. I'm probably the only woman to ever have done that to him, and in doing so, I turned myself into a challenge.

"Hey, slow down."

I pause and look around in surprise. I've been lost in my thoughts, not realizing how far into the garden I pulled him.

"I'm sorry, Dr. Grant," I say, turning to face him.

He smiles at me and shakes his head, his hand lifting to brush aside my hair. "Don't be," he murmurs. "It's beautiful here." He's referring to the rose garden, but his eyes are on me. The way he's looking at me has my heart racing and I look away, unable to hold his gaze.

We walk together, and much to my surprise, he keeps my hand in his, our fingers entwined. His warmth, his touch... I'm enjoying it a little too much. I can't keep my thoughts from drifting, and the small sense of enjoyment I felt is ripped to shreds by the memory of the phone call I overheard.

"Is your girlfriend okay with you walking through a rose garden holding someone else's hand?" I ask, my tone harsh. "Because I wouldn't be."

Dr. Grant pauses and tightens his grip on my hand. I'm tempted to yank my hand out of his, but at the same time I want to hold on to him for as long as I can.

He looks startled by my question, and then he smiles. "My girlfriend? Hmm... yeah, I see how that conversation could've been interpreted that way." Dr. Grant smiles at me, and I hate how sexy he looks, standing here in the moonlight. "I was speaking to my sister in that bar I took you to. She moved to Cali a few months ago, and I went to see her last weekend."

My eyes widen, and he chuckles, the sound making the butterflies in my tummy come alive. I look away, too embarrassed to meet his eyes.

"So... is there anyone who'd be upset about *me* holding *your* hand?"

My heart hammers in my chest and I smile as I shake my head. "No. No one."

"Except your grandfather," he murmurs, his voice so soft I barely missed it. I frown at him, and he shakes his head. "It's nothing. So, who's Gregory? Your ex?"

I nod reluctantly, wishing he hadn't seen us together. I know I have nothing to be embarrassed about, yet somehow I am.

"It sounded like he's willing to invest in your company. Are you going to take him up on that?"

I shake my head. "I don't want to, but I might not have a choice. My grandfather warned every one of our acquaintances not to invest in me, so I'll probably have to accept Gregory's offer."

Dr. Grant tightens his grip on me and turns toward me, his eyes flashing with intensity that sets me ablaze. "So you're going to date him?" he asks, sounding angry.

"What choice do I have?" I ask, my voice breaking.

He cups my cheek, his thumb tracing over my lip, and my breathing turns shallow. "I'll help you."

My eyes widen, a tinge of hope settling deep in my chest. "How?"

"Have you ever heard of Grayson Callahan?"

I laugh. "Who hasn't?" The tech giant has his hands in every tech-related industry, from robotics to corporate software solutions. He's one of my biggest idols, and one of the few people that's out of reach for me, even as an Astor. He didn't come from money, so none of the people that surround me have access to him. He's a recluse, and opportunities to meet him are pretty much nonexistent.

"He's my best friend. He'll help if I ask him to. Besides, he just told me he's dating my *sister*, so I have a feeling he'll be quite eager to do me a favor."

I gasp. "No way. *Grayson Callahan* is your best friend? That can't be true."

He nods, a reassuring smile on his face. This could change everything for me. Having Grayson Callahan backing my company means it'd be an almost instant success. Everything that man touches turns to gold.

"I'll call him tomorrow and ask him about it. He'll likely want you to present your product and you'll need to have a business plan ready."

I nod eagerly. "Of course. I've got an entire investor's package to present him with and I'll work on improving my prototypes too. I have a full set of toys to show him."

Dr. Grant's eyes narrow, and he shakes his head. "You can *show* him the toys. No demonstrating."

I stare up at him in surprise. Is that... jealousy? I blush and look away. "Of course, Dr. Grant."

He places his index finger underneath my chin and tilts my face back up to his. "Noah. Call me Noah."

"Noah," I whisper, my heart skipping a beat. Somehow saying his name feels like a privilege, a sin.

"Good girl," he murmurs, and I swallow hard. The tone of his voice, that look in his eyes... I can just imagine him saying those exact words to me in bed.

"I can't thank you enough," I tell him, hoping my sincerity is evident. "If there's anything at all that I could do for you, please let me know."

Dr. Grant... *Noah* nods. "There is," he says, pulling on my hand. "Dance with me."

Chapter Fifteen

AMARA

His arms wrap around me, and I blink in surprise. This man... he's something else. I look around the moon-lit rose garden, music only just about audible from the ballroom's balconies. A smile spreads across my face as I place my hands against his chest. I slide my palms up, until my arms are wrapped around his neck, enjoying the feel of his muscles.

He twirls me around, and I laugh. I can't even remember the last time I felt this happy. Dr. Grant... he's different from the men I know.

"We could dance in the ballroom, you know?"

He shakes his head and tightens his grip on me. "I doubt your grandfather would be okay with that."

I pause in his arms, confused. Dr. Grant smiles at me and gently brushes my hair out of my face. "I've been told to stay away from you, Amara. Rightfully so, I guess. You don't seem to realize who you are. You shouldn't even be out here with me."

I lock my hands behind his neck, keeping my chest pressed

against his, our bodies flush against each other. "Why not? I'm just a girl, Dr. Grant."

He laughs and shakes his head. "If only," he murmurs. "You're my patient, Harold Astor's granddaughter, and a student at Astor College. The three very things I've been told to stay away from."

I look into his eyes, my heart racing. "And will you... stay away, that is?"

He buries his hand in my hair and cradles my head, his expression making my heart race. "So far I'm not doing a great job at that, am I?"

I smile and shake my head. "Maybe it would help if I'd stop finding trouble."

"Maybe... but I love being the one that saves you."

The way he looks at me makes my heart skip a beat. He's always looked at me this way, as though he sees *me*. He didn't approach me in the ballroom, showing off that he knows me, the way so many others do. Instead, he's dancing with me underneath the stars, just the two of us.

"When I'm with you, I feel a little more human. I might not be *just a girl*, Dr. Grant... but you make me feel like I am. And that feeling? It's addictive. You may need to save me yet again, Doctor. I think I'm developing an addiction."

He chuckles, the sound breaking the silence in the empty rose garden. Despite everything he just reminded me of, despite everything that stands between us... I can't help but wonder what it'd be like to be with him.

"You always catch me off guard," he says, smiling down at me. "Some of the things that come out of your mouth... you might not be the only one battling an emerging addiction."

I smirk at him, unable to help myself. "I'm very good at putting things *into* my mouth too."

He chuckles, but I feel the way he hardens against me. There's no shame in his eyes, though. He's not trying to hide his desire, he just smiles at me. "You're incorrigible," he admonishes.

"You know, Dr. Grant... I'm not always going to be those three things you listed. Once I finish my PhD, I'll no longer be a student, and I'll no longer be listed as one of the college clinic's patients. I might still be an Astor, but if my company succeeds, I won't be at my grandfather's mercy."

He looks into my eyes, and what started as a joke, a challenge... instantly turns into more. His eyes roam over my face, and his hand threads deeper into my hair. "But until then, you're off-limits to me, Amara. Until then, all I'll have are these moments where I find myself alone with you when I shouldn't be."

I look into his eyes, my heart pounding in my chest. "There will be a few more moments," I tell him. "I'm addicted, after all... I'm with you right now, but I think I might need another dose of you soon. And you did say that you'd provide me with medical supervision for my experiments, didn't you?"

Dr. Grant hardens even further, and I swallow hard. He's big. I knew he was big from the very first time we met, but back then I only felt it briefly. Now? Now it feels like he's pressing a steel rod against me. A hard *thick* one, and I can't help but wonder what it'd feel like inside me.

"I did say that... and I also told your grandfather that I'd never deny a patient my care, not even if it's you."

I grin at him. I bet that shocked Grandpa. He's used to people falling in line when he makes the smallest suggestion, but not Dr. Grant. "I need you to care for me, Dr. Grant."

He laughs, his eyes dipping down to my lips. "You're playing with fire, Amara."

"Maybe I am, but you're to blame for setting me ablaze."

He smirks, his eyes dropping to my lips. "Oh baby," he whispers. "I haven't done anything yet."

I'm breathing hard, and so is he. I don't think I've ever wanted a man this badly, and he's barely even touched me.

I rise to my tiptoes, and his breath catches. For a second I think he's going to pull away, but then he leans in, his lips brushing against mine, once, twice, before he finally kisses me.

I moan as my hands thread through his hair and pull him closer, returning his kiss. His tongue brushes over my lips, and I open up for him, wanting more of what he's doing to me. Another moan escapes my lips as he deepens the kiss, his hands roaming over my body.

He tries to pull back, but each time he lasts a mere second before his lips are back on mine. I smile against his lips, and Dr. Grant pulls away, his forehead dropping to mine.

"Fuck. I didn't mean to do that, Amara... but damn it, you're impossible to resist."

I giggle and look up at him. Seeing him looking at me like that, his eyes filled with lust and affection... yeah, this salvages my wrecked night.

"Noah," I whisper. He groans and pulls me back to him, kissing me hard and rough, his touch different to before. I can feel how hard I'm making him, and knowing he wants me that badly drives me crazy.

He pulls away abruptly and turns around, taking a few steps away from me. I stare at him, lost for words as he pulls a hand through his hair.

"Fuck," he groans. He clears his throat before turning back to me, his eyes filled with regret. "I'm sorry, Amara. I swear to God, I'm not trying to lead you on. I'm not messing with you."

I nod and walk up to him, placing my hands palms flat on his chest. "I know. I know that, Noah. I know how much there is at stake for you. I know what my grandfather is like. This is just a moment between you and me. It's just a kiss."

He walks up to me and cups my cheek, his touch at odds with the way he's clenching his jaw. "It's more than that and you know it." I look away, unable to hold his gaze. "What is it about you, Amara? You captivate me like no one ever has before. I know I need to walk away, but all I want to do is kiss you again. I want to slide my hands down your body and find out if you're wearing underwear tonight, or if you skipped it again. I want to feel you quiver against my fingers, my name on your lips. I want you in a maddening all-consuming way, and I can't figure out what it is about you."

I rise to my tiptoes and press a kiss to his cheek, my heart racing. "I'm afraid we suffer from the same affliction, Dr. Grant. It's an addiction."

He laughs and brushes my hair out of my face gently. "You'll be my downfall, Amara Astor. I just know it."

I look into his eyes, hoping that he's wrong and knowing that he isn't. My grandfather wants me with Gregory. He'd never accept Noah. He might be a doctor, but that won't be enough for Grandpa. If things go further between us and he finds out, Noah will lose out on the future he could have.

I saw the way Grandpa personally introduced him to his friends. He sees something in Noah, and I can't stand in the way of that.

Chapter Sixteen

AMARA

Three days. I've been thinking about whether or not to confront my grandfather for three days. Part of me thinks it won't matter, but a larger part of me is refusing to go down without a fight. I hesitate in front of his office door, but this just isn't something I can let go.

Grandpa is seated behind his large mahogany desk, the scent of the cigars he loves so much permeating the air. He looks up when I close the door behind me, his expression guarded.

When did he stop smiling when he sees me? When I was a little girl, this was my favorite room in the whole world, because it's where my granddad always was. He was my hero. I might have grown up without a father, but Grandpa made sure I never felt the loss. He was always there. He attended every ballet performance and every violin recital when I was little, and when I grew older and started to choose science fairs over the dancing and acting classes my mother tried to force me to go to, it was Grandpa that sided with me. He and I were always on the same side, a united front. When did that change?

"You're sabotaging me."

He drops his pen and sighs as he looks up at me. The way he looks at me hurts. That expression... it's like I'm a nuisance, like I'm wasting his time. Maybe I am. It's highly doubtful he'll change his mind after all.

"Why would you do that to me? Why would you stop me from finding an investor for my company? I'm not asking you for your support because you've made it clear you won't give me that, and I'm certainly not asking you for money either. So why? Why are you actively trying to sabotage me? I'm your *granddaughter*. Shouldn't you want to see me succeed?"

Grandpa crosses his arms over his chest and stares at me in silence, the way he used to when I was throwing a tantrum as a child. Is that what he thinks this is? Does he think my company is my way of rebelling?

I run a hand through my hair and inhale shakily. "I'm trying so hard to stand on my own two feet, Grandpa. I'm trying my best to be independent, to grow a company by myself. I'm trying to chase my dreams and I'm working my ass off to do it. Why would you not want this for me? I get you not supporting me, but why would you try to curb my growth?"

"Amara, how long are you going to keep this up? I worked to grow our business for most of my life, and I'll be damned if I watch you throw your inheritance away over some silly company. I agree that there's a lot of money to be made in adult toys, but if that's what you want to do, you can easily purchase a few existing companies and grow the Astor business that way. You and Adrian are my heirs, Amara. You need to get your shit together and start learning how to run our business, because your cousin has no intention of returning to the States to help you. That little company of yours will not prepare you. I worked for years to grow our business into what it is. I've paved a clear path for you and for generations to come. I worked as hard as I did so you don't have to, Amara. The last thing I want to do is see you struggle the way I did, when there's a road to success ahead of you that most would kill for."

"Grandpa... you've never asked me what I want to do, you know? You've always assumed that I'd naturally learn to fill your shoes, but I can't. I'm not like you. I'm much more comfortable in a lab, inventing products, utilizing my creativity. I'm not a leader. I never will be, and I'm okay with that. It doesn't mean that I won't be successful. It just means I won't be the next *you*."

"Not a leader," he repeats, looking away in disgust. "You can learn, Amara — and you *will*. You must. I've never asked anything of you but this. You need to learn how to manage the company. Gregory will help you once you're married."

I shake my head, wishing there was a way to make him see. "Grandpa, I won't ever marry Gregory. I won't. I have dreams of my own that I want to pursue. I'm not asking you to support me, I'm just asking that you don't stand in my way."

He stares at me, his disappointment evident. "You'll give up on those dreams when you realize how hard life really is — but by the time that happens I might not be here anymore, Amara. I won't be there to teach you all you need to know. Stop this foolishness. I didn't work myself to the bone only for you to now abandon all we've got. You're not a child anymore and I'm done entertaining you. You want to follow your dreams? You'll do so without my support, and without those in my network. It won't take you long to realize that the dreams you have are a luxury, one you can't afford without me and all I've built."

He picks his pen back up and stares down at his documents, silently dismissing me. I don't know what I expected when I came in here. I knew he wouldn't budge, and I knew he'd never even attempt to see things from my point of view.

He won't let me deviate from the path he thinks I should walk. He's never going to let me build a future of my own choosing.

Part of me worries that he's right, that I'll eventually end up caving. Someday I might find myself sitting behind his desk, and it wouldn't be a bad life. Far from it. It just wouldn't be the one I chose for myself, and the thought of that scares me.

I'm not the right person to take over from him. I'm not smart enough, and I'm definitely not a leader. I can't be his heir. I'm not qualified. I'm not like my cousin Adrian — who doesn't want the job either. At least he's well-equipped for it. I'm not.

I can't command people the way my grandfather does. I'm good at what I do. I'm an excellent researcher and an even better engineer... but a leader? That's something I'll never be, and eventually Grandpa will have to face that fact.

Chapter Seventeen

NOAH

I run a hand through my hair, frustrated. All I've been able to think about lately is Amara. It's almost like Mr. Astor has some sort of sixth sense, because he's kept me so busy that I haven't had a chance to see her since the ball.

I've been working myself to the bone. Mr. Astor wasn't joking when he told me he'd help me with my career. In the last two weeks, I've had lunch with him twice, and he's introduced me to countless people that I'd otherwise never have access to. He seems to be actively working on acquiring existing medical practices to add to his investment portfolio, and he wants me to run them. It's an insane chance, and I'd be crazy to pass it up.

"Sending in your next patient."

I glance at the phone on my desk, having developed a love-hate relationship with the intercom feature. I love my job, but man, I'm tired.

The door opens, and I freeze in my seat when Amara walks in. I haven't seen her since the ball, and it's been for the best. I'm putting my future at risk by getting involved with her, yet when she's standing in front of me, I can't resist her.

I rise from my seat, surprised to see her in my office. I texted her to let her know Gray would meet with her, but I've barely spoken to her since. Gray couldn't commit to anything until his current projects wrap up, and I hope Amara will be able to wait. The thought of her turning to Gregory terrifies me. It isn't something I should be thinking about at all if I value my career prospects... but I can't keep her off my mind.

"Amara."

She nods as she closes the door behind her. "Hi, Dr. Grant."

"What brings you here today," I ask, trying my hardest to act professional, when all I can think about is how beautiful she looks in that red flowing summer dress. The way it highlights her breasts, that tiny waist... fuck. Her long red hair flows to her waist, and I can't tear my eyes away. My eyes drop to her lips, memories flooding me. The way her lips felt against mine, the way she sighed, the way she fit into my arms so perfectly.

She holds up a bag and smiles at me. "I came to return your jacket. I'm sorry it took me so long." She puts the bag down next to my desk and hesitates before she sits down opposite me. "But I also... well, do you remember when you told me not to test my prototypes without medical supervision?"

I swallow hard and nod. The mere memory of her coming on my hand has my cock hardening. Fucking hell.

"So... I developed something new in anticipation of meeting Grayson Callahan. I wanted to have a full set of toys to show him."

She grabs her bag and takes out something that can only really be described as a contraption. It looks a bit like a dildo, but there's a piece sticking out at the front. Interesting.

She glances at me, her cheeks bright red. "Will you help me test it?"

I pull on my tie, suddenly feeling hot. "And how would I assist you, exactly?"

She grins at me, a hint of nervousness in her eyes. "I... well, I'd just test it and you'd just sit here and make sure you can intervene if anything goes wrong. Maybe time orgasms. I'd pay you for your time as though it's a regular consultation, of course."

My cock is so fucking hard that it hurts. She wants me to sit here and watch her get off? Amara looks away and bites down on her lip before shaking her head. "I'm sorry," she says, grabbing her toy. "This is a terrible idea. I shouldn't be doing this. I saw the way my grandfather introduced you to his business partners, and I know what's at stake for you. I don't know what I was thinking. I guess I wasn't really thinking at all. I should ask someone else for help."

Someone else? A vision of her with Gregory comes to mind, and I rise from my seat, barely able to restrain my sudden anger. Amara pauses halfway to the door and turns to look at me, her expression a mixture of embarrassment and hope.

"Sit," I tell her, tipping my head toward the patient bed in my office. She looks down at the floor as she walks toward it, and I lock my office door. I need to stay away from her. My future depends on it. But I'll be damned if I let her walk out now. She's not testing any of these toys of hers with anyone but me. Over my dead body.

"I told you I'd help you, didn't I? I'd never turn a patient away, Amara."

She nods, biting down on her lip as she walks over to the bed in the sectioned-off corner. Her hands tremble as she sticks her dildo device to the leather bed using the suction grip she built into it. What the fuck is this thing? Looks like it's meant to be ridden.

I walk up to her and study it curiously. "So, what would you like me to do? How can I help?"

Amara trembles, as though her nerves are getting the best of her, and I raise my hand to her face gently. "Hey," I murmur, pushing her hair behind her ear. "It's okay. It's just me."

She gulps and looks into my eyes, nodding slowly. "Yes, okay," she whispers. "Okay, so if I was alone, I'd just put on some lube and insert it, but I'm too nervous to even function. I'm not sure..."

My cock fucking jerks at those words. "All right," I tell her. "I'll help you. Just sit back."

She reaches into her handbag and pulls out the biggest bottle of lube I've ever seen. I frown involuntarily, trying my hardest to push away thoughts of her with other men. She's so into these toys of hers that it's likely she leads a far more active sex life than I do, and the thought of her in anyone else's arms sends a burst of pure violence through me.

Amara sits back as I unscrew the bottle of lube, suddenly feeling angry at myself. She's here because I'm someone she trusts. Because she's conducting an experiment. I'm betraying her trust with the thoughts I'm having, and I need to get myself in check.

My heart rate fucking skyrockets when she pulls her red dress up her thighs, until it settles above her hips, exposing her bare, smooth pussy. No underwear again. I'm starting to think she doesn't wear any at all.

I swallow hard as I squirt some of the gel onto my fingers and lean into her, my cock jerking when the tips of my fingers come into touch with her pussy. Amara gasps, her eyes finding mine.

"It's cold," she whispers, and I bite down on my lip, spreading out the gel and getting a feel of her pussy. I slip a finger into her, enjoying the feel of her. Her breathing turns shallow as I finger fuck her like that under the guise of lubricating her.

"I forgot to wear gloves," I tell her, not a single part of me truly feeling guilty. Nah. I've wanted to feel her pussy without any barriers ever since she first came on my hand.

"It's okay," she says, her voice husky. I slip another finger into her, and her eyes fall closed. She lifts her hips and pushes against my hand harder, and I bite back a smile as I pull my hand away, eliciting a whimper from her.

"I think you're ready."

She nods, her lips parted and her eyes on mine. She's so

fucking sexy, and I fucking wish she was riding my dick instead of this damn plastic toy.

Amara rises to her knees and grabs the ends of her dress, pulling it up so she can see. I watch as she lowers her pussy onto her toy, gasping when the tip slips into her. If she's gasping like this on that toy, she's going to be in pain sliding onto my cock.

Amara lowers herself fully and breathes in deeply, trying to steady herself. I watch her in fascination as she clicks on one of the buttons, turning it on. Amara shimmies back and forth, a frown on her face, as though she isn't comfortable. She reaches in front of her, and her dress escapes her grip, frustrating her further.

I grab it and lift it up for her, my cock straining against my suit trousers. "It might be easier to take this off," I say, my voice husky.

She nods and raises her arms, and I pull her dress over her head, exposing her body. Fucking hell. She's wearing a bright red lace bra that contrasts against her skin beautifully. Those tits... perfection.

I place her dress next to her, trying my best to control my desire. I want her flat on her back, my cock sinking deep inside her. Instead, I'm standing here, watching her fuck a plastic toy.

"The clit stimulator isn't working," she says, frustrated. I lean in and fiddle with it, pushing it toward her until she finally gasps in delight.

"It needs an adjustor, a hinge of some sort, so it can be adapted to different bodies," I tell her.

She nods and reaches for me, her hands resting on my shoulders. "I knew asking you for help would be a great idea."

She keeps her hands pressed against my chest, her eyes on mine as her body gently sways, and I could fucking come like this. This woman... she'll be the death of me.

"How does that feel?"

She nods. "Good. I don't think it'll require much more work, but I was going after triple stimulation and I'm not really getting it. The clit part is definitely failing, but I'm also not really getting the G-spot friction I was after. The part that works well is the thrusting."

I grit my teeth, oddly jealous of this damn thing that's pushing up and down inside her. "I bet it isn't as good as my cock would be," I say, without thinking. I regret my words instantly. I'm trying so hard to be professional with her, but I keep losing my composure around her.

Amara's cheeks redden and her eyes widen as I cup her cheek, my thumb tracing over the edge of her lips. I want to kiss her. I want her lips on mine.

Amara squirms, clearly wanting to come, but her invention is letting her down. I reach for her and push aside the front part of her toy, replacing it with my thumb.

She moans when I swirl my thumb over her clit, teasing her, slowly increasing the pace. I take my time with her, building her up, then pulling away, doing to her what she's doing to me — keeping her on the edge.

"Dr. Grant," she whimpers, and I smirk as I thread my hand through her hair.

I pull her closer, my lips hovering over hers. "What did I tell you to call me?"

"Noah," she moans, and the way my name sounds on her lips, fuck me. She's my every fantasy come to life. Those lips of hers. I want them wrapped around my cock.

"Good girl," I whisper. I smile and kiss the edge of her lips, teasing her. Amara tilts her head, her lips brushing against mine. My eyes fall closed as I give in, kissing her the way I've been wanting to from the moment she walked into my office.

She moans and opens up for me, deepening the kiss. The way she moves against me, practically riding my hand as she fucks my mouth with that tongue of hers... fucking insane. I increase the pressure on her clit and get her close, only to pull away seconds before she comes, my lips lingering on hers.

She pulls away to look at me, her lips swollen and parted, her expression silently begging for more, and I give it to her. I increase the pace and watch her come on my hand again, enjoying it far more than I did last time. The way she moans... fuck. I think I could come just at the sound of her. I watch her as wave after wave rocks her body, until she finally smiles relaxedly, her gaze filled with an expression I can't even name. Ecstasy, perhaps.

She turns her little toy off, reality catching up on her. I smile as I lift my fingers to my face, licking them slowly, getting a taste of her. She moans when my lips close around my fingers, and I smirk.

"Delicious," I whisper.

Amara is breathing hard, and her eyes drop to my trousers. She startles me when she reaches for me and places her hand over my cock. Her eyes widen and she looks up at me. "You're big," she whispers. "How big are you exactly?"

I frown. "Um, in inches?"

She nods, and I can't help but grin. "I have no idea. Can't say I've ever taken a ruler to my cock, Amara."

She nods and lets go of me as she lifts herself off her toy. It's coated in her wetness, and I grin as she takes a napkin out of her bag to wipe it clean. She came prepared, huh?

"I'll have to thank you somehow," she says. "I have something in mind for you. You know how I like suction? I'll make you something."

"Hmm... suction? Sounds like you're trying to rope me into being a test subject, Amara."

She blushes and shrugs unapologetically. "Fine. That's true. You'll help me, won't you?"

My eyes drop to her lips. "Depends. If you're going to attach some weird thing to my cock, are you going to give me real lips to compare the feeling to?"

Amara's eyes darken with desire, and I know I'm taking this too far, but I can't help myself. I can't resist. She licks her lips, and my eyes follow her every move. She's beautiful. Fucking hell. I could come to the mere thought of her wrapping those lips of hers around my dick.

"Maybe," she says, hopping off the bed. "If you're lucky."

She grabs her dress and pulls it over her head in a rush. Within seconds she's standing by the door, looking back at me with rosy cheeks, a satisfied look in her eyes.

"Thank you, Dr. Grant... Noah."

And then she's gone, leaving me standing here with the bluest fucking balls ever.

Chapter Eighteen

NOAH

I'm nervous as I stare up at the Astor mansion. Mr. Astor invited me for dinner, and it all just feels weird to me. So far I've mentally been able to keep Amara and her grandfather separate, but tonight two different parts of my life will collide, whether I like it or not.

Things between her and me have been strange. We're both trying to stay away from each other despite the undeniable attraction, an unspoken agreement in place. I know that's what is best for both of us, yet I live for the times she gives in to temptation, the times she'll find an excuse to see me. Her visit to my office is still fresh on my mind, and it won't be easy to have her next to me and smile at her grandfather innocently, when I just know having my hands on her is all I'm going to be thinking about.

So far, I've had lunch with Mr. Astor a handful of times, but he's never once invited me to his home. Not until today. I don't know what to expect. I can't read that man at all. He's taking all the steps that are required to build the medical empire he has in mind and he truly seems to be putting me in charge of it, but it all seems calculated somehow. Something about him makes me feel uncomfortable... but maybe it's just the fact that I keep touching his granddaughter in ways he'd deem unforgivable.

I brace myself before I walk in, not even remotely surprised when I'm greeted by a butler. The way the Astors live... it's surreal. This is the world Amara lives in. The world she grew up in.

I follow the butler to the dining room, and my heart skips a beat when I hear laughter that I recognize. Amara. As expected, she's here. I should've texted her to let her know I'd be there tonight, but it seemed weird somehow. She and I text occasionally, but it's usually about her toys and her meeting with Grayson. We rarely discuss her grandfather. Part of me wants to keep my relationship with her separate from the business relationship I'm developing with Mr. Astor. I know it's impossible, but I'm delaying the inevitable.

The doors open, and I tense when I find the source of Amara's laughter staring down at her with adoration filling his eyes. Gregory. The same guy that offered to invest in her. Her ex. I stare at the two of them, and she looks up at me, her eyes widening in disbelief when they land on me.

"Dr. Grant," she says politely, hiding her shock. I'm only barely able to suppress the disappointment and anger I feel, seeing her standing here with *him*. I guess waiting to meet with Grayson was taking too long. I have no right to the disappointment I'm feeling, but that sure as shit isn't stopping me.

I tear my eyes away from her and school my features when Mr. Astor walks up to me, two women behind him. I smile politely and shake his hand.

"Noah," he says, turning. "I understand you've already met my daughter, Charlotte. Someday, I'll introduce you to my son too. He lives in England, but I believe he's visiting with his son this Christmas. You would get on great with my grandson."

I smile at the thought of that. It's strange, because the Astors intimidate me, but at the same time they make me feel so welcome amongst them.

"Noah," Charlotte says, taking my hand in hers. "It's so good to see you again. I'm sorry I missed you at the ball. I kept meaning to come say hi, but before I realized it, the night was over. You looked great in the tux. It fit just the way I expected it to."

"Thank you again for that, Ms. Astor," I say, feeling just a little awkward.

"I'm sure my father has already told you this, but we consider you family, so please do just call me Char."

I nod, even though the thought of that makes me cringe inwardly. These aren't people I should get comfortable with at all.

"Please, allow me to introduce Kim Jones."

The woman standing behind Ms. Astor straightens and offers me her hand. "We've met before, at the charity ball."

I nod, recognition hitting me. She's a famous cardiovascular surgeon that's equally renowned for her beauty. What is she doing here tonight?

"Come, kids. Let's eat. I'm starving," Mr. Astor says, leading his daughter to the table. We follow him, and it soon becomes apparent that I'm being set up with Kim, while Amara is with Gregory.

I grit my teeth as we sit down, and Mr. Astor clears his throat. "Noah, this is Gregory. His family is in oil, and Amara and he have been dating for years now."

Years, huh? So they've got history. I guess she took him up on that offer to take her out on a date. I wonder if he knows that I made his girlfriend moan my name last week.

"Greg, this is Noah. He's going to be managing the medical arm of the Astor portfolio."

He nods at me and wraps his arm around the back of Amara's chair, a smug smile on his face. I glance at her, but her eyes are on her plate.

The devastation I feel is debilitating and I swallow hard. I shouldn't give a fuck about what she does, who she's seeing, but I fucking hate this. I hate that I never stood a chance, that I never will. Not that it matters. Maybe this was all a game to her, or maybe she truly sees me as nothing but a doctor.

Gregory leans into her and whispers into her ear, making her smile, and my heart fucking tightens. I tear my gaze away and turn to Kim instead, trying my best to focus on her.

"It's great to see you again," I tell her, and her eyes light up.

She pushes her long dark hair behind her ear and smiles at me. "I didn't think you'd remember me. We only spoke to each other briefly."

I nod and return her smile. "You're hard to forget." She's the youngest surgeon I know. Hell, she's the same age as I am. From what I gathered, she graduated early and then breezed through med school. Kim is nothing short of amazing, and she's exactly the kind of person I need to get acquainted with. She's going places. Whereas I... I'm tempted to settle for the bare minimum. Part of me fears reaching for greatness, but seeing Kim achieve it with such grace inspires me.

Mr. Astor clears his throat and smiles at the two of us. "You two are well-matched," he says. "Why don't you take Kim out for dinner, Noah? You should get to know each other better. You're in the same field, after all."

I bite back a smile at his lack of subtlety, and Kim grins, equally amused. I'm about to agree when I look up and find Amara staring at me, her eyes blazing with what looks a lot like anger.

Chapter Nineteen

Amara

She's hard to forget? Is that what he just said? When did he even meet Kim? I grit my teeth and watch the two of them interact. Grandpa is blatantly setting them up, and what my grandfather wants, he gets.

My heart twists painfully when Dr. Grant smiles at her. She's beautiful, with her caramel skin tone and her thick dark hair. He looks mesmerized, and it kills me. Jealousy claws at me, and I resist the urge to draw his attention away from Kim.

I tense when Grandpa suggests that the two of them go out for dinner. The idea of Kim having a part of him I'll never have... I hate it.

"Dinner sounds lovely," I say without thinking. "Let's make it a double date."

Gregory sits up, his gaze burning, but my eyes are on Noah. His expression is unreadable, and for a second I think he'll dismiss my idea. But then he glances at Gregory, and something flickers through his eyes.

"A double date, huh?" he says, his words slow, drawn out. He looks into my eyes as he nods. "Sounds... lovely."

I inhale shakily, relief and anger clashing within me. I'm annoyed he wants to go on a date with Kim at all, yet relieved he won't be alone with her. The idea of that sickens me. Him having her in his arms, smiling at her... No.

Kim grins, oblivious. She places her hand on Noah's arm, her touch lingering as though she's admiring the muscles underneath her touch, and I grit my teeth. "Oh, why don't we visit my family's vineyard?" she asks, her fingertips trailing over Noah's arm.

He turns to look at her, an intimate smile on his face. "Your family owns a vineyard? I've never been to one, so I'd love to go."

Gregory wraps his arm around my waist and pulls me into him, his lips grazing over my ear. "A double date, huh? We haven't done that in years."

I nod and force a smile onto my face. The last thing I want to do is give Greg any ideas, but it's too late now. Grandpa ambushed me by inviting him over tonight without even informing me, and I just made things so much worse by mentioning a double date. Grandpa is acting like I never asked him to stop standing in my way, like I didn't tell him I'd never marry Gregory. I should've known my words would fall on deaf ears.

I won't be able to get myself out of this situation... but I don't want to. I'd rather suffer through a day with Gregory than leave Noah alone with Kim.

"I haven't been to your family's vineyard in years," Greg tells Kim, and I breathe a sigh of relief when she drags her eyes away from Noah's, breaking whatever spell she had him under.

"Yeah, when was the last time we hung out?" she asks, eying the two of us. "It's been a few years, hasn't it?"

Gregory smiles and presses a kiss to my shoulder the way he used to back when we were dating. "I have some fond memories of that vineyard. It'd be good to revisit those."

My cheeks heat in mortification and Noah tenses. He locks

his jaw and looks away, as though Gregory is getting on his nerves. Maybe he isn't as unaffected as he pretends to be. Maybe this thing I'm feeling... is mutual.

"Excuse me," he says, rising from his seat.

I jump out of mine too. "Oh, I'll show you the way to the bathroom," I tell him. "I need to grab my phone from my room, anyway."

Grandpa stares at me, but I ignore his gaze. He took it too far by inviting Gregory over tonight. Setting Noah up with Kim is just adding insult to injury. There's no way I'm sitting back and letting this happen.

Noah is quiet as we walk down the corridor, his shoulders tense. He isn't smiling at me the way he usually would. He isn't even looking at me.

"I didn't expect you to be here tonight," I murmur.

He nods, but otherwise he doesn't engage with me at all, and it frustrates me. I don't even know what I want from him... a reaction, I guess.

I grab his arm as we turn the corner, and he pauses, his eyes dropping to where I'm touching him. He looks angry, and that just confuses me.

"Are you mad at me?" I ask, my voice soft.

He smiles humorlessly and tilts his head. "Now, why would I be mad at you, Ms. Astor?"

Ms. Astor. So we're back to that, huh? He pulls his arm out of my grip and keeps walking in the direction we were going. I follow behind him, feeling helpless. "It's this way," I say, pointing to my bedroom door. Noah nods and walks in, freezing when he realizes where I led him to.

He turns to walk back out, but I close the door and lean back against it. "You can use my bathroom," I tell him, tipping my head toward the door behind him. "But I'm not letting you go back to the dining room until you tell me why you look so angry."

He laughs and walks up to me, his hands wrapping around

my waist. "And you think you'll be able to stop me? Amara, I can lift you up with ease," he says, and he does.

I gasp as he lifts me into the air and place my hands on his shoulders. He's about to move me out of the way, but I'm not letting him go that easily. I can't stand this feeling, this distance between us.

I wrap my legs around his waist, and he freezes. Noah swallows hard, but the anger in his eyes doesn't diminish in the slightest.

"What would your boyfriend think if he saw us now, Amara?" he asks, pushing me against the door roughly, closing the remaining distance between us so my breasts are pressing against his chest.

I tighten my legs around his waist, my breathing turning shallow. I can feel him hardening against me, and it's got me biting down on my lip in an effort to suppress the sudden need I feel.

"What would he think if he knew I had my fingers buried in your pussy just a week ago? I doubt he'd be happy to know that I helped you test some of your toys, that I tasted that hot pussy of yours. Tell me, what would he think?"

He's breathing as hard as I am, and I smile, realization dawning. "You're jealous."

Noah grits his teeth and stares me down. "Is this just a fucking game to you? Some rich people bullshit?"

I tense, my smile melting away. "No. God, Noah. No." I see it now. There's not just anger in his eyes. There's hurt and insecurity too. I'm definitely not the only one that feels something between us. He's right there with me. "He's not my boyfriend, Noah. I didn't know he'd be here tonight, either. I'm as surprised as you are. I swear I haven't seen him since that night at the ball. This is all my grandfather's doing. I stayed quiet because of the relationship Gregory's father has with my grandfather — because of the respect I have for my grandfather despite his actions tonight."

He looks into my eyes as though he's looking for a trace of a lie, and I breathe a sigh of relief when his shoulders relax. Noah drops his head to my shoulder, his lips grazing against my neck, sending an involuntary tremble down my spine.

"The double date?" he whispers against my skin.

I grimace, suddenly embarrassed. "I... I didn't..."

Noah chuckles and straightens to look at me. "I love this shade of red on you," he murmurs, and it just makes me blush even harder.

I swallow hard when his hands move down to my ass. He grabs onto me tightly and a soft moan escapes my lips. Noah smirks and leans in, his lips hovering over mine. I don't hesitate to thread my hands through his hair and pull him closer. His lips find mine, and I moan, needing more of him. Noah gives me what I want and deepens the kiss, driving me crazy with the way he moves his body against mine.

He carries me to my bed and carefully puts me down before kneeling down in front of the bed. "I have a bad habit of falling to my knees in front of you," he whispers, pressing a kiss to my inner thigh. A soft moan escapes my lips and he smirks as he separates my legs. "I was wondering if you were wearing any underwear tonight. I'm pleased to find that you aren't." He presses a kiss on top of my pussy, his breath tickling me, turning me on further.

Noah teases me with his tongue, circling it around my clit before flicking his tongue over it. He gets me close within minutes, and then he pulls away.

"Don't stop," I beg, and he smiles as he shakes his head, pulling my dress back over my hips before he rises to his feet.

"I've wanted more ever since I first got a taste of you in my office," he tells me, his eyes on mine. "But you don't get to come. This is punishment for making me jealous. For roping me into a date I don't want to go on."

I stare at him in disbelief. "You are the *worst*, Dr. Grant. It's a good thing I have toys in my bedroom."

He smirks and shakes his head. "Yeah, but you have no time. We've been gone for too long already."

I stare at him in frustration, and he laughs as he grabs my hand and pulls me to the door. "We need to go back, Amara. We've been gone for far too long."

I nod reluctantly and tighten my grip on his hand, my eyes on his. "You're not mad anymore, are you? I promise you, I didn't know he'd be here."

He shakes his head and cups my cheek gently. "I'm not mad at you, beautiful. I shouldn't have let my emotions get the best of me today. You and I... your grandfather holds my entire future in his hands."

I drop my forehead against his shoulder, and Noah wraps his arms around me, holding me tightly. "I know that," I whisper. "I know."

He's right, of course. Grandpa has plans for us both, and they don't involve us being together. I could risk my own future, but I can't ask it of Noah. We're playing with fire, and we both know it.

Chapter Twenty

NOAH

I should be looking forward to today since I've never been to a vineyard before, but I'm dreading it. I'm not looking forward to seeing Amara with Gregory. Knowing that he's her *date*... I can't fucking stand it, but I have no choice.

It's important that I build relationships that can advance my career. Mr. Astor is offering me the opportunity of a lifetime, and I'd be crazy to walk away from that, yet I can't shake the dread I feel.

My phone buzzes and I glance at it in surprise when Amara's name pops up. I feel bad for wishing that she's texting because she's canceling, but I can't help it. I don't want to see her with him.

Amara: *do you think you could pick me up?*

I stare at my phone in surprise. I assumed she'd get to the vineyard with Gregory, and I smile as I text her back.

Noah: *Sure. I'll be there in ten minutes.*

I'm grinning as I walk to my car, and I'm still grinning by the time I pull up in front of her house. Just the thought of getting to have her to myself for the two hours that it takes to drive there makes me smile. I bet she somehow knew that Kim is spending the weekend there — that's she's already there, and I'd be making my way there alone. I keep telling myself that I'll stay away from her, yet I can't resist stealing these moments with her.

I step out of the car when Amara walks out of the house, and I open the car door for her. She smiles up at me, her eyes twinkling, and my heart starts to race. I'm smiling like a fool as I walk back around the car. I should probably be worried about Mr. Astor hearing about me picking her up, but all I can think about is Amara.

I glance at her as I get behind the wheel, my smile falling when I take a good look at her. She's in another one of those flowing dresses of hers, a white one this time. The way the top of it hugs her breasts makes it almost impossible to look away. "You look beautiful," I murmur, wondering if she dressed up for Gregory. He's the one that gets to call her his today. She's *his* date.

Amara's eyes roam over my arms, taking in the black t-shirt I'm wearing. "So do you. You look good, I mean. It's rare to see you looking so casual. It's a good look on you."

She looks as dismayed as I do and the atmosphere is tense between us, the silence heavy. Amara fiddles with the radio for a good twenty minutes, her hand trembling just slightly each time she changes the channel.

"What's wrong? You seem... I don't know. Nervous?"

She looks up at me, her cheeks blazing. "Could you pull up over there?"

I frown and do as she asks, parking on the side of an empty road. We've only been driving for half an hour, but it already feels like we're somewhere else entirely.

"What's wrong?" I ask her again, turning to face her.

Amara looks into my eyes, and that expression of hers... she drives me insane without even touching me.

"There's something I wanted to try today. Something I wanted your help with."

My heart hammers in my chest, and I run a hand through my hair. "Another toy?"

She nods. "I thought today would be the perfect time to test something new. I've been working on this for a while now. It's not that original, this one, but it's fun and I think it's a must-have for my collection. I want to know how unobtrusive it is, how it'll feel, how long I can wear it comfortably."

I look away, feeling conflicted. "No."

"No?" she repeats, confused. "I thought you said you wanted me to do this under medical supervision. I... I don't understand. Was I wrong?"

I turn back to face her and shake my head. "You're not wrong. I told you I'd help you, and I meant it. But not today."

Something flashes through her eyes, and it hits me straight in the chest. She wraps her arms around herself and looks out the window. "Oh, okay. I get it," she murmurs. "It's fine. Today is not a working day for you, after all. Besides, I doubt you want to feel like you'll need to keep an eye on me when it's Kim you want to be focusing on."

"I don't think you do," I tell her against better judgment. "I don't think you get it."

Her eyes meet mine, and the pain I see in them guts me. This thing between us... it's bigger than either of us wants it to be, yet neither of us can fight it.

"I'll be damned if I have you turned on all fucking day, when you'll be with your damn ex. When you're coming, when that pussy of yours is squeezing whatever crazy fucking toy you've invented, I want you to be with me. I want your thoughts filled only with *me*. No one else."

Amara looks at me, her skin flushed, her lips slightly parted. Fucking hell. I wish I could grab her hair and yank her toward me. I want those full lips of hers against mine. I've never wanted to kiss a woman more than I do right now. It's so fucked up that it's her I want when I'm on my way to a date with another woman.

Amara smiles shyly and looks down. She looks flustered, and I like that look on her. I watch her as she bends forward, taking something out of her bag. She grabs my hand and places a small remote control in it. It's no bigger than a credit card, but thicker.

"The toy?" she whispers. "It comes with a remote control. You'd be in charge all day. My every orgasm would be yours. I'd be at your mercy, unable to think of anything but you." She swallows hard and closes my fingers around the device. "And while you're toying with me like that... you won't be able to think of anything else either. When you know how wet I am for you, how badly I want to come for you... you won't be able to focus on anyone but me."

I lean in and cup her cheek, my thumb tracing over her bottom lip. "You'll be mine all day, even if you aren't on my arm. Your pussy will be mine."

She nods, her breathing irregular. I wonder if she's been as jealous as I've been, thinking about today. Does she just want to test a toy, or does she want to keep me spellbound?

"Show me."

Her little sigh of relief gives her away. She's worried about Kim. Clever little fox. She's calling me on my promise to provide her with medical supervision, but in doing so, she's also making sure Kim will never stand a chance.

Amara pulls out a toy and holds it up for me. It's similar to her last design, but bigger. I smile to myself, thinking about the multiple times I'll be able to make her come with this.

"Fine."

She grins at me as I hold up her toy, inspecting it. It looks far more robust than her previous ones. The rubber is thick, and it's sealed properly. There shouldn't be any safety concerns, but then she probably knows that.

I turn to look at her, taking in the rapid rising and falling of her chest, her parted lips and those flushed cheeks. "Tell me. Are you already wet?" Amara's eyes widen ever so slightly, and I smirk when she nods hesitantly. "Of course you are," I whisper, leaning in.

I trail my hand down her dress until I've got the edge of it between my fingers. A soft gasp escapes her lips when I slip my hand underneath the fabric, taking my time moving my fingers up. The way she looks at me... fuck.

"Part those thighs for me, baby."

She obeys, and my eyes fall closed when the tips of my fingers reach her pussy. Soaking wet, as expected — and no underwear, again. I push two fingers into her, making her moan. "Just making sure you're wet enough for insertion," I tell her. "All part of the medical supervision I'm providing you with."

She nods. "Of course, Dr. Grant."

My cock fucking jerks at those words. When *she* calls me Doctor, it's different. That voice of hers, her tone. Fuck.

"Yeah, I think you're ready." I pull my fingers away reluctantly and grab her toy, wishing it was my cock slipping into her, and not this fucking thing.

Amara gasps when it's in place, and I smirk. "Are you sure this'll stay in place without underwear?" I ask, a little concerned. "I'm all about playing with you, Amara... but I don't want this slipping out of you in public."

She nods, a sweet smile on her face. "Don't worry, Noah. I've pre-tested this. It won't slip out, I promise."

I grin and look away. She doesn't even realize she's giving herself away, does she? Pre-tested it... then what does she need *me* for?

I grab the remote and click a few of the buttons as she explains to me what each of them does. Every gasp that escapes her lips thrills me, and I'm suddenly looking forward to today. Even as she smiles at Gregory, it'll be me that's in control of her pleasure.

Chapter Twenty-One

NOAH

Kim smiles when she spots me, but that smile rapidly melts away when she notices Amara right behind me. She looks between the two of us in confusion and forces a smile onto her face as she walks up to me.

Amara and I both tense when she throws herself in my arms and hugs me tightly. "It's so good to see you," she says, smiling up at me before she turns to give Amara air kisses. "How come you two drove here together? I thought you'd be coming with Gregory."

The only one she's coming with is *me*, I think to myself. Amara looks at me knowingly when I smirk and shakes her head. I shrug unapologetically in response.

Our silent exchange doesn't go unnoticed, and Kim frowns, making me feel bad instantly. If nothing else, I'd like to be friends with her, and I'd hate to make her feel bad when she's gone out of her way to host us today.

"He should be here any minute," Amara says. "He had some work to finish up."

Kim nods and wraps her hand around my arm. "Come on, let me show you around. Greg knows the way, he'll be able to find us just fine."

I nod and let her lead me along, feeling somewhat self-conscious. I can feel Amara's eyes on me, and even though I told her she and I can't be together... even though I'm willing myself to believe it too, I don't want to hurt her. There's something between us, and it's not just lust. It's more than that. I can't stand the thought of her smiling at Gregory, and the look on her face as she stares at the hand Kim is touching me with tells me she feels the same way.

I slip my hand into my pocket, my fingers grazing over the remote control she gave me. I glance at her and smirk as I turn her device on. Her eyes widen and she looks down. Perfect.

Amara is quiet as Kim gives us a tour of the vineyard, and neither one of us can focus as she tells us about their grapes and the history of this place. All I can think about is that I want to get Amara alone. I guess her little scheme is working, because she's all I can think about.

Amara and I both breathe a sigh of relief when we reach a clearing where a table has been set up. "It's beautiful," Amara murmurs, and I have to agree. Adequate shading thanks to the trees, a decadent spread, and chairs that look incredibly comfortable.

"I thought we might do a wine tasting," Kim says, looking up at me. She's leaning into me, clearly being flirtatious, but I struggle to play along. I know this is what I need to do to further my career. I need to schmooze with whoever Mr. Astor sets me up with, and he clearly wants me with Kim. I'm fairly confident he intends to formally pair us up... but it's his granddaughter I want instead.

I nod at Kim and pull out her chair for her. She beams up at me, and I smile at her. She's a wonderful woman, and had I not been enchanted with Amara, she'd be perfect for me. I understand why Mr. Astor wants us together. We're both doctors. We're both young and ambitious.

I catch Amara gritting her teeth as she sits down next to Kim, and I sigh. I feel so fucking helpless. No matter what I do, I'm in the wrong. Technically Kim is my date, but Amara... what is she even?

I sit down opposite Kim, and she leans into me as she pushes a wine glass my way. "Try this, Noah."

I smile at her and take a sip. "Wow. That's good."

She nods in satisfaction and pulls the glass back, lifting it to her own lips, the gesture intimate. She's beautiful, and she's brilliant... but fuck. She isn't Amara. Amara, who is staring at Kim's glass as though she's willing it to shatter.

I slip my hand back into my pocket and increase the vibrations of her toy, distracting her. I regret it the second I see Gregory walking up to us, his eyes on Amara. He looks as enthralled as I am, and I regret putting that blush on her cheeks.

"Sorry I'm late, sweetheart," he says, leaning in. I tense, a surge of violence rushing through me at the thought of him kissing her. His lips graze her cheek instead of her lips, but that does nothing to settle my instant anger.

He nods at me before turning his attention to Kim. "I can't believe the three of us are back here, together. When was the last time Amara and I were here? It must've been three years ago." He chuckles and glances at Amara. "Yeah... I vividly remember the last time we were here," he adds, his tone suggestive. Amara's eyes widen, and my heart twists painfully. I might have her turned on right now, but he knows her body in ways I don't. He's had her in ways I'll never have her.

"Ugh, don't remind me. It was so obvious I walked in on you guys," Kim says, shaking her head. She turns to look at me. "Those two... they're rabbits, I tell you. If they end up going missing today, don't go looking for them. You'll never be able to unsee what you walk in on."

I force a smile onto my face, pushing down the pain and jealousy. Amara... she isn't mine. She never will be. These feelings, they're fucked up.

"Maybe we should reenact that, honey. Scar Kim a little further." Gregory laughs, and Amara grits her teeth as though she's biting back her response, her cheeks bright red.

What the fuck am I doing with her? What am I doing? She's my patient *and* she's Harold Astor's granddaughter.

A man like Gregory... that's who she'll end up with. An oil magnate. Someone filthy rich, someone who understands her world. Someone that can maintain the lifestyle she's used to. Before today I'd never even been to a vineyard. Stuff like this isn't part of my life and it probably never will be. She might find me interesting now, but the novelty will wear off, and she'll move on. Meanwhile, I'll have thrown every opportunity away for her, and I'll be left with nothing but regrets and memories.

"Excuse me for a minute," I tell Kim, rising to my feet. I force myself to keep my feelings in check, but I'm failing. My thoughts are spiraling as I make my way to the bathrooms we passed earlier. What the fuck am I even doing?

"Noah."

I pause at the sound of her voice and turn toward her. Amara is standing next to one of the trees, and I walk over to her, anger coursing through my veins. She takes a step back, until she's pressed against the tree behind her.

"Rabbits, huh?" I say through gritted teeth, my hand wrapping around the back of her neck, my thumb resting against her throat.

"He never should have said that. He's purposely being a dick," she tells me, her gaze pleading.

"He knows your body in ways I never will. Your pussy is dripping wet for me, yet I don't know how it feels wrapped around my cock. He does. Tell me, is it his name you used to moan? Did you come for him the way you do for me?"

She shakes her head, her eyes blazing with desperation and sincerity. "Never, Noah. Not once. I swear. I've never come for him the way I do for you. It's why I create the toys. No man has ever made me..."

I stare at her and pull my hand up until my thumb traces over her lips. That pretty little mouth of hers falls open, her tongue darting out to wet her lips.

"Has he ever had your mouth?"

She shakes her head, her eyes wide. "The thought never appealed to me. Not with him."

I pull her around the tree so we're both out of view. "Get on your knees," I tell her, leaning back against the tree.

Amara's cheeks turn crimson as she does as I say, pulling her white dress up before kneeling in front of me. Her eyes drop to my trousers and I bite back a moan when she unbuckles my belt. I want her so fucking badly.

I slide my hand into my pocket to grab the remote just seconds before she pulls my jeans down, taking my boxer shorts right along with it. Her movements are impatient, and I can't help but chuckle.

"Look at you, princess. Fucking look at you, on your knees in the middle of a vineyard, and there's nowhere else you'd rather be, huh?"

Amara smiles at me as she grabs my cock, her grip tight. My eyes fall closed at her touch. "Fuck," I groan.

Amara chuckles, and when I glance down, I find her looking at me. Her eyes never leave mine as she brings her lips closer, taking her time, teasing me.

I smirk as I increase the vibrations of her toy, enjoying the way her expression changes instantly. "None of this bullshit, Amara," I warn her. "Suck my cock like the good girl you are."

Her lips close around me and I moan, unable to keep quiet. Her mouth is so fucking hot and tight. I watch her as she takes me in deeper and I bury a hand in her hair, fisting it tightly as her head moves up and down.

"I'll make you come while you're choking on my cock," I tell her, pulling her head closer, until I hit the back of her throat. I expected her to choke, but she takes it eagerly. I almost fucking come when she swallows, the sensation foreign on my cock.

I fiddle with the remote control she gave me, barely able to focus when she sucks me off this good. She moans when I increase the pressure on her clit, and the vibrations of her voice take me right to the edge.

I grab her head and hold her still as I thrust in and out of her mouth, quickening the pace. "Look at you, baby. Look at you taking my cock. You're such a good fucking girl, aren't you?"

She moans, her eyes glazed over with lust. The way she tangles her tongue around my cock, keeping me under her control even when I try to take it away from her... fucking unreal.

Her moans get louder, and I barely hold on as her eyes fall closed, her body swaying as her orgasm rushes through her. I pull out of her mouth just in time, making a mess of her face and dress.

Amara lifts her hand to her face, her fingers tracing over the liquid staining her skin. She rises to her feet with a smile on her face. I reach for her, pulling her dress up and using the edges to clean her up with.

"You're going to walk around like that, baby, with your clothes stained, reminding you of who the fuck you belong to."

She nods, and I lean in, pulling her toward me roughly. I kiss her, pouring every trace of lingering anger into it. She's breathless by the time I pull away, and I smile. "Your mouth is mine, princess." I reach down and pull her dress up, my hand finding its way between her legs. I push her toy in deeper, wishing I could replace it with my fingers. "This pussy is too, you hear me?"

"Yes, Noah," she says, her eyes still filled with desire. "But you'd better remember it too. Don't even dream of flirting with Kim if you want any more of this."

I smile at her, loving this side of her. I had her on her knees just a few minutes ago, and she's already putting me back in my place. This girl... I don't think I'll ever get enough of her.

Chapter Twenty-Two

AMARA

I'm trembling as Noah leads me back to the clearing, desperate for him. The toy isn't enough. I want him deep inside me. I want him close, his body on mine. I've never wanted anyone the way I want him, and he doesn't even seem to realize it. He has nothing to worry about with Gregory. Nothing at all. I wish I could make him see that.

Kim looks up at me when she spots us, her gaze questioning. I can't help but smirk, and the jealousy I see in her eyes gives me a strange sense of satisfaction. It's odd, because the feeling is at war with the guilt I simultaneously feel. I've never been possessive, but it's different with Noah. I'll take any opportunity I can get to make it clear he's off-limits to her, even when I know better. It's irrational, and it's crazy, but I can't help it.

My entire body feels sensitive as I sit down next to Gregory. Noah made me come so hard that I can barely even take the subtle vibrations he kept on. The way he held my head as he thrust into my mouth, the anger in his eyes, the danger he radiated. I want more of it. I'm so tempted to provoke him further, to make him lose control again. I want more of the man he keeps hidden from the world.

"Where were you?"

I turn to Gregory and sigh. "Got lost," I lie. "The bathrooms weren't where they were years ago, and this place is a maze."

He glances at Noah and then back at me, and I smile sweetly. I might want to mess with Noah, but never at the expense of his future. I don't trust Gregory, and there's no way I'm putting Noah at risk.

"Yeah, it is a bit of a maze, isn't it?"

I nod and lean back as he wraps his arm around the back of my chair. My eyes meet Noah's and the look in his eyes has me clenching my thighs. He looks angry, seeing me sitting here with Greg, and Noah angry is a sight to behold. I glance down and grab my phone to send him a text.

Amara: *you're sexy when you're jealous. I'm tempted to provoke you further.*

Noah blinks in surprise when his phone buzzes, and the edges of his lips turn up into a reluctant smile when he sees my message.

Noah: *baby, I strongly advise against that. I'm a doctor. I can think of at least twelve ways to permanently injure your little boyfriend and make it look like an accident.*

I smile as I put my phone away, even more turned on than I was before. I'm used to powerful men, but Noah is different. I doubt his threats are empty, yet he doesn't scare me in the slightest. On the contrary, he makes me feel safer than anyone else ever has.

"So, you're a doctor, aren't you? You work for the Astors?" Greg says, an irritatingly smug smile on his face.

Noah nods and smiles back, holding his gaze. It's subtle, but I notice the way Greg tenses. Noah puts him on edge, and it isn't just because of me. "I do," he says simply.

Greg clenches his jaw, clearly irritated that he didn't get more of a response from Noah.

"How nice of the Astors to treat you so well. I'm not surprised, though. They're prone to taking on charity cases."

I've never thought highly of Greg, and I only ever dated him because my grandfather pushed us together. It seems like the small amount of respect I had for him was misplaced, though. My opinion of him is sinking by the second.

Noah smiles relaxedly. "Indeed. It's incredibly nice of them. What about you? What do you do?"

Greg relaxes, thinking he's got the upper hand, but he's wrong. He's missing the angry glint hidden in Noah's eyes, the clenched jaw despite his smile.

"I'm the COO of Zilium Oil," he says proudly. "It's one of the largest oil companies in the country."

Noah nods and smiles. "How nice that your daddy gave you a job. Being charitable must be a rich people trait." He says it so calmly and with such seriousness that it takes Greg a few seconds to realize what he said, and I bite back a smile.

I can see Greg struggling to come up with a retort and failing. No one has ever been rude to his face, and seeing his incredulous expression is priceless.

Noah takes a leisurely sip of his wine, dismissing Greg without a second thought, and my heart swells with pride. I've been worried about this trip, about Noah feeling out of his depth, but he's handling himself just fine. I should've known he would.

Kim leans into him under the guise of asking about the wine, her chest grazing against Noah's arm, and all my amusement drains away. Noah looks up, his eyes meeting mine, and something in his expression puts me at ease.

"He's going to pay for that," Greg murmurs, leaning into me. I tear my eyes away from Noah to look at Greg and shake my head.

"No. He won't. My grandfather adores him, and so does my mother. Grandpa is grooming him to take over an entire division of Astor Inc. If anything, Grandpa would just love him more for the way he carries himself."

I jump when the vibrations of my toy increase suddenly and glance at Noah, but he's looking at Kim, a serious expression on his face as he listens to her talk about the way her wine is made. I smile as I turn back to Greg. So Noah doesn't like me speaking to him, huh?

I love seeing him jealous. I know Noah isn't mine, but when he acts this way it feels like he is. It feels like he cares, like this is more than just lust.

"He's still nothing but a little worker bee. Keep that in mind, Amara. Your grandfather might want to use him for his potential, but that doesn't make him one of us. He'll never be one of us. I see the way you keep looking at him. Play with the help all you want, but a man like him can't provide for you. A man like *me* can."

I'm speechless for just a moment, and then I burst out laughing. "Greg," I say, my voice soft. "I don't need a man to provide for me. I need someone that respects me, that'll put me first. Someone that can make me laugh with him — not *at* him. I need someone that understands me and that supports my dreams and ambitions. Someone that will grow with me. A man like *you* will never be what I want."

He grits his teeth, a humorless smile on his face. "I might not be what you want right now, but you'll want me, Amara. You'll need me, and you'll come begging for another chance."

I smile at him, thoroughly amused. "You're insane. I've bitten my tongue for weeks now, purely out of respect for the relationship your father has with my grandfather. Don't push me, Gregory. You won't like the consequences."

Greg crosses his arms over each other and stares me down. "You might be an Astor, but you're nothing without your grandfather. You'll learn your place eventually. I can be patient, Amara. For you, I will be."

"This is exactly why you'll never have me. The type of man that I'd choose to be with would help me stand on my own two feet, instead of counting on my reliance on him. You don't get it,

Greg, and you never will. Because of that, you'll never have me. You never did."

I rise to my feet, needing a bit of space. "I think I've had a bit too much sun," I murmur.

Noah looks up at me and nods as he gets up. "I'll drive you home. I'm fully booked tomorrow, so I need to get back anyway."

I nod and thank Kim in a rush, walking away before Greg can insist that he drive me back himself. I can't stand to be in his presence for another second.

I hear Noah rush after me, and I exhale in relief when he falls into step at my side. "What did he say?" he asks, his tone tense.

I glance up at him, wondering what to say. I decide on the truth. "That I'll end up back with him. That he'll wait for me while I'm 'messing around with the help' or something like that."

Noah grimaces as he opens the car door for me, and I can't help but wonder if I should've just kept that conversation to myself. He seems tired as he gets behind the wheel, or maybe that isn't even the right word. He's weary.

"Is that what you're doing?" he asks, keeping his eyes on the road as we drive out of the massive estate.

"No. God no. Of course not," I say, the words tumbling out of my mouth in a rush.

Noah glances at me briefly and sighs. "He's not wrong. With me you'd never have the life you live right now. Even if we both worked our asses off, I doubt we'd ever be this rich." He runs a hand through his hair and shakes his head. "What am I even saying? *We*? There is no we."

I stare at him, my heart twisting painfully. "I... Noah, I don't need any of this. I grew up without it, and I can do without it."

He looks at me and shakes his head. "Your grandfather is offering me the opportunity of a lifetime, Amara. What you and I are doing... it's stupid. I admit that I want you. I want you more than I've ever wanted anyone else, but you and I can't happen. We're already taking it too far, and you know it."

I nod and stare out the window. "I know, Noah. I can't help

it. I can't stay away. I've never felt this way before. I know what's at risk. Trust me, I know. Despite that, I just can't help myself."

He tightens his grip on the wheel and nods. "Me too, baby," he murmurs. "But we need to stop before this gets out of hand. Today... the way I touched you. Fuck. Do you know what your grandfather would do to me if he ever found out? We have to stop."

I bite down on my lip and look down at my lap. I'd single-handedly destroy Noah's future if we keep doing this. "I know," I whisper, wishing there was another way and knowing that there isn't.

Chapter Twenty-Three

AMARA

"You've been quiet and absentminded all week. What's wrong, babe?" Leia asks.

I hesitate before answering her. "Noah has been avoiding me since that day at the vineyard. I've been to his clinic twice, and both times he wasn't there. Or so I've been told. He's not answering my text messages either."

Leia sighs and lies down on her bed, next to me. "Babe, what are you even doing? He told you that you two can't be together. He literally told you that your psycho grandfather holds his future in his hands. What are you doing?"

I grab her pink teddy bear and wrap my arms around it, feeling torn. "I don't know, Leia... I just really like him. I've never felt anything like this before. I swear I'm not playing any games, it's not a thrill or whatever you think it is. It's not that at all. I just... when I'm with him I'm happy, and I think he feels the same way."

She looks into my eyes and nods. "Yeah, I've never seen you this crazy about anyone. Is it worth it, though?"

"I don't know," I tell her honestly. "Grandpa seems to be grooming him to take on quite a sizable portion of my family's portfolio, so he clearly values Noah."

Leia stares me down and purses her lips. "But does he value Noah enough to let you be with him? From what you told me, it doesn't sound like your grandfather will let you walk down the same road that your mother chose. Noah might be a doctor, and he might be wonderful, but compared to your family, he's still just a normal man. He still has student debt and probably lives paycheck to paycheck."

"What's wrong with that?" I ask defensively. Noah is a *doctor*. Sure, it's still early in his career, but it's an honorable profession. He's nothing like my father, who won't stop texting me. His weekly messages just add to my distress. I haven't told Leia about him, and it feels strange to keep something from her. But this... this I can't tell her. It would change the way she looks at me, and I can't bear the thought of that happening. I spent years building a life I could be proud of. I won't let Dad take that from me all over again.

"Nothing," Leia says carefully. "There's nothing wrong with it, but his life and yours differ too much. He has a promising future, for sure... but it hinges on him not getting involved with you. I don't doubt that your grandfather will ruin him if you two get together. Is that a risk worth taking?"

"No," I whisper. I'm being selfish, and I know it. There's definitely something between us, something stronger than anything I've ever felt before... but that's all it is. We aren't in a relationship, and Noah has made it clear he doesn't intend to pursue me. I can't expect it from him either. I can't stand up to my grandfather myself, so how could I ask him to?

Leia wraps her arm around me, and I drop my head to her shoulder, feeling defeated. "I just can't take it, Leia. The way Noah looked when Gregory so blatantly reminded him of our history, and then the look on his face when I told him about what

Greg told me... I don't know. He looked so hurt, and I just want to speak to him. I just want to reassure him."

Leia sighs and shakes her head. "I get it, babe. I do. But maybe this is for the best, you know?"

"Yeah, maybe," I murmur. I wish this was easier. The feelings I've got for him are getting stronger every day, and it's becoming hard to fight this thing between us. I fell for him just a little when he caught me in the rain, then even further during the ball. Every interaction with him since then has just cemented those feelings. I know letting go is what's best for him, but it's hard. This doesn't feel like a simple crush. It's not just infatuation.

"Talking about elusive men, have you tracked down the one-night-stand you were so obsessed with?" I ask, changing the topic.

The way she smiles cheers me up instantly. The way I feel about Noah... that's how Leia feels about this mystery man.

"No, but I will. God, Amara. He was so delicious. I won't rest until I have him between my legs again. That man knows how to fuck. Ugh, and that cock. I need more of it."

I burst out laughing and shake my head. "Did you go back to the bar you met him at?"

She nods. "Every night for a month straight. He wasn't there. I'm not surprised, to be honest. His accent was unfamiliar. He sounded a little British? It wasn't a strong accent, but it was there. I doubt he's from around here."

"That bastard," I mutter. "I can't believe he ghosted you."

Leia frowns and throws her arm over her face. "It's worse than that, though. He actually gave me the wrong number. I'm not trying to be cliche or any of that. You *know* I'm not like that. But this was just different. It might have only been one night, but the connection we had was insane."

I nod in understanding. "Yeah, I get that." I might never have slept with Noah, but the way he makes me feel... I've never felt anything like it before.

"I don't even know what it was about that night. I guess it was just the way he managed to cheer me up when I was convinced that forcing even one more smile that day would shatter my heart. He made me smile until it hurt for all the right reasons, and then he took me to watch the stars, reminding me of how beautiful life can be. We just talked, you know? I don't think either of us even really expected it to turn into more, but when it did... wow."

She wraps her arms around herself and sighs. "I guess that's why it hurts so much that he gave me the wrong phone number. It's because I thought he felt that same connection, and I guess he didn't. It was just sex to him."

I open my arms and Leia rolls toward me, until I've got her wrapped in my embrace. She inhales shakily, as though she's keeping in her tears, and I rub her back gently. "Fuck both of them," I whisper.

Chapter Twenty-Four

NOAH

"Well done, son," Mr. Astor says. I smile at him, a sense of pride washing over me. He's been working me to the bone all week. I've barely had time to sleep between work, the endless dinners and lunches he asks me to attend, and the site visits we've been doing together.

I didn't expect him to be so involved in his new acquisitions, but he's personally reviewed every single aspect of the three clinics we bought.

"I got the hang of it after the first two," I tell him. He's been teaching me what to look out for in acquisitions, how to negotiate, and how to put together a growth plan to turn businesses around and make them more profitable, which is ultimately what he wants for his portfolio.

"You won't need me to accompany you anymore soon. I'll leave you in charge of growing the business. I'd like to own another seven clinics in three months' time. There'll be a lot to learn."

I nod, oddly nervous. He offered me a performance-based contract, meaning I get a cut of the profits of each of his clinics. The more profitable I can make them, the more I'll earn.

"Working at the college clinic helps," I tell him honestly. "Seeing how that's run, being there to make operational changes and seeing how they impact the clinic... that type of hands-on experience is invaluable."

He grins as he opens his car door, and I rush to get to the passenger door. He's always been friendly, but I'm not crazy enough to get too comfortable with him. "I knew I was right to put my faith in you, Noah."

I smile back at him in gratitude. "This opportunity you're giving me, I'm beyond grateful for it, Mr. Astor."

He shakes his head as he puts the car into gear. "You needn't be, Noah. And call me Harold, please. We're hardly strangers, are we?"

I nod, feeling a little out of place. My life has changed so much in the span of a few months. The trajectory I'm on isn't one I could've ever gotten to by myself. No matter how hard I work, by myself this would never be achievable.

"It's late. How about dinner at my place? You'd probably eat alone otherwise, wouldn't you? Besides, my daughter has been asking about you. She's convinced that I'm overworking you. I think it'd be good for her to see you."

My first instinct is to decline. Dinner at his house means facing Amara. She and I haven't spoken since that day at the vineyard. I haven't seen her at all, but that hasn't kept her off my mind. I'm trying to distance myself from her, but it seems like an impossible task.

Everything reminds me of her. She's so deeply entrenched in my life. I can't go to work without thinking of her in my office, I can't go to the gym without thinking of the time I caught her crying in the rain, and then there's her grandfather... she's everywhere.

I'm absentminded by the time we get to the Astor mansion. I'm not ready to see her. I've only just about managed to convince myself to stay away, but I'm weak. One look at her and my resolve will crumble. I won't be able to remind myself that I can never provide her with the life she has now. And if I give in, I'll lose my only chance at an extraordinary future.

"You all right, son?"

I nod and force a smile onto my face as we walk toward the dining room. If Mr. Astor notices, he doesn't say anything.

A pang of disappointment hits me right in the chest when I walk into the room to find that Amara isn't there. It's just her mother.

"Charlotte," I say, greeting her. She rises from her seat and hugs me, startling me.

"How are you, sweetheart?" she asks, pulling out a seat for me the way my mother used to do. I stare at her in surprise, my heart twisting painfully. I've done a very good job at pushing down the pain that haunted me for so long, but every once in a while, something happens that reopens the wounds.

Charlotte smiles at me, but there's a hint of worry in her eyes. I grit my teeth as I sit down. I'm trying, but I can't recall what my mother's laughter sounds like. The memories are fading, and it's killing me.

"What's wrong?" Charlotte asks, her tone higher than usual, a hint of panic in it.

I shake my head and force a smile onto my face. "It's nothing. I'm sorry. For a moment, you reminded me of my mother."

Her eyes widen, and she looks away in understanding. I know the Astors looked into me, into my background, so she knows how my parents were killed. I'm not after sympathy, though. It's taken my sister and me years to heal as much of our battered hearts as we could, and I don't want to take a step back.

"Excuse me for a minute," I tell her, needing a moment to compose myself. As the years pass, it becomes easier to hang onto the good memories and to let go of the pain, but tonight I'm struggling. Maybe it's the loneliness I've been feeling, maybe it's the way both Charlotte and Harold have welcomed me into their family, each of them in their own way. Maybe it's a combination of it all. Either way, the pain is hitting me hard tonight.

I look up in confusion when I realize where I am. I walked into Amara's bedroom without thinking. It shouldn't surprise me. This is, after all, where she took me last time. Besides, if I'm truly honest with myself, I'm longing for her tonight. I want her snark, her smiles.

I sit down on her bed and smile to myself. I can just imagine her lying here, testing out her toys. I wonder if she ever thinks of me.

My fingers trail over her pillow and my eyes fall closed. I wish I could have her in my arms tonight. Falling asleep with her, what would that be like?

I tense when her bedroom door opens. Amara gasps, her initial shock quickly making way for confusion.

"Noah," she murmurs, and the way she says my name tugs at my broken heart. I drink her in, my eyes roaming over her body. She looks beautiful tonight. "What are you doing here?"

I rise from her bed and cross the room, pausing right in front of her. "Your grandfather invited me over for dinner."

She looks into my eyes, and the look in her eyes soothes my soul. "That doesn't explain why you're in my bedroom."

My eyes drop to her lips, and I grit my teeth when I notice the edges of her lipstick are smudged. I cup her face and brush my thumb over the barely visible stains. She tenses underneath my touch, her eyes widening.

"Where were you tonight?" I ask, unable to keep the question buried.

She blinks and looks away, as though she can't face me. I laugh humorlessly and let go of her, taking a step away. I've been fucked up over her, and all the while I thought she felt the same way. I guess I was wrong.

"I apologize for intruding," I tell her, pasting on my physician-face.

I move to walk past her, but before I can, she grabs my hand. "Noah," she whispers, and I stop in my tracks.

Chapter Twenty-Five

AMARA

"Noah," I whisper, my hand wrapped around his. Something is wrong. I can feel it right down to my bones. That look in his eyes... he's hurting. "What happened?"

He stares at me, but it's like he sees straight through me. Noah shakes his head, a polite smile on his face.

"Leia," I tell him. "I've been with Leia all evening. That's where I've been every single evening for the last week. We've been watching movies and drinking far too much wine. Too much pizza too, come to think of it."

His shoulders sag in relief, and though he tries to hide it, it's clear some of his worries are put to rest.

"But where have *you* been, Noah? You haven't been replying to any of my text messages, and every time I went to your office, I was told you weren't there."

My tone is sharp, the accusation clear. Noah takes a step closer to me, and I take a step away, my back hitting the door. The way we're standing here together... this is exactly how we were just a few weeks ago, when he lifted me into his arms.

"I've been trying to stay away from you, Amara. The more your grandfather mentors me, the more I stand to lose by getting involved with you."

I gulp and nod. "I know," I whisper. I do know that, but I selfishly still want him to take the risk. I want him for myself. "But my grandfather isn't keeping you from being friends with me, is he?"

"Friends? You want to be friends?" He laughs humorlessly and cups my cheek. "Do you ask all your friends to help you test sex toys? What do you even need me for when you have Gregory? He was right, you know? Eventually you'll end up with a guy just like him."

"Noah, the things he said... I'm sorry. I think he somehow feels threatened by you."

He grits his teeth and closes the distance between us, his body pressing against mine. "I can't stop thinking about what he said. Tell me... did you fuck him in that vineyard, Amara?"

I look away, unable to answer him. "It was years ago, Noah. He and I are over."

He slides his hand down and turns my face back to his. "Sure as fuck doesn't seem like it's over. He was here for dinner with you, and he was your date at the vineyard. Your family seems to believe you're still dating him, and he clearly still wants you. What kind of fucking game are you playing, huh? I don't know what's going through your mind, but I'm not playing along."

I look up at him, my eyes blazing. "I'm not playing any games, Noah."

"No? Aren't you?" He asks, his hand sliding down to cup the back of my neck. "Asking me to test toys with you, crashing the date your grandfather set up for me, ensuring that at all times you're the only one I can think of. You do that, knowing that I can never have you. This is all fun and games for you, isn't it? A bit of excitement, toying with one of your grandfather's employees. You do it, knowing that when you're ready, you'll be able to move on with a guy just like Gregory. Someone that can give you the world, someone that can give you the life you're accustomed to and that can support your dreams. That person will never be me, and you know it. This might all seem like a bit of fun to you, but it's my future you're playing with."

I place my hands on his chest, palms flat against him. I can't tell whether I want to push him away or slide my hands up so I can hug him. "Aren't you? Aren't you the person that's supporting my dreams? My own grandfather is blocking every avenue available to me, and it's you, Noah. It's you that's making my dreams happen. You. No one else." I inhale shakily, wishing he could see what I see when I look at him. "The only truth to everything you just said is that getting involved with me means risking your future, and I'd never ask that of you, Noah. I know how powerful my grandfather is — I know it better than anyone else. With his support, you'll go further than you can even dream of, and I'd never ask you to risk that."

I look into his eyes, my hands sliding up his chest the way I've been wanting to. He tenses as I wrap my arms around his neck. "But don't do this, please. Don't shut me out like this. Don't punish me for my past, or for who my family is. I understand that you and I... we can't happen. I know that. But please, Noah. All I'm asking for here is your friendship. Can you give me that much? If it burdens you too much, I'll stop asking for your help with the toys. I'll stop, Noah. But please... please don't push me away like this."

Noah drops his forehead to mine, his eyes falling closed. "Don't stop," he whispers. "I can't stand the thought of you testing those damn things with anyone but me, and I meant what I said: you need medical supervision, Amara." He pulls away slightly and presses a featherlight kiss to my forehead. "We can be friends. I'm sure we can manage that."

Noah takes a step away, and it takes all of me to tear my eyes away from his. All I want to do is take a step closer and feel his lips against mine. I want his hands on my body, his hand wrapped into my hair. I want him. All of him.

"Come on," he says, running a hand through his hair. "I've been gone for far too long. Your grandfather is going to come looking for me soon, and he's not going to be happy to find me in your bedroom."

I nod and follow him to the dining room in silence. My heart feels like it's in disarray. Noah is right here with me, yet somehow I miss him. I can't pinpoint what it is about these last few days, but it's like something is standing between us now. That day at the vineyard changed things, and it wasn't for the better.

"Why are you two together?" Grandpa's voice is harsh, and the way his eyes flash with anger makes me flinch. My eyes meet Mom's, and I'm surprised to find worry in them. Both of them have supported Noah like he's family, yet they worry about me being alone with him for just a few minutes? What do they think he'll do to me? Ravish me? I wish.

"I ran into Amara in the hallway," Noah says, smiling politely, completely unfazed. Grandpa stares him down, but Noah doesn't even flinch.

I follow his lead and sit down at the dining table, ignoring the way my mother's gaze burns into me. I was hoping that the way they've been supporting Noah meant they approved of him, but that doesn't seem to be the case.

"How did your date with Kim go?" Grandpa asks Noah, smiling tightly. "You should call her and follow up. The two of you are perfect together, and I want her to be in charge of the new hospital we're planning to acquire."

I sit in silence, looking up only to thank the staff when they serve me food. Noah and I are on different paths, and if I want what's best for him, I need to make sure I don't become an obstacle.

Chapter Twenty-Six

Noah

I stare at my phone, my heart overflowing with emotions I didn't realize I was capable of. I sit down on the sofa, my eyes trailing over the family pictures surrounding me, a smile hurting my cheeks.

Grayson wants to propose to Aria. Those two... neither of them led easy lives. For a moment, when they first told me they were dating, I worried it'd lead to mutual destruction. I couldn't be more happy that they proved me wrong.

Aria getting married... the thought of it fills me with happiness and loneliness all at once. I didn't think either Aria or I would ever get married. Both of us are too broken, too haunted. Yet here she is, making me proud. She couldn't have found a more perfect person to be her husband.

I stare at the phone in my hands, a different sense of loneliness washing over me. This is the best news I've received in years, and there's no one to share it with. For years, all I focused on was my education and Aria's upbringing. It left me with little to no time to make friends or socialize. I didn't notice how lonely I was when

Aria still lived at home, but now that she's gone, it's hitting me hard. Gray proposing means she won't come back.

I look around the house, seeing it through different eyes. It suddenly feels too big, too quiet. I'm so used to being alone and battling demons, presenting the world with the person my parents would want me to be while I suffer in silence... but tonight I don't want to.

I tighten my grip on my phone, hesitating for a brief moment as I scroll through my contacts, pausing on Amara's name. The darkness within me isn't something I've ever wanted to subject someone to. Not until now. Not until Amara. Amara changed everything the second she walked into my office with those flushed cheeks of hers, her blue eyes sparkling.

Since she walked into my life, the loneliness has become too much to bear. I long for her with a desperation that's foreign to me. I bite down on my lip as I fight the urge to call her. It's a losing battle.

She picks up almost instantly, startling me. "Hey," I say, my voice soft.

"Hi," she replies. "I'm surprised you called."

I sigh and run a hand through my hair. I've tried to stay away from her, but I barely lasted two weeks. "I just got some great news, and you were the first person I wanted to share it with," I murmur, realizing that it's true. She flashed through my mind the second Grayson hung up the phone.

"Oh, what happened?" she asks, her tone lighter.

I smile to myself as I lean back on the sofa. "Grayson wants to propose to my sister. He asked for my help to set everything up."

"Oh my gosh!" she says, genuinely sounding excited, and my smile broadens. This is what I love about her most. Her heart. She doesn't even know Aria or Gray, but she's genuinely happy for them.

"My sister and I have this tradition of sorts," I murmur. "She bakes me a themed birthday cake every year, and I thought it'd be nice if I made her an engagement cake. What do you think?"

"That would be amazing, Noah. Oh! You could make it in the shape of an engagement ring! How nice would that be?"

I chuckle and shake my head. "I think that might be beyond me. I was going for something edible."

Amara sighs, and my eyes fall closed. I miss her. These two weeks without her have been horrible. "I'll help you. I love baking," she says hesitantly.

"Would you really? Gray told me they're flying in tomorrow, so I wanted to make the cake today. Do you... do you think you could come over to help me?"

I half expect her to say no. She hasn't texted me since I saw her at her house, and I don't blame her. She and I... we're impossible.

"Yes, text me the address. I'll be there in twenty minutes."

"You're the best," I tell her, a mix of giddiness and nerves washing over me. I'm excited to see her. It's only been two weeks, but it feels like a lifetime.

I'm restless as I text her the address, looking around the house to check if there's anything I need to tidy up. I frown when I realize that I barely even use the house. All I do is eat and sleep. I don't even remember the last time I watched TV.

The doorbell rings, snapping me out of my thoughts. I'm oddly nervous as I open the door, but my every thought melts away when my eyes land on her. She's beautiful. She always looks stunning, but she looks especially breathtaking in the black dress she's wearing tonight.

"Hey," she says, and that smile... it makes my heart skip a beat. Amara's eyes roam over my body and I take a step back, swallowing hard.

"Hey," I murmur.

She walks into the house, and her floral scent lingers as she walks past me. Amara pauses in the hallway, her eyes drifting over the family photos. "Wow," she says, tracing the edge of one of the photos with her fingertips. "You look just like your dad. I'd love to meet him one day. And that must be your sister? She looks just like your mom."

I look up at the photo of the four of us and swallow hard. "Yeah, that's my sister," I say, my voice soft.

Amara turns to look at me, her brows raised. "What's wrong?" she asks, her confusion obvious. So she doesn't know, huh? I assumed she knew about my past, like her mother and grandfather do.

"It's nothing, sweetheart. Come on, I'll show you around."

Amara holds up a grocery bag and grins. "I brought supplies. Show me where to put them."

I nod and lead her to the kitchen, suddenly feeling self-conscious. My house is nice enough, but it's nothing like hers. It's tiny in comparison, and most of our things Aria found at garage sales. I can't help but wonder if she's comparing me to Gregory. I can't even imagine what type of place that guy must live in, and I know I don't measure up. Today it's more clear than usual that she and I are from very different worlds, and it doesn't sit well with me.

"You're quiet," Amara says as we walk into the kitchen. "Aren't you excited about the proposal?"

I turn to look at her, taking in her blue eyes and her red hair, the freckles on her nose that are only ever visible when she isn't wearing makeup. She's beautiful. Everything about her is beautiful, right down to her soul. She deserves the best the world has to offer, and I'm not it.

"I'm excited, and a little sad too. I always expected Aria to come back home, you know? And now she won't. I miss her. She's the only family member I've got left, and I guess I'm feeling a little lonely. I'm happy for her, though. She deserves this."

Amara's eyes widen in shock. "I'm so sorry, Noah. I see... that's why you looked so sad when I asked about your parents in the hallway. I didn't realize."

I lean in and brush her hair out of her face, my fingers lingering longer than they should. "I don't talk about my parents, so there's no way you could've known. They passed away when I was quite young," I tell her as I unpack the groceries she brought.

I frown at one of the tiny bottles she brought. "What's this for?" I ask, wanting to change the subject. I hate talking about my parents, because it always leads to pity, and I don't want it from Amara.

She stares at me and bites down on her lip, hesitating before she forces a smile onto her face. "Noah, that's vanilla. Are you kidding me? How were you going to bake a cake without it?"

I smile sheepishly. "I was just going to google it and hope for the best."

Amara looks outraged, and I can't help but chuckle. She leans in and snatches the bottle from me. "Okay," she says, shaking her head, "you clearly cannot be trusted with this."

She bumps her hip against mine, and I move aside to give her more space at the kitchen counter. She smiles at me and I sigh. I want this. I want this with her. I want to stand in the kitchen with her, doing the most mundane tasks. I want her in my house, in my space. Fucking hell. I can see Amara being my wife.

Chapter Twenty-Seven

Amara

My hands tremble as I grab the measuring cup and fill it with flour. I'm nervous, being this close to Noah. Things have been strange between us, and I can't quite figure out where we stand. He and I being friends... I can't see it happening. The chemistry between us is impossible to ignore.

Noah moves behind me, placing his hands on either side of me as he leans over me, his chin on top of my shoulder. He watches my every move with such intensity you'd think I'm creating art instead of baking a simple cake.

"I thought we agreed to be friends," I whisper, unable to help myself.

Noah tenses and moves away, turning around to lean against the counter, facing me. "You're right. I'm sorry."

I look away, unable to hold his gaze. His expression is filled with the same heartache I'm feeling, and I hate feeling this helpless. I hate knowing that being with me could destroy his future. This thing between us... how could something that feels so good be so destructive?

"I forgot to tell you this because of the news about the proposal, but Gray also mentioned that his project wrapped up, and he's available to meet with you now. We could go as early as next week if you want to."

I gasp, almost dropping the cup of milk in my hands. "No way!"

Noah smiles, and the look in his eyes has my heart skipping a beat. It's a knowing, intimate look. "Yeah," he says. "You're going to do amazing. I just know he's going to be so impressed."

"You really think so?"

He nods, and there isn't a doubt in his eyes. He truly believes in me, more so than anyone else ever has, my own family included.

"Thank you," I whisper. "I really wish I could kiss you right now."

Noah's eyes drop to my lips and for a second I think he's going to lean in and kiss me, but then he looks away and grabs the milk. "I'd better actually help with this cake," he mutters.

He throws the milk in the blender and turns it on before I can stop him. "Noah, no!" I yell, just as the mixture goes flying everywhere, soaking us both before I manage to turn it off.

He looks perplexed, flour all over his face and hair as he turns to look at me and finds me just as messy. The horror on his face has a giggle rising up my throat, and I burst out laughing.

"Oh shit," Noah says, frantically looking around the kitchen. He grabs a towel and presses it to my face, trying his best to clean off the stickiness and failing. "Why would it do that? Why would it just fucking explode?"

I giggle and wipe away a layer of flour from his forehead. "You're supposed to put the lid on, genius."

He hangs his head, and I grin to myself. He's so incredibly cute. "It's okay, Noah," I tell him. "It'll wash off."

He nods and tips his head toward the staircase. "Let me show you to the bathroom," he says, his cheeks pink. Dr. Grant, embarrassed. I never thought I'd see the day.

I'm quiet as I follow him up, my heart beating loudly. It's

131

hard to even explain the distance between us. It's like we only just met, when we've known each other for months.

"Here you go," Noah says, holding the door to the bathroom open for me. I smile awkwardly as I walk in, leaning back against the door the second it falls closed. I raise a hand to my chest, willing my heart to stop racing.

I take a steadying breath as I undress, feeling oddly vulnerable. There's something about being naked in Noah's house, knowing he isn't far away. My hands tremble as I step into the shower, letting the water wet my hair. I smile to myself as chunks of sticky flour fall down and lean back against the wall. I've never seen him so flustered. For a while, I wondered if I meant anything to him at all. If, perhaps, he was just playing games with me. Now I know better. There's nothing I can do with that information, and it doesn't make our situation even remotely better, but it puts me at ease nonetheless.

I inhale deeply as I shampoo my hair, enjoying how much everything smells like Noah. By the time I step out of the shower, I'm grinning to myself, feeling happier than I have in weeks. I grab the clean towel Noah got me and dry off before wrapping it around me, suddenly feeling self-conscious. My clothes are soaked and filthy, and I forgot to ask Noah for a change of clothes.

I clutch my towel tightly as I walk out, finding Noah standing outside the door, leaning back against the wall. His eyes widen when he sees me, and the way his gaze travels up and down my body has my cheeks heating. He's in gray sweats with a white tee, and this casual look is even hotter on him than his doctor's coat.

Noah clears his throat awkwardly and holds out a t-shirt for me. "I got you this," he murmurs. "But you can look through my sister's clothes if you want. She wouldn't mind."

I shake my head and grab the t-shirt before rushing back into the bathroom, my heart running wild. What's wrong with me? I've walked into his office with a sex toy stuck inside me, but *now* I'm nervous?

I swallow hard as Noah's t-shirt falls over my body, covering up most of me. It doesn't hide my nipples, though. Those are still clearly visible through his t-shirt, and it's making me even more nervous.

I hesitate before walking out of the bathroom, feeling naked despite the t-shirt that covers my body. Noah clenches his jaw and looks away, but his gaze travels back to my body every few seconds. I can't help but smile when I realize how hard he is. Those gray sweats don't help him hide his erection in the slightest.

"Let me wash your clothes," he says, holding out his hands. I hand him my clothes and he rushes off with them, disappearing around the corner. A soft chuckle escapes my lips as I make my way back down. We're both nervous around each other. It's weird, but it also makes me giddy. I haven't felt this way since I was a teenager.

By the time Noah comes back down, I've got the cake base in the oven, safely out of his reach.

"Oh no," he says, his expression crestfallen. "I wanted to help with that."

I smile at him and nod. "You can help decorate it later. It'll be done in an hour."

He nods and tips his head toward the living room. I follow him quietly, feeling out of place. I feel like I'm intruding by being in his home.

Noah hands me the remote as he sits down on the sofa, patting the seat next to his. I join him, conscious of the way my clothes ride up. I'm barely paying attention as I scroll through the different tv shows, and I end up clicking on Modern Family, one of my favorite shows.

Noah smiles in approval and leans back, his gaze fixed to the TV, almost as though he's avoiding looking at me.

"Hey," I murmur. "Will you tell me about your sister? I'm a little nervous about meeting her."

He turns to look at me, his eyes lingering on my lips. "My little sister... she's my hero," he says, a sweet smile on his face. "She practically raised herself, you know? Aria is the sweetest and most hardworking person I know. She's an actual genius. Both she and Gray are software engineers. I can barely make sense of what she's saying half the time, and the things she can do with a computer, it's insane. I'm pretty sure she's doing illegal shit half the time, and has been for years, but I've never worried about her because she's got a heart of gold, and I just know that despite her incredible skills, she'd never abuse them."

I nod, even more curious about Aria Grant. I tried googling her, but there was even less information available about her than there was about Noah.

"She's going to love you," he says, a knowing look in his eyes. "Be warned, though... I've never introduced a woman to my sister, and she's going to overreact. Even if I tell her we're just friends, she won't believe me for a second."

I grin as I try to form a picture of Aria. "I think I'm going to like her," I tell him, and he nods.

"I think so too. How do you feel about meeting Gray next week? Are you ready?"

I nod. "I think so. I'm as ready as I'll ever be."

"Good. I'll book our tickets then."

Noah hesitates and bites down on his lip, glancing at me with an expression I can't read.

"What is it?" I ask, my voice soft. The way he's looking at me has my heart racing.

"I can't get you off my mind, Amara. I'm trying to be friends with you, but all I can think about is how beautiful you look, sitting here wearing my t-shirt. I want to push you over so I can lean in and kiss you. I'm always thinking about you, and I just don't think these feelings are going to disappear." He runs a hand through his hair and sighs. "One week," he whispers. "If you feel the same way, then why don't we spend one week together while we're visiting Aria and Gray? It's probably a terrible idea and while I sincerely hope it'll help us get these feelings in check, it'll probably just fuck us over even worse. Despite that, I can't stop thinking about what it'd be like to hold your hand, to take you out on a date, to kiss you in public without worrying that your grandfather might find out."

I force myself to look away, but I can't help the way the edges of my lips turn up into a reluctant smile. "You know we shouldn't."

"I know," he whispers.

Noah turns back to look at me, his eyes filled with the same desire I'm feeling. "One week. Just you and me, far away from everything. I'm not asking for anything, but I'm tired of being here. For just one single week I want to know what it'd be like if you weren't who you are, and I'm just a guy that can love you freely. This thing between us won't go away. Let's give ourselves one week. After that... after that we'll go back to being friends."

My heart aches at his words, and I inhale shakily. "I want nothing more, Noah," I whisper, and I do. I'd rather be with him for a week than wonder what it'd be like for the rest of my life. "One week."

He nods, and when he smiles, his happiness is reflected in his eyes. I haven't seen him smile like that in such a long time, and I want more of those smiles of his. Even if it's just for one single week.

Chapter Twenty-Eight

Amara

"I'm nervous," I say, my voice shaking. I hide behind Noah, and he smiles indulgently. We've barely seen each other in the week since I helped him bake Aria's cake, and for the most part, we've managed to stay friends. This trip is bound to change things. Not just with Noah, but also with my career and my company. I'm terrified. I'm scared of messing things up with Noah, of being unable to find an investor, of Grayson disliking me. It's been an endless spiral of overthinking things.

"It's okay," he reassures me. "Aria and Gray are both super chill."

I roll my eyes as we wait for the front door to open. "Do you even realize who your best friend is? He's Grayson freaking Callahan."

Noah eyes me suspiciously. "I guess it's a good thing he's already engaged to my sister."

I laugh, and he smiles indulgently. My smile melts off my face when the door opens, a truly stunning dark-haired woman standing in front of us. Her eyes are identical to Noah's, and the similarity becomes even more clear when she smiles.

"Come in," she says, stepping back as she opens the door wider. Noah walks in, and I rush to follow him, feeling entirely out of place.

When he said we'd be visiting, I assumed we'd be staying in a hotel. I didn't realize he expected us to stay at Grayson Callahan's *house*. I'm worried the rumors about Grayson are true, and that my presence here will make him uncomfortable. Almost every article I've ever read about him says he's a recluse that barely speaks.

My heart nearly stops when Grayson walks into the hallway, a smile on his face. I've never seen him in real life, and it almost feels like I'm meeting a superstar. Which I guess he is. I've idolized the man for years.

"Hey buddy," Grayson says, nodding at Noah before turning to look at me. I stare at the floor, flustered. I'm supposed to convince him to invest in my company, but I can barely even look him in the eye.

"Aria, Gray," Noah says, "meet Amara Astor."

I look from Grayson to Aria and timidly offer Aria my hand. "It's lovely to meet you," I stammer, before turning to Grayson and shaking his hand. My palms are sweaty, and I'm both nervous and embarrassed.

"Remember when I told you about that company I thought you should invest in?" Noah tells Grayson. "She's the founder."

"Hmm," Grayson says, glancing at his watch. "I need to get to the office. Something came up. Walk with me and fill me in," he tells Noah, who nods before turning to me. It's clear the two of them want a private moment to talk.

Noah places his lower hand on my back and leans into me, his lips brushing against my ear. "I'll leave you with my sister for just an hour or so, okay? She's very sweet, I promise."

I nod and swallow hard. I've had to socialize with so many

supposedly important people, including high-ranking politicians, but this is different. I actually admire Grayson, and being here has me feeling unlike myself. I've never wanted approval as badly as I do in this moment, and on top of that, I'm scared Noah's sister won't like me.

"I was about to go cake tasting," Aria says. "How about you come with me while the boys catch up? I think I'd have much more fun with you than I would with Noah."

I look at her wide-eyed and nod. I know Noah and I aren't dating, and she'll never become my sister-in-law, but for just this one week, I want to fool myself into believing she could be, that Noah and I could end up together.

Grayson walks up to Aria and leans into her, his hand wrapping around the back of her neck as he tilts her face up for a kiss. "Be good, Nyx," he says, and my heart almost stops.

"Nyx?" I repeat, shocked. The name Nyx is notorious. No one knows who she is, just that she's a woman. Nyx has single-handedly built a vigilante platform where those let down by the justice system can present their case. There are hundreds of volunteers on the platform, and they've solved some insanely big cases. They've even saved some people from death row. I've long wondered who was behind it, and Aria being a software engineer combined with her connection to Grayson makes it obvious. It's her. I might idolize Grayson, but that pales in comparison to my admiration for Nyx.

"It's a nickname," she says, grabbing her handbag. "No one but Gray calls me that, though."

I follow her down to the garage in a daze. "You're Nyx, aren't you? *The* Nyx. It makes sense... Noah told me you're an engineer too."

She looks at me with raised brows as she gets behind the wheel of a brand-new Lamborghini. "You've heard of the Nemesis Platform?"

I smile as I buckle myself in. "Yes. Who hasn't?"

Aria grins, her eyes lighting up with excitement in the same way Noah's do. "You're an engineer too?"

I nod and try my best to explain my educational background. She listens with interest, keeping our conversation going all the way into the bakery.

"So you're almost done with your PhD?" she asks as we sit down in the quaint bakery, and I nod. Aria takes a bite of a slice of cake and pushes it toward me. I take a bite and nearly choke when she grins at me and says, "tell me, how did you meet Noah?"

She seems far more interested in me than in the cake tasting. I blush and look down, unsure what to say. Part of me wants to lie, but I know Noah and his sister are close, so there's a chance she already knows. And if she doesn't, he might tell her himself.

"Well, um... the company Noah asked Grayson Callahan to invest in... it's mine. I, um, well... I founded a company that creates sex toys. I basically use my engineering skills to create unobtrusive yet revolutionary toys."

Aria grins in amusement, and I bite down on my lip, hesitating before I continue. "I... well... I was testing a new invention," I murmur, my cheeks blazing. "It, um... it got stuck in me, so I had to go to the doctor's office to get it removed."

Aria bursts out laughing, clearly already seeing where this story is going. "Dr. Grant... *Noah*, he was startled, to say the least."

"That story was better than anything I could've imagined," Aria says, smiling. "So tell me, what do you think of my brother?"

I look at her wide-eyed, surprised by the question. "I... um, he's a great man. He's helped me countless times, and he does it without ever expecting anything in return. Noah, he's an incredible man, and I'm lucky to have met him."

Aria smiles. "You're in love with my brother, aren't you?"

I fall silent, unsure how to answer that. "Yes," I tell her honestly. "Irrevocably and helplessly. But it isn't quite that simple."

"How so?"

I force a smile onto my face and shake my head. "My grandfather... he's taken an interest in Noah. He's mentoring him and he's offered to let Noah manage the medical side of our investments, so he clearly values Noah. Despite that, he won't accept me being with him. My grandfather is set on me being with my ex, an oil magnate. While Noah, well, my grandfather wants him with another doctor that he keeps pushing Noah's way."

Aria nods. "Interesting. Your grandfather is Harold Astor, correct?"

I nod, surprised she knows about my family, and then it clicks. This is Nyx. She would've dug up everything there is to know about me the moment Noah first mentioned me. She's probably only asking me questions to be polite. Aria doubtless already knew everything I just told her.

"Amara, you should know that you're the only woman Noah has ever introduced me to. He's never asked Grayson for a favor either, not even once. He did that for you."

I nod, and she smiles.

"My brother is smitten with you, and you clearly return his feelings. If there's one thing I've learned, it's that things that are meant to be will find a way."

I nod, hoping that she's right, but knowing better. "Maybe," I murmur. "But not everyone has a grandfather like mine."

She nods. "That's true, and he is an obstacle you'll have to overcome. Your grandfather is controlling and ruthless, but it comes from a good place."

I frown. "You know him?"

Aria leans back and looks away. "It's complicated. Let's just say that the truth has a way of coming to the surface, no matter how well hidden. Just know that Noah isn't alone. Just because Gray and I keep low profiles does not mean we won't wage war over him if need be. All I care about is his happiness, and I haven't seen my brother smile the way he did today in *years*. You make him happy, Amara, and that's all that matters. The rest? The rest we can figure out."

Her words give me hope that I have no business having, but I find myself nodding nonetheless. I want to believe her, even if it's just for this week.

Chapter Twenty-Nine

NOAH

"You know what your sister is like," Grayson says, shaking his head. "She's curious about Amara, and she's going to want to play matchmaker."

I groan, worried my sister will ruin the delicate peace between Amara and I. "Surely this must be the one good thing to come out of you being engaged to my sister? Tell her to knock it off."

Grayson laughs, his disbelief apparent. "You think I can tell Ari anything?"

Right. This is my sister we're talking about. "Fucking hell," I mutter as we walk back into the penthouse.

I'm worried about what this trip might do to Amara and me — what being around Gray and Aria might do to us. They're so happy together, and even I find myself wanting just a small piece of that.

I'm worried about what Aria might have said to Amara while I was away. I know she has the best intentions, but Aria is a dreamer, a hopeless romantic. She'll see things that aren't there, and if left to her own devices, she'll do the one thing I can't have happening: she'll give us hope — she'll make us think we can be together, that things might work out for us. It'd be all too easy to deceive ourselves over here, far away from Harold's influence.

I'm nervous as we walk into the living room, worried about the wreckage Aria might have caused, but I find the two of them sitting on the sofa, smiling. Amara looks up when I walk in, and my heart skips a fucking beat. She's so damn beautiful. Fuck. She smiles at me, and I just stare at her, mesmerized. "Hey," I murmur, ignoring the way my sister is grinning at me.

Aria rises from her seat and stretches. "It's late," she says, a hint of a smile on her face. "You two were gone forever. Amara and I had dinner together, so I'm off to bed. I prepped the guest room for you already."

I hesitate, but before I can tell my sister that I'll sleep on the sofa, she's gone. Gray throws a look my way that screams *I told you so*, and I sigh as he follows her, leaving Amara and me alone. She seems nervous as I walk up to her and jumps off the sofa, her cheeks reddening rapidly. I love seeing her so flustered. Knowing that it's me she's responding to that way, I don't know... it's pretty special.

"Hi," I whisper, walking up to her hesitantly. We said we'd have a week together and there's nothing I'd want more, but I'm scared of ruining the bond we've got now. I'm scared being together might ruin things for us forever.

"Hi," she says, closing the distance between us. I hesitate before deciding to wrap my arms around her. I can't resist her. I never could.

Amara grins, and relief washes over me. Things have been weird between us lately, both of us tiptoeing around each other, pretending like there's nothing between us.

She places her palms flat on my chest, her eyes on me. The way she looks at me, fucking hell. "How was your day?" I murmur. "I'm surprised you survived the day with my sister."

She chuckles, the sound making my heart skip yet another

beat. "Noah! Do you even know who your sister is? How could you not have told me that she's *Nyx*? *The* Nyx."

I tense, surprised. "She told you that?"

Amara nods, her excitement palpable. "I've been such a huge fan of hers for years. I didn't think I'd ever find out who she is. Now that I've met her, I'm even more impressed. She's so... normal, and *sweet*."

I smile at her, a tinge of pride coursing through me. "Yeah, she's amazing. She guards her online identity with an iron fist, though. I'm surprised she admitted that to you."

Amara nods, her expression dreamy. "Wow, Nyx and Grayson Callahan. You have no idea how cool it is that those two are getting married. They're so perfect together."

I chuckle and lean in to kiss her cheek, startling her. "Should I be jealous? Seems like you're a much bigger fan of my sister's than you are of me."

Amara slides her hands up my chest, until she's got them wrapped around me, a smile on her face. "Oh, no. you're still my favorite, Dr. Grant. You always will be."

I smile at her, feeling oddly happy here, far away from everything that's keeping us apart. "Amara," I whisper, her name a plea on my lips. Her eyes widen as I tighten my grip on her. "I know we said we'd have one week together... but I don't want to ruin things, and we've been doing okay at being friends—"

"Kiss me," she says, her eyes filled with the same longing I'm feeling. "Just kiss me, Noah. One week. We'll go back to being friends the second we return, but while we're here, I want to call you mine."

I grin as I lean in, my lips hovering over hers. "I'm yours," I whisper, my lips brushing over hers. A soft moan escapes her lips right before I close the distance between us, kissing her the way I've been wanting to for weeks.

Amara tightens her grip on me and deepens the kiss, her hands roaming over my body. By the time she pulls away, we're both breathless.

"I missed you," she murmurs, her hands dropping to mine. I interlace our fingers and pull her along to the guest room, my eyes never leaving hers.

"Oh yeah?" I ask, leading her into the room. "How much did you miss me? Sounds like you were too busy obsessing over my sister."

The door closes behind us, and Amara turns me around, pushing me against it. "You're so cute when you're jealous," she says, rising to her tiptoes. "I like it. I love watching you lose your mind over me."

She leans in and kisses me, her hands roaming over my body impatiently. She pulls my shirt out of my trousers and slips her hands underneath, the tips of her fingers trailing over my abs.

I bury my hand into her hair and tighten my grip, turning us around so she's got her back against the door.

"You're mine, Amara. This entire week, you're mine," I whisper against her lips, right before I lift her into my arms. Her legs wrap around me, and I push up against her, eliciting a moan from her.

"Yes, Dr. Grant. I'm yours."

She drives me insane when she calls me Dr. Grant, and she knows it. I smirk and pull on her hair, tilting her head so her neck is exposed. I kiss her until I hit a sensitive spot that makes her moan my name.

"Good girl," I whisper. "Say my name."

"Noah," she moans. "I need you. *Please.*" She undoes the buttons of my shirt, pushing it down my shoulders impatiently, and I smile against her skin, pressing a featherlight kiss to her neck. The way she touches me without abandon... I love that about her. There's no holding back with Amara.

I kiss her right below her ear, enjoying the way she rolls her hips against mine every time I hit a sensitive spot.

"I've wanted to fuck you against a door ever since that first time I had you pressed against your bedroom door."

"Then fuck me, Noah."

CATHARINA MAURA

I smirk and push her dress up over her hips. "If I wasn't worried about the noise, I'd take you right here, right now. I won't share any part of you, baby. This moment... it's *ours*."

Amara tightens her legs around my waist as I pull her dress up and over her head. "No underwear, what a surprise."

She smiles and buries her hands in my hair, pulling my lips to hers. "I brought you something," she murmurs against my lips.

I grin and lower her to the floor, taking in the provocative look in her eyes as she slips out of my arms and walks over to her bag.

Amara pulls out a toy, and I chuckle. I should've known. "You came prepared, huh?"

She smiles and walks back to me, her eyes reflecting the same desire I feel. She's fucking beautiful standing in front of me in nothing but that red lace bra.

"It's for *you*. I didn't make this myself. I bought it because I was curious about how it might work and what it'd feel like."

I stare at the contraption in her hands, my brows raised and my cock fucking throbbing. "Whatever it is you've got in mind, I'm down. But first..." I pull her toward me and reach behind her, undoing her bra impatiently. "I've been dreaming about what you'd look like naked," I murmur, pulling her bra away. "But nothing could ever fucking prepare me for this." My eyes roam over her body, and I shake my head in disbelief. "How are you more beautiful than you were in my fantasies?"

She laughs and drops to her knees in front of me, unbuttoning my trousers. "You're not the only one that's been fantasizing," she says, pulling down my trousers, undressing me fully. "The vineyard wasn't enough, Noah. I want more."

I swallow hard as I look down at her, reminded of the way I held her hair that day, the way her pretty little mouth took all of me.

"It's a cock ring," Amara says as she grabs my cock. "You put it on, and it vibrates. It's supposed to keep you hard for ages. See

146

this part here?" she asks, pointing out a little part that sticks out. "This is for me."

She puts it on me, and I groan when she turns it on. "Baby, the mere thought of fucking you has got me close. This thing? Yeah... that's going to make me last even less long."

She laughs and leans in, her tongue teasing the tip of my cock. "No fucking way," I tell her, pulling her up. "I'm taking your pussy."

I lift her into my arms and carry her to the bed, placing her down carefully. "You're already wet for me, aren't you, baby?"

She bites down on her lip and nods. I love that look on her face. So fucking needy.

I spread her legs and kneel between them, kissing her thigh and enjoying the way she quivers. "Noah, please," she begs. "I need you inside me."

I smile as I settle between her legs, the tip of my cock resting against her wetness. "You want this, baby?"

I push just the tip in, and the way Amara gasps has my cock jerking. "Noah," she moans, my name a plea on her lips.

I hold myself up on top of her, my eyes on hers. "I've been dreaming about taking your pussy," I whisper, pushing another inch into her. "In my dreams I've got you screaming my name, coming on my cock the way you did on my fingers."

I push in another inch, enjoying the way she squirms underneath me, the way she tries to move her hips up because she wants more.

"Let me make those dreams come true. Fuck me, Noah," she pleads, and I smile as I thrust all the way into her, the toy she put on me pressing against her.

The way she moans and moves underneath me drives me insane. "You are, baby," I whisper. "You're my every dream come true."

I bury my hands into her hair and hold myself up on my forearms, my lips lowering to hers. I pull back a little, rotating my hips as I push back into her, fucking her slow and hard, our bodies close, my lips never leaving hers.

I pull away a little to look at her, wanting to see her expression as I fuck her, keeping the rhythm steady to make sure that toy of hers stays pushed up against her.

Amara wraps her hands into my hair, her eyes on mine. "I can't," she whispers. "I think I'm already going to come. I've wanted this for so long, and the vibrations..."

I smirk and pull back almost all the way before thrusting back into her, teasing her the way she teased me for months. "You want more, baby? You wanna come for me?"

She nods, her expression pleading. "Please, Noah."

"No," I tell her, pulling almost all the way back. "You won't come until I tell you to."

She squirms underneath me, trying to tilt her hips up to get me closer, and I smile. "So eager. So desperate for my cock. You've tortured me for months, my love. Making me watch you come on my fingers when you know damn well I wanted you on my cock."

I push into her and rotate my hips against her, making the ring around my cock hit her at different angles, getting her close only to pull back just in time.

"Noah, *please*," she begs.

"This pussy is *mine*, and you'll do as I say. You'll come when I tell you to, understood?"

"Yes, Noah," she whispers, a moan escaping her lips as I tilt my hips.

"Good girl," I murmur. "You're so desperate, aren't you? Do you know how many times I've been this desperate for you? Every fucking time you handed me a new toy, Amara." She swallows hard, her eyes on mine. "Every one of those times I imagined this. You underneath me, begging to come all over my cock."

I love the way she pants, the way her eyes never leave mine. I keep the ring around me pressed up against her, tilting ever so slightly whenever she gets too close. The way she looks at me... *fuck*. Words I know I can't ever say to her threaten to spill from my lips, so I kiss her. I lose myself in her, fucking her harder, rougher.

"Come," I whisper against her lips, pulling away to look at her. Amara's muscles squeeze my cock the way I knew they would, and she takes me right along with her, my name on her lips. Wave after wave rocks her body, and I come deep inside her, harder than ever before.

Chapter Thirty

NOAH

I rest my forehead against hers, both of us struggling to catch our breath. Amara giggles and wraps her arms around me.

"That was better than in my fantasies," she whispers.

I laugh and lower my lips to hers, kissing her tenderly. "It was. We didn't use a condom, though. I brought some, but in the heat of the moment..."

She smiles at me and shakes her head before leaning in for a kiss. "It's okay. I'm on the pill, and I'm clean. Considering that you're a doctor, it's probably safe to assume that you are too?"

I nod. "I am. I actually... well, I've never had anyone but you without a condom. No one but you has ever made me feel so out of control. I've never experienced anything like this before."

She smiles at me and nods. "It's the same for me."

I smirk and turn us over, reaching between us to take off the toy she brought. "I like this thing. We're using that again," I murmur, placing it on my nightstand.

Amara giggles and nods. "It *was* good." She settles in my arms, her head on my chest. We lie there together like that, just enjoying this moment, the tips of my fingers running over her skin. She presses a kiss to my neck, and I sigh in contentment. Having her in my arms... it's unreal.

"I'm sorry for leaving you alone today," I whisper as I thread my hand through her hair.

Amara pulls away and smiles at me, her eyes twinkling. "I got to spend the day with Nyx, so I didn't mind it at all. I missed you, though. If I only get to have one week with you, then I want it all. You need to take me on a date, doctor dearest."

I lean in for another kiss, my lips lingering. "I will, baby. Everything I've ever wanted to do with you, we'll do."

Amara nods, her gaze clearing, and I smile to myself, knowing what she's suddenly curious about. "So... you spoke to Grayson?"

I smile smugly and nod. "Yeah, and I can be convinced to tell you all about it."

"Oh yeah?"

I nod, and Amara giggles. "What will it take?"

"How about a kiss, for starters?"

She leans in and presses her lips to my neck, surprising me. She kisses my throat softly, taking her time moving her lips up to my ear. I groan and bury my hand in her hair, tightening my grip on her.

"Playing dirty, are we?"

She laughs, and the sound stirs my cock. "The more you tell me, the more I'll give you," she whispers, her voice husky.

I smirk, my eyes falling closed. This is a trap of my own making, but I don't mind being her prey.

"He asked me all about you. Wouldn't rest until I told him everything I know about you."

"Everything?" She lowers her lips to my chest, and a moan escapes my lips when she sucks down on my skin, marking me as hers.

"Not everything. Some things are only for me to know, Amara."

She pulls her lips away, looking at the damage she did with satisfaction. "What did you tell him?"

"I told him about your educational background, your company, and your family. I told him about your tenacity, your independence and drive."

Amara kisses my abs, and I smile. "What did he say?"

"He seemed impressed. Gray said you can give him a presentation tomorrow. He'd have done it sooner, but he was working on a government project with a tight deadline, and he had a few things going on recently on top of that."

She sits up, her eyes wide. "I'd love to. I can't believe you made this happen for me, Noah. I can't believe this is happening."

I grin at her, my heart overflowing with happiness. "You'd better believe it, baby. You're going to do amazing."

Amara nods, but I see the insecurity in her eyes. "You've got this, Amara. You're incredible, and Gray will recognize that."

"I'm scared, Noah," she whispers, pulling her hands off my body and wrapping them around herself protectively. "This is my last chance. If Grayson doesn't invest, then it's over. I'll probably have to start working for my grandfather and walk the path he paved for me. I'm terrified of failing. If I do, then all my dreams will fade to dust. But at the same time... I don't know. I feel selfish. I confronted my grandfather about him blocking all my investment opportunities, and I don't know... I can kind of see his point. He did work hard, and maybe I *am* being ungrateful by wanting to follow my own dreams."

I pull her down with me, lying down with her head on my chest, my hand brushing over her back. "You're not, baby. You're being brave. I don't doubt for a second that you'll succeed. There are several paths to success, and yours is no less admirable."

She looks up at me, her eyes filled with fear. She's always seemed so fearless to me, so brave. Seeing her this scared and insecure... it's a unique experience. It's a moment I know I'll always cherish, having her in my arms and having the honor of reassuring and consoling her.

Amara inhales deeply, almost as though she's bracing herself. "He thinks I'm being foolish, and my mother agrees."

I keep my arms wrapped around her, stroking her back as she finally truly lets me in and tells me about the day she confronted her grandfather. This is what I wanted with her. With Amara, I want far more than just sex. I want her to be mine in every way. I want to be the one she turns to when she's scared. I want to be her safe haven. Even if it's just for this one week.

So I hold her a little tighter when her voice wavers, and I press kisses to her temple when she sniffs. I keep her close, until she falls asleep in my arms, safe from her fears.

This intimacy between us... I'm not sure I can do without it. I don't think I'll be able to go back to what we used to be.

Chapter Thirty-One

Amara

I sit up in bed, my heart racing as I stare down at Noah. He's still fast asleep, his lashes fluttering as though he's dreaming, and I smile to myself. I didn't think that I would ever get to experience this with him. Falling asleep together, waking up together. They are simple things, but I want them with him. We ended up talking about my grandfather and my upcoming presentation most of the night, and it was oddly perfect. The sex was amazing, but somehow lying in his arms and telling him about my greatest fears felt just as intimate.

I'm glad I get to have him with me today as I present my products to one of my idols. I can't believe he made this happen for me. I didn't think I'd ever be able to escape my grandfather's influence, yet here I am with the man he doesn't want me to be with, about to ask Grayson Callahan to invest in me. Grayson is perhaps one of the very few people my grandfather cannot control.

Noah stirs, his eyes opening slowly. He looks around, disoriented, but then his gaze lands on me and he smiles. "Hey, baby."

He pulls me closer and wraps his arms round me, hugging me tightly. "Excited for your presentation?"

I nod against his chest and snuggle closer. "More nervous than excited," I admit.

Noah threads his hand through my hair and holds me tightly. "You have nothing to be nervous about. You're going to do amazing. Gray's going to love your concept."

"I hope so," I whisper. "This is my only chance to escape my grandfather's influence."

Noah pulls away to look at me, his gaze questioning. "Why is it that you're so intent on gaining independence? There's nothing wrong with it, of course. But it seems like it's about more than you make it out to be."

I nod and look away, unsure how to explain. I tried to last night, but every time I attempted to bring it up I just ended up in tears. "It is. The world my grandfather has shown you isn't the one I grew up. Far from it, actually. You might have heard this already, but my father was a poor man. He was a janitor at Astor College when my mother was a student there. That's how they met. Needless to say, my grandfather didn't approve. He gave my mother a choice: her family or the man she fell in love with. My mother chose to be with my father, and my grandfather disowned her."

I bite down on my lip, my heart aching. "It wasn't the happily ever after they thought they would have. Being disowned meant my mother never got to finish college, and janitors don't make that much money. They were struggling, and things just got worse when I came along. We were very poor, Noah. That type of poverty can lead to desperation."

Noah cups my cheek, his thumb brushing over my skin soothingly. "I never would have guessed. You are elegance itself. I always assumed that you grew up rich."

I shake my head. "If only. If my grandfather hadn't disowned my mother, if she had felt like she could turn to her father for help... then maybe our lives wouldn't have been in pieces. I don't really want to go into it, because even now the memories are painful. I guess what I'm trying to say is that I want to stand on my own two feet. If my grandfather ever casts me out the way he did my mother, if I ever don't fall in line the way he expects me to, then I have to be able to take care of myself. I don't want to live my life at his mercy the way my mother did, the way she still does now. I want more than that. I want to be able to make my own choices, work where I want to work and love whoever I choose."

Noah looks into my eyes, as though he can hear the words I'm keeping in. I want to be able to love *him* without repercussions.

"You're going to do amazing today, baby. Everything you've been working for is going to be worth it. You're going to amaze Grayson. I just know it."

I nod and pull away from him, suddenly feeling vulnerable. I hate thinking about the past, about my dad. I hate feeling helpless and trapped. I can't undo the past, and I can't forgive him for it either.

Noah leans back in bed and watches me as I select an outfit for today. I've been looking forward to today for so long, but talk of the past has drained my excitement.

I don't snap out of my somber mood until Noah leads me to the kitchen, rooting me back in the present. I am at the home of two of my biggest idols. Even if Grayson chooses not to invest in me, this trip still would have been well worth it. In part because I got to spend time with Noah, and in part because I got to meet both Grayson and Nyx.

"Morning," Aria says as we walk in, her eyes shifting between Noah and me in curiosity. She isn't like the mysterious, cold-hearted Nyx I expected. Instead, she's warm and welcoming without being intrusive. She's obviously curious about Noah and me, but all she's really asked about is my feelings.

"Morning," I tell her, unable to keep my cheeks from heating. It's so surreal to me, being here with Grayson and Nyx. Grayson looks at her as though she's all he can see, and the love between them brings a smile to my face. It's been a while since I was so surrounded by love. I forgot how infectious happiness is.

"Gray tells me you'll be giving us a presentation today?" Aria asks as she lifts her mug to her lips. "Why don't we get that out of the way now so you can relax and actually enjoy your time here?"

"Oh, um... yes, of course." I turn to rush back to the bedroom and grab the set of toys I prepared. Aria is right. It's going to be all I can think about otherwise, but I just didn't expect to be show-casing sex toys over breakfast.

I'm nervous as I walk back out, realization dawning. This one rather informal presentation could make or break my career. All eyes are on me as I place my product case on the dining table. I panic for a moment, and then my eyes meet Noah's, and I know I'm going to be okay.

Chapter Thirty-Two

NOAH

I watch Amara as she opens her laptop and talks Aria and Grayson through her business plan. They both listen raptly, giving her all their attention. My heart is filled with gratitude sitting here, just being here in the moment with my three favorite people.

I bite back a smirk when Amara pulls one of her sex toys out of her product case, her expression serious. Grayson looks startled, and I realize he didn't actually expect her to have prototypes on her. I shake my head silently. He should have known better. I wouldn't have asked him to hear her out if I thought she wouldn't come prepared.

Aria grins when Amara explains how one of her toys works, the one she took to the vineyard with her. Meanwhile, Grayson stares at Amara's prototypes with wide eyes, and I bite down on my lip in an effort to keep my laughter in.

It takes Grayson a few moments to compose himself, but once he does, his entire demeanor changes. I've always seen him as my best friend, the guy that would split grocery bills with us because neither of us could afford to both feed ourselves and go to school. Seeing him like this, so in love with my sister and capable of making Amara's dreams come true... It fills my heart with happiness.

I watch Aria and Grayson carefully as Amara wraps up her presentation. Aria smiles at Gray, her eyes twinkling the way they only ever have around him, and then she nods, sending him a pleading gaze. He smiles back at her, the sight so rare that it startles even me. He leans in and brushes her hair out of her face gently, and then he leans back, crossing his arms as he turns to Amara.

"Your concept sounds interesting," he says, taking Aria's hand in his. "We'd be willing to invest."

Amara's shoulders relax and a wide smile spreads across her face. "You won't regret your decision, Grayson." She walks up to me, and I instinctively open up my arm for her. Her happiness is palpable, and I shoot Grayson a grateful glance.

"We?" I ask as Amara drops her head on my shoulder.

Grayson nods. "This particular investment will be underwritten by Grayson and Aria Callahan."

Aria giggles and leans in to press a kiss to Grayson's cheek. "You just wanted to say Aria Callahan, didn't you?"

Grey smiles sheepishly and raises Aria's hand to his lips. "I've never been a patient man, my love."

Amara stares at the two of them, stars in her eyes. It's so clear that she wants what they have, and I guess I do too. I want it with her.

Aria leans over and grabs Amara's hand. "We have to celebrate, but Gray and I have some urgent work to finish. He did something rather foolish involving hacking the airport's video systems not too long ago, and now we've been roped into doing even more government work to avoid repercussions."

I glance at Gray, surprised. He never told me that. I wonder what the story is there.

"Don't you worry," Amara says, squeezing Aria's hand. "Noah can show me around. It'll be fun."

Aria nods and smiles indulgently as she rises from her seat at the table. Gray follows her, leaving me standing here with Amara. The second the two of them disappear behind the door, Amara turns to me and squeals as she grabs my hands, jumping up and down in excitement.

"Oh my God, Noah. Did you hear that? They'll invest! My two heroes are investing in my company!"

She's so excited that she's got tears in her eyes, and I decide here and then that this is my favorite look on her. Happiness looks great on her.

I take a step closer to her and tangle my hand in her hair, pulling her toward me roughly. She moans when my lips come crashing down on hers and rises to her tiptoes to deepen the kiss. Her hands slide up my shoulders until she's got her arms wrapped around my neck, our bodies pressed together. I kiss her fiercely, taking her mouth the way I'd been wanting to throughout her presentation.

"I knew you'd do it," I whisper in between kisses. "I had no doubts."

Amara pulls back to look at me, a dreamy look in her eyes. "You really believe in me, don't you?"

I nod. "Of course. You're the most remarkable person I know, Amara. I know you're going to be hugely successful, and I can't wait to see you flourish."

She smiles at me and rises to her tiptoes to press a kiss to my cheek. "So will you, Noah. You're going to do amazing things. I just know it."

I hope so. I'm sabotaging myself by being here with her, by holding her the way I am, yet I can't deny her. If I truly want to become successful and be on par with Amara, Aria, and Grayson, I'll need to get my priorities straight. But not today. Today is for celebrating victories.

"So, what do you want to do today?" I ask, forcing myself to stay in the present, to enjoy the limited time I have with Amara.

"Honestly? Nothing. I just want to enjoy my time with you."

I take a step closer and cup her cheek as I lean in to kiss her forehead. "I have something in mind. Get ready. We'll leave in ten."

Chapter Thirty-Three

AMARA

I look around with wide eyes, taking in the cherry blossom trees at the park, the water in front of us and the sun shining down on us. "This is perfect," I whisper.

Noah grins at me and holds up the picnic basket he brought. "It's the perfect place to just relax and enjoy our time together."

I watch him as he lays down the blanket he brought and unpacks the wine and snacks we stole from Aria and Gray, before sitting down and offering me his hand. I take it with a smile.

I lean against him, and he wraps his arm around me, the two of us staring at the water. I wonder if he feels the way I do. Is he as happy in this moment as I am?

"I wanted this with you," he says, his voice soft. "When we went to that vineyard... I kept wishing it was just the two of us. I'd have loved to go wine tasting with you, stroll through the place with your hand in mine. I wanted to call you mine then, but I couldn't."

He looks at me in a way he never has before, and my heart skips a beat. Yeah... Noah is feeling exactly what I'm feeling. "I'm yours now," I whisper, wishing it could stay that way. "This day, this moment... it's ours."

He nods and leans in, pressing a lingering kiss to my temple. "I don't want this week to end," he tells me, and I swallow hard, trying my best to push aside the sorrow I feel. Noah raises his hand to my face, his touch gentle as he brushes my hair behind my ear.

I love him. There's no doubt in my mind. The feelings I have for him can't be described in any other way.

I bite down on my lip and rise to my knees before straddling him and settling in his lap. Noah smiles at me and places his hands on my waist, his eyes on mine. The way he looks at me... I'm tempted to believe he loves me too.

"Thank you," I whisper. "For today. For this week."

He looks away, hearing the words I left unsaid. *Thank you for the memories.* I inhale shakily and thread one hand through his hair, cupping his cheek with the other. Noah's eyes meet mine, and the need in them matches my own.

I lean in, my lips hovering over his. I press a featherlight kiss to his lips, once, twice, before kissing him fully.

Noah groans against my lips and tightens his grip on me, kissing me back slowly, deeply. He takes his time with me, his touch different from before. He's got my heart racing, and I find myself wishing that his is too.

He pulls away a little, his forehead dropping to mine. "I don't think I'll ever get enough of you," he whispers. "I'm addicted, well and truly. I need you, Amara. All of you."

His lips drop back to mine, and this time his kiss is more frantic, his desperation as strong as mine. His hands slide up my body, until he's got his thumbs resting underneath my breasts, drawing circles on my skin. "Tell me you're naked underneath this dress," he whispers against my lips. I laugh and nod, enjoying the feel of him underneath me. I love knowing how much he wants me. Everything about this moment is perfect. The desire sizzling between us, the emotions we're both not voicing... I just know this is going to be one of those moments I'll always remember.

Noah smiles and reaches for the picnic bag, taking out the toy we used last night. "I had a feeling you'd seduce me," he says, smirking. "The park is mostly empty, but that could change any second. This thing... I think we could both come without moving much if we use this."

I grin and undo his jeans, covering us both up with my dress. "I corrupted you, Dr. Grant."

He laughs, but his smile melts away when I attach the ring. I chuckle as I turn it on, loving the power I've got over him. "I wanted this too," I tell him. "At the vineyard... I wanted you to bend me over and fuck me right there against that tree. Driving you crazy with my mouth was nice, but it wasn't enough."

I lift myself up and position him underneath me, a teasing smile on my face. "I guess it's only right that you make up for not giving me what I wanted that day," I say, slowly sinking down on him, until he's filling me up.

"I wanted this then," he murmurs. "I always want you. I wanted you from the very second you walked into my office. You're the most beautiful woman I'd ever seen, and I was hooked. With every interaction since then, you've just cemented your place in my mind further. I'm always thinking about you, Amara. I always want you. Fuck, I think you bewitched me, because I sure am fucking addicted to you."

I smile and roll my hips, enjoying the way he bites down on his lip. "The feeling is entirely mutual, Noah."

I wrap my hand in his hair and lean in to kiss him. I don't think I'll ever get tired of kissing Noah. His hands roam over my body, settling on my ass. He squeezes tightly, and I gasp when he lifts me up, only to pull me back down with force, his cock driving me insane.

"How does that feel, baby? Can you feel the vibrations? Is this thing pressing against your clit?"

I nod and rotate my hips, enjoying the way Noah bites down on his lip. I love seeing him lose his mind over me.

He thrusts up, pushing deeper into me, his arms wrapped around me. Sitting here with him, face-to-face with him buried so deep inside me... this is perfection.

"Oh God," I whisper, my hands on his shoulders. There's something about this moment, being out here in the open, barely able to move.

Noah freezes and keeps me still, his lips brushing over my ear. "There's a lady with a stroller heading our way," he whispers, and I giggle, suddenly nervous.

He looks at me, and we both burst out laughing, but Noah's laugh is cut short when his eyes widen. "Fucking hell... when you laugh like that your pussy tightens. Don't make me come with some stranger walking right by us," he warns, and I blush.

"That sounds like a challenge." Noah looks past me, and I watch his face as I tilt my hips back and forth as subtly as I can, giving him the extra friction I know he needs to come.

Noah drops his head to my shoulder, our bodies flush, his lips pressed to my neck. "You'll be the death of me," he whispers. "I can't take it when you move like that."

I'm teasing him, but I'm on the edge myself. I doubt I'll be able to hang on much longer, not with the way he feels inside me, with the way this toy presses against my clit.

I breathe a sigh of relief when I hear the wheels of a stroller pass by us, and I turn to watch the woman walk past us, her eyes fixed on her baby. She glances at us and smiles indulgently. To her it must look like we're hugging... if only she knew. I smile back at her and hide my face against Noah's shoulder, my cheeks blazing.

The second we're out of view, Noah grabs my hair, pulling my lips against his roughly. The way he kisses me gets me close, but it's the way he moves his hips, the way he pulls on my hair... that's what pushes me over the edge.

Noah silences my moans with his lips, and when he pulls

away, he's grinning in satisfaction. "Ride me. Ride me good," he orders.

And I do. I use his cock and the toy to make myself come again, and Noah watches me as I lose control all over again. When my pussy contracts around him, he whispers my name, coming right along with me.

He leans back on his arms, his eyes on mine as we both try to calm our raging hearts. "I didn't think you could get more beautiful. I was wrong," he whispers. "The toy is a keeper."

I smile and wrap my arms around his neck, pulling him back to me. "So are you," I murmur, right before kissing him.

I don't want this week to end. This right here, I don't want this to end... but I know we're on borrowed time.

Chapter Thirty-Four

NOAH

I slip out of bed, glancing at Amara in my bed. The last couple of days have been perfect, and the thought of going back to what we were before terrifies me. I can't see my life without her anymore.

I sigh as I slip out of bed and make my way to the kitchen, surprised to find my sister sitting at the kitchen counter, a fuzzy robe wrapped around her.

"Can't sleep?" she asks.

"How'd you know?"

Aria smiles, a knowing look in her eyes. "You've always been this way. You've never been able to sleep when you're worried, and ever since yesterday you've had that look in your eyes. The one that never used to leave your eyes when we were younger, the gaze that told me you weren't sure if we'd have enough money for groceries, if you'd be able to stay in school."

I sit down next to her, a deep sigh escaping my lips. "I didn't realize you were aware of all of that. I tried so hard to shield you from it, Aria... but I... I failed you. I failed you in so many ways, and I see it more clearly the older I get. I don't know how you turned out so wonderful considering our past, but I'm so incredibly proud of you, kiddo."

She looks at me, her eyes watery. "Noah, I turned out this way *because* of you. Because you taught me to work hard no matter what life throws at us, to value the things we have, and to put family first. If not for you, I don't even know where I'd be now. You are and always have been my role model. I'm proud of you too, you know?"

I look away, unable to hold her gaze. I wish I were the man she thinks I am. She's Nyx, a notorious hacker and vigilante. She built her platform without me even knowing. I didn't realize what she was up to until Grayson mentioned her platform and her username. He didn't realize who she was, but I did. I knew the second I heard the name Nyx. She's brilliant, and so is Grayson. Hell, even Amara is going places. It's just me that's not.

"You're quiet," she murmurs. "Tell me, Noah. What has you so worried? Amara is lovely, and she's as crazy about you as you are about her."

I sigh and turn to face her. "It's not that simple, Ari. I work for her grandfather, and he's made it clear she's off-limits to me. You don't understand... the opportunities Harold Astor is giving me are unreal. I'm not like you, Ari. I can't get where you and Gray are without connections, without help. He's opening doors for me I can't even reach by myself. Being with Amara is guaranteed to ruin my career, and I've worked so hard to get where I am today. But it isn't enough. I don't want to be a salaried worker bee. I don't want to be just another one of Amara's family's employees. I don't want to be *the help*."

She nods. "So let me invest in you. Let's buy you a clinic. Would that help?"

I smile at her. "I love you, Ari, but I need to do this by myself. Besides, a single clinic doesn't compare to what I'm managing now. It'd be slightly better than being a salaried doctor, but it still..."

"Who are you trying to measure up against?" she asks, a frown on her face. "I'm all for ambition and I'll support you in any way I can, but Noah... you're incredible, just as you are. Who is making you feel as though you aren't good enough?"

"You don't understand," I murmur, and she doesn't, she can't. Aria is brilliant in her own right. Even when she was doing an underpaid job she hated, she had her platform and the prestige that came with her pseudonym. If she never found a job she loved, she'd still have left her mark on the world. But I? I'm just doing the bare minimum. I always have been.

She's right to say I compare myself to others, but it's only because I know Amara eventually will. Whether I like it or not, as I am now, I can't give her as much as Gregory could. When it comes down to it, I don't have anything to offer her. I own my home, but I haven't paid off the mortgage yet, and I still have student loans to pay off. I can't maintain the lifestyle she's gotten used to. She tells me she grew up poor, but I know from experience how hard it is to go from being well off to suddenly being poor. When Aria and I lost our parents, our entire life was turned upside down. We were okay, but it was never easy. I can't put Amara through that type of hardship.

"Has Amara... has she told you much about her family?" Aria asks, snapping me out of my thoughts.

I turn to look at her and nod. "I'm quite close to her grandfather, and her mother occasionally drops by my office with lunch. They're both kind good people. It was unexpected, really. They've welcomed me with open arms, and I truly count myself lucky for it."

Aria nods and looks away. "What about her father?"

I shake my head. "All I really know is that he was a janitor, and her mother was disowned for choosing to be with him. He left them when she was younger, and that's all I really know. He's been contacting her recently, and she's been ignoring him. She doesn't like to talk about him. The first time he texted her, she had a full-blown panic attack, so I try not to probe."

Aria nods, her expression pensive. "I see," she murmurs. "Do you love her, Noah?" She turns to look at me, her gaze tense.

"Yes," I say, my voice calm and certain. "There's much I'm not sure about. Hell, I don't even know what my future looks like, but this I know. I love her. I shouldn't, but I do."

Aria smiles. "Then that's all that matters. Amara is not her family. She didn't choose to be born into that family, but she did choose you."

Her words remind me of the words Amara uttered when I tried to distance myself from her. She begged me not to punish her for who her family is. Those words held true then, and they do now too.

"I know she isn't," I murmur, exhausted. "I know, Ari... but I can't escape her family, not right now. I want the future Harold is offering me. I want it with my heart and soul. This opportunity, it's the chance of a lifetime."

Aria smiles at me. "Noah, you can have both, you know?"

I smile and raise my hand to her face, tucking her hair behind her ear. I've always loved Aria's naivety. "I can't, sweetheart. I wish. Harold specifically told me to stay away from her. He doesn't want us together. That man... he's powerful."

Aria crosses her arms. "So am I," she says, her eyes narrowed. "I can find dirt on him. I'll happily destroy him if he threatens your happiness."

I burst out laughing and shake my head. "And ruin the relationship between Amara and her grandfather? You can't, Ari. I'll find a way, okay? I just need some time. I don't know what to do, but I'll find a way."

She nods. "I'm here, you know. My offer stands. It always will. There's nothing I won't do to ensure your happiness, Noah. I see how happy she makes you, and I want that for you. Don't let anyone take that from you."

I nod and cup her cheek, barely recognizing the woman sitting next to me. When did she grow up? She's still that little girl to me... the one that didn't speak for years, the one that'd check all locks in the house three times before going to bed. Yet here she sits, making me more proud than she'd ever realize.

"I won't," I promise her, hoping I can keep that promise.

Chapter Thirty-Five

AMARA

Noah and I are both quiet as we board the plane. I'm not ready for this trip to end, and I don't think he is either. I'm not ready to go back to how things used to be. I don't think I ever will be.

Noah grabs my hand and entwines our fingers, his expression as sullen as mine must be. He seems resigned, and the look in his eyes tears me apart. He looks helpless and bitter, and I hate that I'm doing this to him. To us.

I can't help but wonder if I'm being selfish. I want Noah with my heart and soul, but love isn't meant to be selfish. I should want what's best for him, but I don't want to be without him. I want to continue calling him mine. I want to spend my nights with him, even if we do nothing at all.

My throat closes up as the plane lands, and I will myself not to cry. I've never felt emotions this strong, and I know I never will again. Noah... he will always have my heart.

He holds my hand as we make our way out of the plane. All throughout the airport, he holds my hand in his. He doesn't let go until we reach his car, and even then, it's only to open the door for me. He's barely looked at me, sadness engulfing us both.

I'm tense as Noah walks around the car, his movements slow, as though he too is hoping to postpone the inevitable. He gets behind the wheel and then he finally turns to look at me, his expression a reflection of my broken heart.

I force a smile onto my face and grin at him. "Thank you for a lovely week, Noah. This is exactly what we needed to get this thing between us out of our system. It was perfect."

He frowns, anger flashing through his eyes before he controls it.

"We said we'd be friends, right? We both know that's the logical thing to do. It's what's best for both of us right now. I guess the timing isn't right for us. It happens. Either way, I'm glad to have had a week with you. Let's move on now, Noah. You and I can be friends, I'm sure of it."

He looks at me, his gaze searching. For a moment I falter, for a single moment, I want to reach out and pull him toward me. I want to lose myself in him, but I can't. Noah is the one person I can't be selfish with. He deserves the world, and I refuse to stand in his way. Things might be perfect between us right now, but he hasn't felt my grandfather's wrath just yet. Once he does, once his future crumbles before his eyes, he'll never look at me the same. I'll have single-handedly taken everything he's been working so hard for, and I can't do that. Not to him. No matter how much I want to be with him. The price to pay is one that's too high to bear, and at some point, he'd resent me for all he lost. I saw it in my mother before our lives fell apart, and I can't knowingly lead Noah down the same path. Not when I know how promising his future is, how brilliant he is.

"Friends," he whispers. He grits his teeth, his jaw tensing as he turns away from me. I swallow down my sorrow and paste a smile onto my face. It's too easy to give in now, to risk it all. I can see that he wants to, but I know that if he does, that light in his eyes will eventually dim. As my grandfather throws one obstacle after another at him, he'll end up blaming me for it. I've seen it happen before with friendships my grandfather didn't think were good for me, classmates he didn't want me around. I know what my grandfather is like. If he's capable of blocking every road to the fulfillment of my dreams, then he's capable of doing much worse to Noah. We decided on sharing just a single week together for a reason. We both know what the consequences will be if we don't end things now.

"You really think we can be friends?" he asks, his tone harsh.

I nod, keeping my expression entirely neutral, courtesy of sitting through countless hours of conversations with truly obnoxious people. The mask I was forced to develop throughout the years is ironclad.

Noah laughs, the sounds chilling. He leans in, his index finger tracing over the side of my face, down to my lips, and then down to my throat. "Now that I know what your pussy feels like... what you taste like... nah, I don't think we can be friends, baby."

I swallow hard, a rush of desire coursing through me. I force myself to stay still, to not clench my thighs the way I want to. He's right. Now that I've had him deep inside me, I want more. It isn't even the phenomenal sex, it's the intimacy. I want him kissing me, stroking my back as we fall asleep together. I want to see the look in his eyes as he sinks deep inside me, his eyes never leaving mine as he fucks me. I want him holding my hand, our fingers entwined. I want him pressing kisses to my forehead and smiling at me the way he does. I want it all with him, and walking away is the hardest thing I'll ever do.

"We can. We said we'd spend a week together, and we did. It's enough. This is enough for me, Noah. Let's just be friends. To be honest, I think I prefer it that way. This week has just complicated things between us endlessly. Neither of us needs extra complications in our life right now."

I see hurt flash through his eyes, and I instantly want to take my words back. I bite down on my lip as I swallow down the words I want to say, and Noah's eyes follow my every move.

"Complications, huh," he repeats. "I see. Fine, Amara. As you wish."

I nod, burying my true wishes deep below the shattered remains of my heart as I smile brightly.

Noah looks away and yanks his seatbelt on, his movements rough, angry. I'm terrified I'm hurting him, but I can't see another way. There's no possible outcome where he and I can be happy without sacrificing the future we're building. Being with him means losing my family while Noah loses his career.

Noah is tense as he drives toward my home, parking in the clearing I left my car at. He stares out the window as he shuts down the engine, and silence washes over us. I don't know what to say, and somehow I can't get myself to say goodbye.

"I... thank you. For this week, for everything."

Noah turns to look at me, his eyes roaming over my face and then down my body. He leans in, and my heart starts to race when he reaches for me, his hand tangling into my hair. He pulls me toward him roughly, his lips finding mine.

I moan against his lips, my eyes falling closed. This. I'll miss this. The way he touches me, the way his hands tell me he owns me without the words ever leaving his lips. I kiss him with all I've got, trying my best to burn this moment into my memories, so I'll always have a part of him.

Noah pulls me closer, lifting me out of my seat, and I tumble on top of him, the two of us barely fitting into this small space. His hands roam over my body, every touch and every caress leaving me wanting more.

He pulls away suddenly, his expression angry. "Tell me, Amara. Can you walk away from this? From us?"

I blink, reality crashing down on me. I smile at him, throwing as much charm at him as I can. "Noah," I murmur, my tone seductive. "I make sex toys for a living. I'm *always* down for a good kiss or even a quickie. I've definitely had a lot of fun with you... but it's just a fling, isn't it? Let's not turn it into more than it is. Let's not destroy our friendship, okay?"

He looks at me as though I struck him, his expression pure devastation laced with despair... and then it's gone. He smiles at me the way he did the first time I walked into his office. It's a professional smile without a trace of emotion, and it kills me more than anything he could've said.

"You're right," he says, carefully placing me back in my seat. He handles me so reverently, his touch kind even as I'm breaking both of our hearts. "Thank you for a wonderful week, Amara. It's just what I needed." He pulls away, his arms crossing over each other as though he's forcing himself to keep his hands off me. "I guess I'll see you around."

I nod, my hand on the door handle. "Yeah," I whisper. "See you, Noah."

I swallow down my tears as I open the door, forcing myself to keep it together just a bit longer. Noah steps out of the car and grabs my bag for me, and I take it from him with shaking hands, praying he won't notice.

"Hey," he says, his eyes on the trees behind me. "Let me know when you get home safe, okay?"

I nod and lean in, rising to my tiptoes to press a chaste kiss to his cheek. I allow myself that much before I turn and walk away, leaving my heart in his hands.

Chapter Thirty-Six

NOAH

I glance at the report that came in about our latest acquisition and run a hand through my hair. The numbers aren't looking good, and I'm scared I made a bad call choosing to purchase this specific clinic over another that Harold was considering. He left the decision up to me, and it was clearly a test — one that I appear to have failed.

The door to my office opens and I sit up, not surprised to find Harold walking into my office. I expected him to show up sometime today. If anything, he's later than I expected. He checks in with me every week, and he usually storms in the way he's doing right now, making it clear that he owns this place. There isn't a single detail he misses when it comes to the expansion he's pursuing. It wouldn't have surprised me if he'd been waiting for me in my office this morning.

"You're back," he says, his tone gruff.

I nod. Usually I'd make small talk with him, but today I'm tired. Or rather than tired, I guess I'm drained. I haven't felt like myself since Amara stepped in her car and drove away. Her words keep resounding in my head, and everything else seems irrelevant. I can't help but run through every interaction I've had with her, every memory we made, wondering how she truly feels about me.

"Where were you? I came in to see you last week, and the receptionist told me you took a week off? You told me you'd only be away for a weekend. I couldn't reach you either."

I smile at him, but it feels forced even to me. "I went to see my sister. She just got engaged. I ended up staying longer than I expected."

He looks surprised, and his eyes soften. "Oh," he says, his tone far less antagonistic. "That's wonderful news. Please tell her congratulations on my behalf."

I nod and turn back to the paperwork on my desk. I've always been grateful to Harold for giving me a chance, for mentoring me... but today I can barely stand to see him. Today, more than ever, I'm reminded of everything I can't have *because* of him, and I just don't know if what he's offering me is worth giving up Amara. I don't think anything ever will be.

Harold sits down opposite me, his gaze searching. "My granddaughter was also away for a week. She stays with her friends often, especially when she's busy at school, but don't you think that's too much of a coincidence?"

I lean back in my seat and cross my arms. "That sounds like something you should be discussing with your granddaughter," I tell him. I'm not in the mood for games or veiled threats. I'm truly exhausted today. My heart is tired of hurting. I'm tired of everything. I'm tired of the loneliness that grips me. I'm tired of tiptoeing around Harold. And I'm really fucking tired of missing Amara.

Harold rises to his feet and crosses his arms, his stance mirroring mine. "I've said it before, and I'll say it again. I'll support you as best as I can, but that is only provided that you stay away from my granddaughter. If I find out that you touched her, you're done. You won't even know what hit you. All you'll see is the damage that will surround you. Damage you could have prevented if you heeded my words."

I stare at him, taking in the anger in his eyes, the small amount of desperation he fails to hide. "Why? Because I'm not good enough for your granddaughter? You say you treat your employees like family, yet you draw the line at one of us actually *becoming* family?"

Harold hesitates, as though he's at a loss for words. He never hesitates, he never falters. I watch him as his expression hardens, intrigued. I've never been able to read him, but today he's revealing human emotion I didn't think he was capable of.

"Think what you will," he tells me. "All that matters is that you understand Amara is not for you. You cannot and never will be with her. My daughter tells me you two are friends of sorts, and that's as much as I'll condone. Don't test me, Noah. There's nothing I won't do to ensure my granddaughter's happiness, and you staying away from her plays a key role in that."

I stare at him in disbelief, completely disillusioned. Part of the reason I struggled so much with my attraction for Amara is the immense respect I had for Harold. I felt terrible going behind his back, doing what I thought would hurt him when he seemed to have my best interests at heart. I was wrong. At the end of the day, I'm just a pawn to him. Just another employee.

"I understand," I tell him, but I don't think I do. I don't think I ever will.

He nods at me as he walks out the door, his usual carefree expression back on his face. "I'll see you next week," he tells me, right before disappearing behind the door.

I stare at it, Amara's words running through my head over and over again. The way she looked at me when she told me that one week was enough, that we shouldn't destroy our friendship. Was our week together just a fling to her, or is she trying to protect me? The way she looked at me... she couldn't have faked that. That's one of the things I love about her most, the way her eyes can't tell a lie. I know we agreed on just one single week, but I don't think I can let her go.

Now that she's shown me what true happiness is... I don't think I can ever settle for less. Consequences be damned.

Chapter Thirty-Seven

AMARA

"Are you sure you're okay?" Leia asks, holding up a screwdriver for me. I nod as I take it from her, trying my best to focus on fixing my malfunctioning product. This lab has become my escape. It's the only place where memories of Noah don't overwhelm me. Losing myself in my work is the only way I'll be able to cope. "Amara, you've barely spoken three words since you got back. You're not okay."

I drop the screwdriver onto the table and turn to face her. "It doesn't matter," I whisper, my voice breaking. I clear my throat and raise my voice. "Whether or not I'm fine doesn't matter, Ley. It's not like I can do anything about it, anyway. I made the right choice — I just didn't think it'd be this hard."

She stares at me, as though she's at a loss for words too. I breathe a sigh of relief when she nods and hands me one of the tiny screws she fabricated for me. If she questioned me about Noah, I don't think I'd be able to take it. I can barely think of him without wanting to cry, and I'm tired of the pain.

"Damn it," I snap. "These damn things are so goddamn tiny!"

Leia tenses next to me, her hip bumping against mine. I don't realize why until I hear his voice.

"Give me that," he says, his voice soft.

For a second I think my heartbreak riddled mind has me hallucinating, but then he smiles at me, his hand wrapping around my waist.

"Noah," I whisper, my voice betraying the disbelief I'm feeling. His grip on me is tight, and he pulls me into him without hesitation. I gasp as I tumble into his arms, my hands on his chest to brace myself. I look up at him, surprised to find him here.

I've been second guessing myself since the moment I stepped out of his car. I've missed him more than I thought was possible. Having him standing here, smiling at me in that way he only ever smiles at *me* soothes my aching heart. "How are you here? *Why* are you here?"

Noah keeps one hand wrapped around my waist while he cups my cheek with the other, his thumb tracing over my lip. "*You're* here, so where else would I be?"

There's no hesitation in his eyes, no doubt. I was so certain that my words would've pushed him away. Yet here he is, standing in my lab.

My eyes drop to the faculty badge around his neck, and I lift it up with a smile. That explains it. I guess being the campus doctor makes him faculty staff. I've never seen him wear this badge before, but then again, he would never have had any use for it. Not until now.

Noah turns to Leia and offers her his hand. "You must be Leia," he says, a charming smile on his face. "We've seen each other before, but we've never officially met. I'm Noah. Amara's boyfriend."

I freeze while Leia smiles at him and shakes his hand. She glances at me wide-eyed, barely able to hide her excitement. "Boyfriend?" she asks, turning to face me. "Is that so?"

I glance at Noah who just stares at me, arms crossed, an expression on his face that dares me to deny his words. I smile at him, my cheeks blazing. "Yes," I tell her, my eyes never leaving Noah's. I thought I lost him when I walked away from him, yet here he is, smiling at me as though I'm all he can see.

Noah wraps his hand around my waist, a satisfied smirk on his face. He leans into me, his lips brushing against my ear. "Good girl," he whispers, and my heart skips a beat.

Leia glances at her phone and then at me, and I just know she's about to make an excuse to leave. She's the world's worst liar. "Oh, I need to go," she says. "My dog got his paws on a roll of toilet paper and TP'ed all of my furniture."

She says it with such a sorrowful expression that I struggle to bite back a smile. How she comes up with this shit is beyond me.

"You don't have a—"

"See ya!" she yells, rushing off. I watch her in amusement, my smile melting away when the door closes behind her.

My heart is racing as I turn to face Noah, my nerves getting the best of me. "Boyfriend?" I murmur.

He picks up the screwdriver, his eyes on my prototype. "Yes. You're mine," he tells me. I watch him as he leans in and works on my toy, as though he didn't just say something crazy.

"I... um, what?"

Noah tightens the last of four tiny screws, taking seconds to do what would've taken me minutes, his hands far steadier than mine. He sighs as he drops the screwdriver onto the table.

"I'm tired, Amara. I'm tired of fighting this thing between us. I'm tired of missing you. I'm tired of pretending like I'm not completely fucking crazy about you. I'm done. You're mine, and you know it. Let's stop pretending like you're not."

Noah takes a step closer to me, and my breath hitches. He looks at me, daring me to object, to tell him no. As if I ever would. I want this just as badly as he does.

He smiles when he realizes I'm not going to fight him on this, and my heart skips a beat when he leans in, his hand wrapping into my hair. I instinctively rise to my tiptoes, meeting him half-way. Noah's lips come crashing down on mine, and I sigh in relief at his touch. I didn't think I'd ever get to have him this close again.

He tightens his grip on my hair, his touch possessive. A rush of desire runs through me, and I push against him, wanting to be closer to him. Noah pulls away just slightly, smiling against my lips. "You're mine," he whispers. "Say it."

I tilt my head, capturing his bottom lip between my teeth, punishing him for teasing me, for withholding more of his touch. "I'm yours, Noah. I've been yours since the day I walked into your office."

He cups my cheek, his eyes on mine. "I'm in love with you," he whispers. "I'm so fucking crazy about you. I love you, Amara."

My eyes widen, and a smile spreads across my face. "I love you more."

Noah shakes his head. "Impossible."

"Take me home with you and I'll show you," I whisper.

Noah chuckles and nods as he pulls away, his hand slipping down my arm until our fingers are entwined. We're both smiling as he leads me out of the lab, my hand in his. I didn't think I'd get to do this ever again. I didn't think I'd ever again get to walk around with my hand in his.

"Thank you," I tell him as he leads me to his car.

Noah frowns, confused, and I smile.

"Thank you for doing what I didn't have the courage to do. I've missed you too, Noah. I've thought of you every single second since I walked away, wondering how it could possibly be the right decision when it felt so wrong."

He twists me around and presses me against his car, his arms on either side of me. "I'll never let you go again," he says, his eyes blazing. "No more games. No caving to pressure from your family. No denying what's between us. You're mine."

I smile and lean in for a kiss. "So, I guess that makes me your girlfriend?"

He laughs and meets me halfway, his lips finding mine. "That sounds too juvenile to describe how I feel about you. You're so much more than that... but for now I'll settle for being your boyfriend."

He smirks before kissing me, his hands moving over my body with the same need I'm feeling. Something this good can't be wrong. I've been miserable since walking away, but I'm done being scared. I want this with him.

This. This thing between us. It's worth fighting for.

Chapter Thirty-Eight

NOAH

Amara is quiet as we walk into my house, and suddenly I find myself second-guessing my decision to go after her. I don't want to pressure her into anything she isn't ready for.

"Hey," I murmur, my hand brushing against hers before I entwine our fingers. "Are you okay?"

Amara turns to look at me, her eyes filled with an expression I can't quite describe. Fear. Worry. Trepidation. "I'm scared," she whispers. "I'm so in love with you, Noah... but I can't just pretend like that'll be enough. Being with me is going to cost you everything, and I'm scared. It might seem worth it now, but it won't be for long."

I take a step closer to her, and she takes a step back, leaning back against the wall. The pictures Aria and I hung in the hallway are right above her head, and I take a moment to look at them before facing her.

"I get it," I tell her. "I'm scared too, baby. I admire your grand-father, and he's taught me a lot in a very short amount of time. I know I'll go far with his support, but is a good career enough? I've lived my entire life cast in shadows of the past, haunted by pain and misery. If there's one lesson I've learned, it's that there's nothing more precious than *happiness*. That's not something I can buy, and it's not something your grandfather can help me achieve. It's something I can only have when I'm with you. When it comes down to it, I'll always choose happiness over money, Amara."

She places her hands against my chest and slides them up, until she's got me wrapped in her embrace. "You say that now, but I'm scared you'll change your mind. I'm scared you'll end up resenting me for everything I'm taking from you."

I smile at her and drop my forehead to hers. "You aren't taking anything from me, my love. If anything, you're giving me more than I ever thought I'd have. You're everything to me, Amara. I knew what I was getting into when I walked into that lab. I vow to you right here and now, I will never blame you for any of the consequences we'll face. We're in this together now. Whatever happens, we'll face it together."

She looks into my eyes, a glimmer of hope lighting up her expression. She smiles at me, and I breathe a sigh of relief. "The mere thought of walking away from you... of letting you go. It won't happen, Amara. I can't ever go back to the emptiness that filled my life before you walked into it."

She rises to her tiptoes and presses a soft, lingering kiss to my cheek. "You have me now, Noah. I'll never leave you."

I nod and pull her closer, my lips finding hers. She sighs happily when I kiss her, and I can't help but smile against her lips. "I missed you so much," I whisper, pulling her toward the living room, my lips never leaving hers for more than a second. "You've been all I've been able to think about."

Amara pushes against my chest, pushing me in the direction of the sofa, and I smile as I fall back onto it. She stands in front of me and I lean back, mesmerized. I can't believe I let her walk away. I never should've let her get into her car.

Amara grins as she climbs onto my lap, straddling me. "I

missed you too, Noah. So much. Just being here with you is so surreal. I thought I'd have to live on the memories we made last week, and it killed me."

I pull her against me, my lips inches away from hers. "You won't have to, baby. We'll spend the rest of our lives making memories together."

She looks at me with wide eyes, and I smirk. I guess it technically is too soon to tell, but when you know, *you know*. Someday, this beautiful woman in my lap is going to be my wife.

"Come here," I whisper.

Amara leans in, her lips brushing against mine, and I wrap my hand into her hair, throwing every ounce of feeling into my touch. She moans against my lips, opening up for me. The way she moves on top of me... *fuck*.

She pulls away to look at me, her gaze heated. I'll never tire of seeing that look in her eyes. Amara smirks as she leans in to press feather soft kisses to my neck, driving me crazy. I tangle my hand into her hair and pull her back up, kissing that smirk off her lips. "My turn," I whisper.

A soft moan escapes her lips when I kiss her neck, my teeth grazing past a sensitive part of her skin. She tilts her head, exposing more of her neck. "Don't stop," she pleads, and I chuckle.

I kiss her collarbone, taking my time as I move lower. We've always been in a rush, but not tonight. She's finally mine now, and I intend to show her what that entails. "I love you," I whisper, before sucking down on her skin, leaving a mark.

Amara gasps, and the sound of her has me rock hard. I love the way her body responds to mine, the desire that's on display for me. My hands roam over her body, and her eyes fall closed when my fingers find their way underneath her dress. "Let me guess," I murmur. "No underwear?" My fingers brush over her thigh, and I chuckle when I realize I'm right. "Already wet for me, as expected. Tell me, Amara. How badly do you want my cock?"

She looks into my eyes, her gaze heated. "You know I want it," she admits. Her voice has always turned me on, but right now it drives me half mad.

I slip my fingers between her thighs, biting down on my lip when I realize she's soaking wet. Fuck. I tease her, my thumb twirling around her clit the way I did back when she walked into my office with a toy to test. I watch her as her cheeks flush and her breathing quickens, soft moans escaping her lips.

"Noah, I need you... please. I need to feel you inside me."

Her hands move to my trousers and she pulls on it impatiently. I lean back and watch her, enjoying the urgency of her touch, her blatant need. My eyes fall closed when she wraps her hand around my cock.

She doesn't hesitate as she lifts her hips, aligning my cock right where she wants it. Amara looks into my eyes as she sinks down on me, her lips falling open when she sits down in my lap, my cock so fucking deep inside her. "Oh God," she moans, and I smile as I lean back, watching my girlfriend ride me.

I wrap my hands around her hips and push up, thrusting deep into her, moving with her. Her dress is bunched up around her hips, and I pull it up further, revealing her bare tits. I pull her dress over her head and drop it to the floor before leaning in, teasing her nipples, enjoying the moans that leave her lips.

"I was going to take my time with you, baby. I wanted to undress you, take you to bed... I wanted to fucking worship you, but damn... I have no self-control when it comes to you."

She laughs and wraps her hands into my hair, pulling me closer roughly. "Self-control is overrated," she whispers, her lips hovering over mine.

I kiss her slowly, deeply, her tongue tangling with mine. This girl... she kisses the way she sucks cock. I swear I could come just from her kissing me. Combine that with the way she's fucking me and I'm ready to blow.

"You're fucking killing me," I whisper against her lips, leaning back to watch her. "You're so fucking tight, baby. I fucking love watching you take my cock like that."

I hold her by her hips and thrust up, hard. Every fucking moan that leaves her lips gets me closer. The way she's riding me is clearly getting her closer and closer, and it's a fucking sight to behold.

She smiles and picks up the pace, her movements turning more frantic, her moans getting louder. Amara's eyes fall closed just seconds before her muscles contract around me, and I watch her come all over my cock. The way she smiles at me when she opens her eyes almost makes me lose it. I've never felt anything like this. Sex has never been about an emotional connection for me, but everything is different with Amara.

I grab her ass and thrust deeper into her, taking her hard. I need her with an intensity that's foreign to me, but fuck if it doesn't feel good.

"I love watching you fuck me, boyfriend dearest."

That fucking does it for me. Having her call me her boyfriend? Yeah. My eyes fall closed as I lose control, coming deep inside my girl. She slows her pace, longing out my orgasm, milking the fuck out of me. "Fucking hell," I groan, my forehead dropping to hers. "I couldn't hold on any longer. Why the fuck do you always make me lose my mind, huh?"

She giggles and threads her hand through my hair, pulling my face to hers. She kisses me slowly, and my heart skips a fucking beat. I'm so in love with her, it's unreal. Our love will cost us, but it's worth it.

Chapter Thirty-Nine

Amara

I stare at the prototype in my hands, unable to keep my thoughts off Noah. I bite back a smile as I tighten the last screw and turn the toy on. I'd love to see the look on Noah's face if I walk into his office with this toy in my hands, asking him to help me test it. Besides, it'd be the perfect excuse to see him at work... and to have his hands on me.

Things between us have been perfect. We've been keeping our relationship quiet, neither of us sure how my family will react and both of us too scared of what's at stake. It's something we'll have to start thinking about soon, but for now I'm enjoying spending my evenings with him. I just wish I could have his nights too. I hate having to get into my car at night, when what I want to do is fall asleep in his arms.

I grin as I put the toy in my bag and walk out of the lab. My heart is racing at the mere thought of seeing Noah again, even though I saw him last night. I can't wait to see him smile at me and feed my addiction. A burst of giddiness rushes through me at the thought of his golden-brown eyes sparkling with thinly veiled desire.

I'm lost in thought as I walk out of the building, impatient to see him. I didn't think I could fall even harder, yet somehow every day that's exactly what I do.

"Amara?"

I freeze at the sound of a voice I know all too well. A voice I haven't heard in years. A shiver runs down my spine as I turn around.

"Dad," I whisper, the word escaping my lips without me realizing. His eyes light up, and I look away as my heart constricts painfully, every hint of joy and excitement leaching out of me.

"Amara," he says again, his voice trembling ever so slightly. He looks older, but he looks healthy and much stronger than I remember him being. There's a haunted look in his eyes that didn't use to be there. In most of my memories, he was smiling at me. My father stands before me now, both of us strangers to each other.

"You grew up beautifully, like I always knew you would. You look just like your mother."

I grimace, hurt by the reminder of the years he missed. He should have been there to watch me grow up. He should've been there to guide me as I built up my life, but instead he left me scrambling for the pieces of what used to be.

"What are you doing here?" I ask, my voice soft.

He looks down at his feet and clasps his hands together, hunching forward as though he's *nervous*. "I don't know, darling. I know you don't want to see me. You haven't been replying to my text messages. I wasn't going to bother you. I just wanted to see you. I wanted to see how my little girl grew up, if you looked happy. I wasn't going to speak to you, but then you walked my way with the biggest smile on your face, your eyes sparkling like they did when you were a kid... and I couldn't help myself. I just wanted to say hi."

I stare at him, unsure what to say. A thousand emotions are

fighting for dominance within me, and I can't tell whether I'm angry or sad. A bit of both, I guess.

"You should've been there, Dad. Our lives would look so different if you hadn't done what you did. Nothing will ever excuse it. Nothing will ever make it better. The damage can't be undone. You wrecked two families, and I'll never forgive you for it. Never."

He looks away, clearly stricken by my words, and it kills me. I don't want this to hurt. I want to be angry at him, but now that he's standing in front of me, all I feel is heartbreak and regret laced with longing for the life we could've had.

"I know, sweetheart. I'll never forgive myself either. Not a day goes by that I don't wish I could go back in time and make better choices. I paid the price for my actions, and I'll pay for as long as I live. Every time you refuse to reply to my messages I'm paying, Amara."

Intense devastation threatens to close up my throat, tears imminent. I don't want to cry in front of him. I don't ever want to cry over him again.

"I just want to know if you're happy, Amara. Are you doing okay? I'm not here to ruin your life any further. I'll respect your wishes. If you don't want to see me or hear from me, I won't keep pestering you."

A fat teardrop rolls down my cheek, and I swipe it away angrily. "I'm not happy. Not truly. You took my happiness with you the day you left us. I work hard, and I study hard. I've done well. I do all the things I think I should. I'm building an unshakeable foundation for myself so I won't ever be in a vulnerable position. I'm doing okay, but I'm not as happy as I could've been. You left me scarred, Dad."

I refuse to lie just to appease him. He doesn't deserve white lies. He wrecked me, and it's only fair that he knows it.

Dad inhales deeply, his eyes falling closed. "I'm sorry, Amara. I've never said this to you, but losing you is my biggest regret in life. You are and have always been the light in my life. I'm proud of you. You're doing well, and you grew up to be everything I hoped you'd be. You're hardworking, intelligent, beautiful. I always knew you'd be an amazing woman, but you've exceeded my expectations. I'm so very proud of you."

I grit my teeth and straighten my back in anger. "You're sorry? I don't need your apologies, Dad. I don't want them. I don't want your sugarcoated words. I can't do this. I'm not doing this. I'm not going to stand here and pretend like you aren't a monster."

I swallow down a sob and turn to walk away, my heart in pieces.

"Amara," he calls. "Tell me, sweetheart. Do you want me to stop contacting you? I want to do what's best for you."

I turn back to look at him, his bright blue eyes identical to mine. Everyone always thinks I got my blue eyes from my mother, until they meet my father.

"I don't know," I tell him honestly. I'm not so immature that I'll cut him off entirely when I haven't made a decision yet, but I don't want to be rushed into choosing either. "I don't know what I need. All I know is that I can't do this right now."

Dad nods, a sad expression on his face as I turn and walk away, the way he once did.

Chapter Forty

NOAH

My phone rings and I smile when I see that it's Amara. "Hey you," I say, grinning to myself.

"Noah," she whispers, her voice sounding off. She sounds the way she did when I found her standing in the rain, heartbroken and lost.

"What happened?"

She laughs, the sound hollow. "How did you know?"

"I just do."

Amara sighs, and I lean back in my seat behind my desk. "I know you're at work, and you probably have at least another hour to go, but is there any chance you could meet me at the bar you took me to that time... when you found me in the rain. I... I can wait."

I check my schedule, finding three more patients on the roster. "Absolutely. I'll be there in ten, okay?"

"Thank you, Noah," she whispers, her tone a little lighter. I'm not sure what's going on, but something clearly happened.

I rise from my seat the second she ends the call, overcome with worry. I can't stop thinking about what might have happened. Something with her company, maybe? It's the one thing she intensely cares about. It can't be about us. If Harold found out, he'd be standing in my office right now.

"Georgia, cancel my remaining consultations. I have a personal emergency I need to attend to."

She jumps up from her seat, her eyes widening. I notice the concern in her eyes, and the curiosity, but I don't know what to tell her. I haven't told the girls about Amara and me because I don't want to have to listen to their objections, and I don't trust Maddie to keep her mouth shut. Georgia nods at me, and I force a polite smile on my face as I walk out.

I'm impatient as I drive over to the bar Amara is waiting at. I hate the idea of her waiting, but more so, I hate the thought of her hurting and sitting in that bar by herself. I want to be there for her, no matter what might be going on.

I'm restless by the time I walk into the bar, and it's not until my eyes find hers that I relax. She's in a booth this time, instead of by the bar. Amara smiles at me, but for the first time since I met her, that beautiful smile of hers doesn't reach her eyes.

I walk toward her, and her eyes never leave mine. She's done this to me from the very first moment we met. She captivates me with a single look.

"Hey," I say, my voice soft.

"Hi," she replies, her voice shaky.

I slide into the booth, taking in the way she's trembling ever so slightly. "Do you want to talk about it or do you want a hug?"

She looks into my eyes, and then she smiles. "A hug, please."

I open up my arms for her and she moves closer, resting her head on top of my shoulder, her lips brushing against my neck. I close my arms around her and hold her tightly.

"Sometimes, when my sister has a bad day, all she really needs is a hug. I've been told that I'm a bit of a problem-solver, so my first instinct is to ask you what's wrong and find a way to fix it... but she taught me that it can wait."

Amara sighs and snuggles closer. "Aria is a wise woman."

I nod. "She is."

Amara pulls away a little to look at me, her expression unreadable. "Did you... did you tell her about us?"

I nod and thread my hand through her hair. "Of course. She was so happy, it was kinda cute. Even Grayson seemed excited for us. I think he actually likes you, you know?"

Amara grins at me, a hint of relief in her eyes. I guess it's just as hard on her to keep our relationship a secret as it is for me. "I wondered, but I didn't really dare ask before. How do you feel about your best friend being with your sister?"

I look away, unsure how to answer. "It's complicated. They're both very broken individuals, and at the start I wasn't sure if they'd be each other's destruction or salvation. I knew it could only ever be either of those two. There's no middle ground with them, and that's what worried me. The last thing I wanted is for either of them to get hurt. My worries were misplaced, though. They're happy together, and I'm happy for them."

She blinks, drawing my attention to her ridiculously long lashes. She's beautiful. Every little thing about her is just beautiful.

"They're lucky to have you, you know?"

I frown, wishing that was true. Both Aria and Gray have given me far more than I've ever given them. Aria practically raised herself. And Gray? He's something else altogether. I never understood why a man so brilliant and so reclusive chose me to be friends with. Compared to either Aria or Gray, I'm solidly mediocre. I work hard, but I'm not a genius like both of them are.

I sigh and lean in, cupping her cheek gently. "So, do you want to talk about what upset you today?" She's been avoiding the topic, and while I don't want to push her, I'm concerned.

Amara pulls away, and I instantly miss her touch. "I ran into my father," she whispers, almost as though she can't bear to say it out loud. "It just feels like it reopened so many wounds. I thought I'd healed, but just seeing him took me back to a time that I'd prefer to forget altogether. He asked me if I wanted him to stop contacting me, and I didn't know what to say, Noah. I always thought my answer would be a resounding yes, but when it came down to it, I couldn't say it."

I bite down on my lip and nod, unsure of what to say. She hasn't told me much about her father, and I get it, so I don't probe. I hate talking about my parents too. Right now, in this moment, I wish she'd let me in, though. I wish I knew more about him, so I could find the right words to say.

"I won't pretend to know what that's like, Amara... but you seem conflicted. You wouldn't feel that way if part of you didn't want him in your life. I know he's hurt you, and I know he left you, but he's back now, isn't he? I guess the question is whether you think you can forgive him, and whether you want him in your life going forward. I can't tell you the answer to that, but I can tell you I'd give the world to speak to my father one last time. All parents are different, but you have yours... and if even a small part of you wants him in your life, then at least think about it carefully before you decide."

Amara looks down at her hands, her entire demeanor turning vulnerable. I lean back and take a sip of the cocktail in front of her as she mulls over my words. This seems like a sore subject for her, and all I want to do is console her and support her, but I worry I might've said the wrong thing. It's hard for me to understand what she's going through, because there's nothing I wouldn't do to have the luxury of arguing with my parents.

"It's complicated, Noah. My father made a lot of bad choices, and our family suffered for it. Not just ours. He destroyed multiple lives alongside his own, and some of the things he did are simply unforgivable. I know they are, and part of me wants to punish him for everything Mom and I went through, but he's my *Dad*. Seeing him was painful because it reminded me of everything I missed out on, everything *he* missed out on."

I wrap my hand around her waist and pull her against me, her head dropping to my shoulder. "I know you're hurt, and I can't possibly understand what you're going through, but whatever you choose to do, make sure that you aren't hurting yourself with your own choices just because they seem like the right ones."

Amara nods, a tear dropping down her cheek. "I don't know what to do, Noah."

I press a kiss on top of her head. "You don't need to figure it out right now, baby. Take your time."

She nods, and I hold her as she tries to compose herself. I hope she'll let me in someday. I hope I'll one day have the strength to tell her about my parents without breaking down. I hope we can heal each other. But above all, I hope that someday, she and I can both let go of the past.

Chapter Forty-One

NOAH

I stare up at the Astor mansion, wrecked with guilt. I've been avoiding this for as long as I could, but Harold is no longer taking no for an answer, and neither is Charlotte.

She invites me over for dinner at least once a month, and usually I love her for it. Tonight I'm feeling conflicted. I'm dating Amara behind their backs, and I'm about to walk in with a smile on my face, pretending like I'm not counting down the seconds until I can get her alone. I feel strangely out of it as I walk in, almost numb. I guess I'm just resigned.

I need to speak to Amara. There's no way we can keep our relationship a secret much longer. They'll find out eventually, and I'd much rather they hear it from us. I know she's scared, but I don't think I can do this for much longer. I want to take her on dates without having to worry that we'll be seen together. I want to kiss her in public and hold her hand. I want it all with her, and we can't commit to each other fully when there's still so much standing between us.

"You're here, darling," Charlotte says when I walk into the

dining room, a bright smile on her face. I try my hardest to keep my eyes on her, but all I can see is Amara looking way too fucking stunning in that dark green dress she's wearing, her long red hair flowing down her body. I can't wait to get her out of that dress.

Charlotte rises from her chair at the dining table, and I smile as I walk up to her. She hugs me tightly and then leans back to look at me, grinning. "It feels like I haven't seen you in forever. How have you been, sweetheart?" She pulls my seat out for me, and I sit down opposite Amara.

"That's because he *hasn't* been here in a while," Harold says, taking the seat next to mine. "Have I been keeping you too busy, boy?"

I smile at him and shake my head. "Not at all. I enjoy working with you, Harold. You know that."

He nods and looks at his daughter with a raised brow, and my heart squeezes tightly. Harold is so gentle with his family, and being around them always reminds me of what I'm missing. I wish I could introduce Amara to my parents. My mother would have loved her, and my father would have adored her. It's all I can think about throughout dinner.

"You all right, sweetheart? You barely touched your food," Charlotte says.

I smile at her as the staff clears the table. "It was lovely, as always. I'm just tired, that's all."

Harold glances at me, his brows raised. "What's got you so tired? Or rather... *who*?" I tense, forcing myself not to look at Amara, and Harold chuckles. "I guess things worked out for Kim and you. She's a lovely girl, and she'll bring your career to new heights."

Amara's expression drops, and I look down when I see a flash of hurt in her eyes. I'm tempted to tell Harold everything right now, but I can't do that without Amara's consent. This is something we'll have to do together. We need to be on the same page.

"No, it's not Kim. I'm genuinely just tired." It's not a lie. Amara and I have been spending our evenings together, and when she leaves, we end up on the phone for hours before going to bed. I've barely been sleeping, but I don't mind it at all. Every minute I get to spend with her is precious.

Amara rises to her feet the second the table is cleared, and I look up at her to find her avoiding my gaze. "I'm tired," she says. "I'm going to bed early."

She walks away, leaving us staring after her. She seems annoyed, and all I want to do is go after her and make sure she's okay, but I can't.

"What's wrong with her?" Harold asks his daughter.

Charlotte shakes her head. "Who knows? I think she's been busy with school. She's probably just tired."

It isn't that. I'm guessing that she's mad because Harold brought up Kim, but there's nothing I can do about that until she gives me permission to tell him about us.

"I'd better get going," I say as I rise from my seat. "Dinner was lovely as always," I tell Charlotte.

She smiles as I walk up to her and presses a kiss to my cheek while Harold claps me on the back. I'm torn as I walk out of the dining room. I know I should walk out and get into my car, but I can't. Not when I know Amara is upset.

I bite down on my lip and hesitate in the hallway, turning to walk toward her bedroom instead of the exit. It's stupid, and I know it, but I can't stay away.

I pause in front of her bedroom door, looking around to make sure there's no staff around. I find Amara sitting on her bed, her knees pulled to her chest. She looks up at me, surprised. Her surprise is swiftly replaced by sadness, though.

I lean back against her door, a smile on my face. "Hi, baby."

She purses her lips and stares at me as she rises to her feet. "*Kim* again?" she says, her eyes flashing with possessiveness. I smile to myself. She's so fucking sexy when she looks at me like that, but I don't have the guts to tell her that right now.

"Has Grandpa been making you see her? Has she been there any of the times you went for lunch with him?"

She pauses in front of me and places her palms on my chest. Her eyes are flashing with anger, and I just can't help myself. I thread my hand through her hair and pull her closer, kissing her the way I wanted to when I first walked into the dining room.

Amara kisses me back, her body melting against mine for just a second before she pushes against me, her eyes narrowed.

"You didn't answer my question."

I chuckle and cup her cheek. I fucking adore her. "No, baby. I haven't seen her since that day at the vineyard. I only have eyes for you, you know that."

Her anger diminishes just slightly, but it doesn't dissipate. I grab her and turn us around, pushing her against the door. "I'm more than happy to tell your grandfather all about us. That'll shut him up."

Amara looks at me, her eyes brimming with fear and insecurity. "You know we can't."

I lean in, my lips brushing against her. I kiss the edge of her lips, teasing her. Amara tilts her head, and I smile against her lips before kissing her. I pull away to look at her, unsure how to reason with her. "He'll find out eventually, baby... and it'll make him stop talking about Kim altogether."

"I'm not ready," she says, her voice soft. "I'm not ready yet, Noah. I'm not ready to face the consequences of loving you."

I nod at her and sigh. I'll respect her decision for now, but we can't keep this up. We have to tell Harold before he finds out.

Amara rises to her tiptoes to kiss me, and my worries fade away. The power she holds over me is insane. "Noah, I don't even want you thinking about her," she says, her gaze accusatory. Her hands run down my body, and my eyes fall closed.

I smile at her and cup her cheek, my thumb brushing over her lips. "My thoughts are always filled with *you*. Always."

"Prove it." Amara's hands run down to my suit trousers, and I groan when she grabs my cock.

"Here? Now?"

She nods. "Everyone thinks I went to bed. I want your hands on my body, Noah. I want your thoughts filled with me."

I chuckle as I lift her into my arms. "Oh baby, don't you fucking tempt me. You know I've been wanting to fuck you against this goddamn door forever now."

She smirks at me provocatively and wraps her legs around me. I lean in and kiss her, and the way she moves against me drives me insane.

Amara gasps when I reach underneath her dress and drag my thumb over her clit, teasing her. I'm really starting to appreciate this not wearing underwear thing. I kiss her and play with her, enjoying the way she just gets wetter and wetter for me. I love the way she moves her hips, the way she makes it so clear she wants me deep inside her.

She yanks on my belt, her movements frantic, and I grin. I hold her up as she grabs my cock and aligns it. She looks at me pleadingly, and I'm tempted to tease her, to withhold what she wants, but I can't. I'm too desperate for her.

Amara moans as I push into her, and I wrap my hand over her mouth. "Quiet, baby. Your grandfather and mother are probably only a few doors away."

She nods, and I let go of her, placing my hands on her hips instead. I pull back, only to thrust back into her, *hard*. I fuck her like that, up against her door in her childhood bedroom. She's biting down on her lip, trying to keep her moans in, and she's never looked sexier.

"Look at you," I whisper. "Your grandfather just bid us good-night, and here you are just minutes later, taking my cock up against your door."

Amara leans in and kisses me, her touch punishing. "You're no better," she tells me, her lips moving to my neck. She kisses me right below my ear, sending a shiver running down my spine. "You're the one fucking me in my grandfather's house. Tell me, babe... how good is my pussy?"

I laugh, I can't help it. I love everything about this woman. "Best I ever had," I whisper.

"The only one you'll ever have," she warns me, and I grab her hair, pulling her lips back to mine. I kiss her, and the way she moves her body against mine, the way her tongue tangles with mine... fucking hell. She's fucking me with her goddamn mouth. This woman. She'll be the death of me.

I fuck her hard, rotating my hips against her the way she likes it. "You want to come all over my cock, don't you?"

She moans, and I shake my head as I wrap my hand over her mouth, warning her with my expression. The way she looks at me, with desperation and lust warring in her eyes... she's close. I smile as I fuck her harder, enjoying the way I'm keeping her on the edge.

"I'm going to make a mess of your pussy, baby. I'm going to come so fucking deep inside you, you'll have wetness leaking down your thighs all night. You'll go to bed like that, with a reminder of me in my absence."

She moans, and I tighten my grip on her face, pressing my hand against her lips harder. "Shh," I whisper. "If you can't be quiet you don't get to come."

She nods, her gaze pleading, and I smile as I increase my pace. I fuck her harder, keeping her at an angle that makes my cock brush against her clit every time I push back into her. The way she moves her body against mine... *fuck*.

It doesn't take Amara long to lose control, and when her muscles contract around my cock, I lose it too. I come deep inside her, barely able to suppress my own moans.

She smiles at me, and my heart skips a beat. "I'm so fucking obsessed with you," I whisper, and she laughs.

"I love you, Noah."

I press a kiss to her forehead, my heart racing. "I love you too, baby."

I pull back to look at her and cup her face. "I want this with you, Amara. I'm done hiding. I want to be with you openly. I'm done sneaking around. We have to tell your grandfather. *Soon.*"

She looks at me, her expression resigned. She inhales deeply, and then she nods. "Okay, babe. We'll tell him soon."

I nod. I have no idea how Harold is going to respond, but there's no escaping this. I'm not letting Amara go, and I'm ready to truly be with her — fully, wholeheartedly, openly.

Chapter Forty-Two

Noah

I smile to myself as I flip through my files, eager for this day to end so I can go home to Amara. The last couple of weeks have been perfect. Truly being able to call her mine changed everything for me. I didn't think I could fall any further for her, but I did.

I sit up in surprise when my office door slams open, my eyes wide. Harold walks in, his expression chilling. The way he looks at me... he *knows*.

I'm resigned when he throws a stack of photos onto my desk, all of them of Amara and me. There are photos of us in Cali and then there are some of us walking in and out of my house, my arms around her. He's even got a few photos of us kissing. How? How did Amara and I not realize we were being watched?

"I warned you," Harold says. "I offered you my support, my guidance, my network. I offered you all I could, Noah. I asked you for one simple thing in return. All I asked of you was that you stay away from my granddaughter." His voice breaks, and his expression betrays genuine hurt I wasn't expecting. It was never my intention to hurt him, to let him down.

"Harold, I..." I don't even know what to say to him. There's nothing I can say that'll make this better.

"You betrayed me, Noah, and in doing so you're ruining your entire life. I had great plans for you. I thought of you as family. I supported you like you were one of my own."

He turns away and runs a hand through his hair, his usually broad straight shoulders slumped. I swallow hard, trying my best to suppress the sorrow I feel. I knew this day would come. I knew he'd eventually find out, and I've been ready to face the consequences from the moment I decided to go after Amara.

"I'm sorry for breaking your trust," I tell him. "But I won't apologize for loving your granddaughter. I'm well aware that I don't deserve her, but I'll never stop trying to give her the best of me."

He looks at me, his eyes flashing with rage. "The best of you? What is that exactly, Noah? You're broken, and you know it. You're half the man you could be, haunted by your past. You can't offer Amara what she deserves, and you'll break her heart. Your love for her will never overshadow the pain you live with."

I laugh, the sound humorless. "You think you know me just because you've read my résumé, because you ran a background check? You know nothing about me, Harold."

He shakes his head and looks down at his feet before looking up at me. "You're fired, Noah. You're fired on grounds of fraternizing with a patient, in addition to breaking regulation by getting involved with a student while employed as faculty staff. Effective immediately."

I knew it was coming, but it still hurts. I inhale shakily and nod. "Very well. Fire me, Harold. But that won't keep me away from Amara. I knew what I was getting into with her. I knew it'd cost me everything. I'll bear the consequences."

He stares me down, a hint of pain shining through his anger. "This is nothing yet, Noah. You have no idea what you got into. I warned you, over and over again. You'll regret being with her. You'll end up wishing you never set your eyes on my granddaughter. And when that day comes... it'll shatter my little girl's heart beyond repair."

He runs a shaky hand through his hair, his face contorted with barely concealed desperation. "Walk away now," he says. "Walk away now and I'll leave you be. I'll even write you a recommendation letter so you'll be able to walk into a cushy job anywhere you please. Leave her. Leave Amara, and I'll get you any job you want and one million dollars on top of it. Enough for you to do whatever the hell you please for years to come."

He looks at me, his expression pleading, and I grit my teeth. "Do you love her?" I ask him. "Or is Amara just a tool to you, an asset? Do you care about her happiness at all?"

Harold smiles, even though his eyes convey misery. "More than you'll ever know. More than *she'll* ever know. I love my granddaughter, Noah. If you love her too, then walk away now and let her have the happiness I know she'd eventually find without you."

"Happiness as defined by you? And what is that, Harold? Married to a man she doesn't even like, giving up on her company and her dreams? No. Amara isn't alone anymore, Harold. If you so much as try to take away her smile, you'll have to go through me."

He shakes his head and sighs. "Go through you? Noah, you'll be the reason she'll lose her smile. You're the reason I'll lose my granddaughter. You'll alienate her from her family by refusing to leave her, and in the end, it'll be you that'll wreck her happiness. You think you love her, but when it comes down to it, that love won't stand the test of time. You'll falter, and you'll do irreparable damage." He holds his hands up and looks me in the eye, his gaze intense, unwavering. "I'll get down on my knees and beg you if I must, Noah. Leave her."

I shake my head. "No. She's the single best thing that ever happened to me, and I know she's happy with me too. You already took my job. I have nothing left to lose, Harold. I won't let her go."

He nods. "Then you leave me no choice. You'll leave her eventually. You won't be able to find a job. You will never work as a doctor again, Noah. You won't be able to support Amara. Soon, you won't even be able to put food on the table. Let's see how long you can live like that. We'll talk again. Soon."

I smile at him. "No, we won't."

Harold looks around my office and shakes his head. "You have no idea what you're throwing away. You don't even realize how much more you'll lose by defying me today, but you will. Eventually you will, and you'll leave her. I'll be counting down the days."

He turns and walks out of my office, and I slump into my seat as the door closes behind him. My eyes fall closed as I fight to keep the desperation at bay. He's right. He's Harold Astor, and I'm nothing, no one. There's every chance I won't be able to support Amara, that I truly won't be able to put food on the table, and when that happens... I'll lose her.

Chapter Forty-Three

Amara

"Is it true?" my mother asks. I look up, finding her standing in my doorway, her eyes flashing with anger.

I frown, unsure what I've done to anger her this time. There's always something. I'm always letting her down one way or another. "You'll have to elaborate, mother."

She crosses her arms over each other, a hint of sorrow behind the anger in her eyes. "Noah," she says simply.

My first instinct is to deny everything, to hide it from her the way I hide everything I care about. But I can't. Not this time. I can't lie about Noah.

"Yes, it's true," I tell her, my voice soft. "We're dating."

"Dating?" she repeats. "You stood right here in this room when you promised me that you'd never get involved with him, that you two would never be more than friends."

I rise to my feet, my body tense. "Mom, he makes me happy. When I'm with him, I'm happier than I've been in years. He makes me feel like myself again. Mom. Why wouldn't you want

She swallows hard, and I freeze when she visibly blinks away tears in her eyes. "Do you have any idea what you've done?" she asks. "Grandpa fired him. Noah was going places, Amara. You ruined his future, all because you couldn't stay away. Because you wanted something that wasn't meant for you and pursued it without caring about what it'd cost Noah, what it'll cost *you*. There's no happy ending here, Amara. No matter how much you think you love him, there's no scenario in which you two end up happily married."

I stare at her in shock, her words slowly registering. "Grandpa *fired* him? Why would he do that? Why would he put so much effort into mentoring Noah only to fire him?"

Mom stares at me, barely able to hide the flash of disgust in her eyes. "Because of *you*. Because of your selfishness. Noah promised your grandfather that he'd stay away from you, and he broke that promise. You know full well Grandpa operates under a zero-tolerance policy. Noah broke his trust, and it'll cost him everything."

I shake my head. "No. No way. I saw how the two of them were together. Grandpa cares about him. He wouldn't..."

"But he did. He did, Amara, and it's your fault. You took a risk, counting on Grandpa to forgive you two, but he won't. He'll never let you be with Noah. I warned you. I pleaded with you. You promised me you wouldn't get involved with him, and yet here we are. Your relationship with Noah is done regardless of how hard you fight to be with him, because he'll never forgive you for taking away the opportunities he had, the life that would've laid ahead of him if not for *you*. It might take time, it might even take years, but it'll happen."

I glare at her, swallowing down my own tears. "Noah isn't like you, Mom. He won't resent me the way you resented Dad. He's a better person than you'll ever be — and he's talented. He doesn't need Grandpa."

Mom laughs, her eyes filled with disbelief. "You're so naïve, Amara. You have no idea what you've done. You have no idea what your grandfather will do to Noah because of you. Noah will never work as a doctor again. Not unless he leaves you. What do you think he'll choose? You, or the career he worked for all his life? Did you know Noah's father was a doctor? This isn't just a job to him. It's his father's legacy. Do you think he'll leave that behind for you?"

I look away, my heart squeezing painfully. I didn't know that. I didn't know Noah became a doctor because of his father. He never speaks of his parents. A hint of unease settles deep within me. I cling onto my faith in us, but part of me can't help but fear that my mother is right. My love for Noah might lead to his ruin.

"Leave him, Amara. Walk away now, and your grandfather will spare him."

"Is that what Grandpa told you, back when you chose to be with Dad?"

Her expression falters, and for a moment understanding flashes through her eyes. "It isn't the same, Amara... but even so, I should've done as I was asked. I should've seen that my father wanted what was best for me, the way I want what's best for *you*. For both of you. Leave him and let him live up to his endless potential. Please, Amara. Don't let your selfishness ruin both your lives."

A tear runs down my cheek as I open my lips to tell her I'll never leave Noah, but my words remain stuck in my throat. Fear unlike anything I've ever felt renders me speechless. I can take responsibility for myself, for the consequences I'll face because of my choices... but I can't drag Noah down with me. I genuinely didn't think Grandpa would fire him. I expected there to be tension between them, and I expected grandpa to disapprove... but I didn't expect this.

"Is he home?" I ask, my voice soft.

Mom nods. "He's in his office."

I nod and walk past her, my heart feeling strangely tender, almost as though it knows it's moments away from breaking. I swallow hard as I raise my hand to my grandfather's office door.

It's a room he and I share so many fond memories in. I'm the only one that was ever allowed to disturb him while he was working from home, and he'd always drop everything to play with me when I was little, or to help me with homework when I insisted on his help instead of my tutor's as I grew older.

I brace myself as I knock on his door, not waiting for him to call me in. My entire body is tense as I walk in, and when Grandpa looks up at me with a resigned look in his eyes, I've got the answers to questions I don't want to ask.

I ask anyway.

"Did you fire Noah?" My voice breaks, and I clench my jaw, willing myself to keep it together.

He nods. "I warned him, Amara. He broke my trust."

I look down, unable to face him, unable to hide the pain that's slowly tearing through me.

"Why? Why are you doing this to him? To us?"

Grandpa looks at me, his expression solemn, not a hint of regret in his eyes. There's no remorse. But then again, I never should have expected it from him.

"He did this to himself, Amara."

I sniff, holding back my tears as best as I can. My lungs are burning, but I refuse to cry. "He gave you everything. He worked himself to the bone for you. He looked up to you, Grandpa. You were his hero. How could you? All because he *loves* me?"

Grandpa looks away when a stray tear runs down my cheek, and I swipe at it angrily. I can't be weak. Not right now.

"I warned Noah. He knew my support hinged on him staying away from you, and he didn't. He knew what the consequences would be, Amara. All I did was keep my word."

"Your word," I whisper. "What about your promises to me? All my life you've promised me you'd always be there for me, that you'd always be in my corner. Can't you see that you doing this to Noah is killing me? It's me you're hurting, Grandpa... far more so than Noah. I love him, Grandpa."

He shakes his head and sighs. "Love? You can't love him, Amara. You don't even know him."

I stare at him in disbelief. "Grandpa, if you love me at all, even just a little... then please don't do this to him. It's my heart you're breaking, not his."

His eyes fall closed, and he inhales shakily. "Amara," he says, his voice soft, pleading. "I love you more than anything. I always will."

"Then why are you doing this to me? Wasn't it enough to cut my company off from funding? Wasn't it enough to destroy my dreams? Why are you going after every single thing that makes me happy, just because it doesn't fit in with your idea of who I'm supposed to be?"

Grandpa stares at me, almost as though he's at a loss for words. "Do you want to save him, Amara? Do you want to safeguard Noah's future? Walk away. Leave him, and he won't face repercussions for defying me."

I shake my head. "Do this, and you'll lose me. I will never forgive you."

He sighs and looks out the window. "You will," he murmurs. "But by then it'll be too late."

I stare at him, too tired to argue with him, to decrypt his words. Instead, I turn and walk away, looking back at him as I reach his office door.

"Goodbye, Grandpa," I whisper, my voice breaking. I walk away, truly putting myself and my happiness first for the first time in my life.

Chapter Forty-Four

Noah

I look up when I hear the front door opening, a reluctant smile lifting the edges of my lips up. I rise to my feet when I hear her footsteps heading my way. Amara rounds the corner, her eyes finding mine, and I freeze when a tear drops down her cheek. She sniffs and bites down on her lip, trying her best to keep from falling apart, but I see the pain in those beautiful blue eyes of hers.

"I'm so sorry," she says, her voice breaking. She chokes back a sob, and I rush up to her, taking her into my arms. "I'm sorry, Noah. This... it's... it's all my fault."

I hold her tightly, my hand running over her back soothingly. "I've been trying to think of a way to tell you, but I guess you've already heard the news."

She nods, her grip on me tightening. I inhale deeply as I drop my forehead to hers. "Don't cry, baby," I whisper. "My heart can't take it. You're killing me."

She sniffs and looks up at me through her tears. "I did this," she murmurs. "I did this to you."

I cup her cheeks and swipe at her tears with my thumbs. "I'm a grown man, Amara. I knew what I was getting into when I showed up at your lab after you so vehemently pushed me away, trying to do the right thing. I could've let you walk away then, but I didn't. Being with you is worth anything. It's worth risking everything. Besides... I'm a doctor, baby. I'll be okay. I'll find something. It may take a while, but I'll be okay. It was just a job."

She shakes her head, her eyes falling closed. "It's not that simple, Noah. My grandpa... he won't let you find another job."

I lean in and press a lingering kiss to her forehead, my eyes falling closed as my heart fills with love for the woman in front of me. She's more hurt than I am. To have someone hurting on my behalf the way she does... it's something I didn't think I'd ever experience outside of my family.

"Baby, your grandfather isn't all-powerful. I found you an investor, didn't I? I can find myself a job. Everything is going to be okay."

She nods, her eyes filled with hope. The sooner I find something, the better. I can tell this is going to be hard on Amara. She's going to keep blaming herself until I find something new. It'll hurt her more than it'll ever hurt me.

I grab her chin and tilt her face toward mine, leaning in for a kiss. Amara sighs when my lips meet hers, and I smile against her lips, right before deepening the kiss. She opens up for me, her tongue brushing against mine. The way she kisses me is different tonight. Her touch is filled with desperation, with sadness.

I lift her into my arms and carry her to the staircase, pausing when I notice the bags in the hallway. I glance at her, and the look in her eyes has my heart working overtime.

"I left," she tells me. "I'm done being a pawn in my grandfather's games. I warned him that if he did this to you... he'd lose me. I meant it."

I carry her up the stairs quietly, unsure what to say, what to feel. Amara's eyes are filled with insecurity by the time I place her down on my bed. "Amara," I murmur, settling on top of her, my forehead against hers. "I don't want to be the reason you lose your family. I'll be okay. I promise you, I'll be fine. Don't ruin your relationship with your grandfather because of me. I have no family other than Aria, baby. Your grandfather may have his flaws, but he loves you. He's only trying to protect you, in his own twisted way. He wants what's best for you, and I can't fault him for thinking you can do better than me... because you can."

"No," she snaps. "I hate that you can't see yourself through my eyes. Noah, you're the most amazing man I've ever met. You're the best person I know, and I'm honored I get to be with you. I wish you could see that. I wish you could see how amazing you are, how lucky I am to be with you."

I smile at her and thread my hand through her hair, my eyes on hers. "I love you, Amara. I really do. But so does your grandfather. Don't alienate your family over me. I'd give the world to have a family of my own, so don't walk away from yours so easily."

She looks at me, her eyes brimming with sincerity. "*I'm* your family now, Noah. And if my grandfather wants to, he can be part of our family too — as soon as he accepts us being together. This isn't just about you, babe. It's about *me* too. It's about me choosing my own path and pursuing my own happiness. I've had enough, Noah. He can either support the road I've chosen, or he'll have to get out of my way. I'm done trying to please my family at the expense of my happiness. I won't sacrifice you."

I stare at her, my heart overflowing with happiness, gratitude and love, all blended into what can only be described as pure *bliss*. I never thought I'd experience this... someone putting me first the way Amara does. "I love you," I tell her. "You're everything, Amara. Everything I've ever wished for, and then some."

She smiles at me, and that look in her eyes just makes me fall even deeper. "You're more," she whispers. "More than I ever hoped for. More than I deserve."

I lean in and kiss her, taking my time with her, kissing away her every worry, every hint of sorrow, until I'm all she can think about.

"Noah," she whispers, and her voice sends a thrill down my spine the way it did the first time I met her.

I lean in, my lips brushing over hers. "I love you," I whisper before kissing her. Amara moans against my lips and threads her hand through my hair. The way she moves underneath me drives me insane. No one can do this to me but her. She's the only person that can make my mood shift from worry and sadness to pure bliss within seconds.

My hands roam over her body, teasing her, stroking her. I love the way she moans for me, the way she looks at me with lust-filled eyes. "I want you," she whispers. "I need you close, Noah."

I slip my hand between her thighs, not surprised to find her wet already. I watch her as her lips fall open when I run my index finger over her, teasing her, staying away from where she wants me. "Please," she whispers, and I give her what she wants. I've got her close within minutes, but she shakes her head. "I want to come with you inside me, babe. I want *you*."

I smile as I pull away to undress. Amara leans back and watches me as I unbutton my shirt, dropping it to the floor. She smirks and pulls her dress over her head when I reach for my belt. Before long, we're both naked, and I grin as I lean over her.

Amara's hands run over my body, and she looks up at me impatiently. I can't help but chuckle. "I fucking adore you," I whisper as I push the tip of my cock into her, loving the way her lips fall open. "You aren't leaving my bed tonight, baby. From now on, all your nights are mine."

I push all the way into her, and the way she moans my name is music to my ears. I pull back only to thrust into her again, slowly, deeply, over and over again. I take my time with her, driving her crazy, fucking her at that angle she loves.

It doesn't take long before her breathing turns shallow and her cheeks flush, her eyes filled with lust. She's close, and I watch her as I push her over the edge. Her muscles contract around my cock, and just that is enough to make me come right along with her.

My eyes fall closed, and I drop my forehead to hers. "I'm crazy about you," I whisper.

Amara wraps her arms around me, her grip tight. "I love you," she whispers. "You and I... we'll be okay."

I nod and press a kiss to her forehead. We will be. So long as I've got her, I'll be fine.

Chapter Forty-Five

Noah

I stare at my laptop screen, feeling entirely disillusioned. I've lost count of the amount of job rejections I've received so far. I wasn't even able to get to the interview stage for any of my applications.

I knew Harold wouldn't make it easy on me, but I underestimated his influence. I'm starting to fear that he was right, and I'll never work as a doctor again. I look up and glance at Amara. The way she keeps her eyes on her own laptop combined with her rigid spine tells me she knows I just received another rejection.

She tries to hide her fears and the guilt she feels, but she's transparent to me. It's in the way she's lost in thought so often, the way she looks at me as though she expects me to one day look back at her with regret in my eyes. It'll never happen. She isn't to blame for the situation we're in, but I'm starting to worry.

It's been six weeks. Six weeks of contacting everyone Harold ever introduced me to in addition to everyone I know in the industry. Six weeks of constant applications and endless rejections. My savings won't last long, not with mortgage payments and student loan repayments.

Amara is working as hard as she can, but realistically her company won't be profitable for another year, if she even manages to make her company profitable at all — most companies aren't in their first year, and we both know it. Harold cut her off, and I know it kills her to have to depend on me. What happens when my savings run out?

I bite down on my lip as I rise to my feet, remembering the one person I haven't called yet. Dr. Johnson. He's retired, so I didn't think of him instantly, but if nothing else, he might have some connections I can reach out to.

Amara looks at me as I walk out of the living room, and I force a smile onto my face. I'm not fooling her, though. She can tell that I'm losing hope, and it's hitting her harder than it is me.

I stare at the photos in the hallway, my gaze settling on a photo of my father and me. I'm wearing his doctor's coat, a stethoscope that's far too big for me around my neck. I must've been six years old. Even back then, all I wanted was to follow in my father's footsteps. I worked my ass off for over a decade to become a general practitioner, nearly giving up multiple times during my residency. I fought through the poverty Aria and I were surrounded by, I fought to stay in school. I won't give up now.

I sigh as I scroll through my contacts. You'd think it'd get easier after six weeks of this shit, but it doesn't. I force a smile onto my face as I press dial. I'm not even sure why I do it, but it helps me put myself into *polite physician* mode, even when I know no one can see me.

"Noah? It's so good to hear from you," Dr. Johnson says, and my heart warms at the sound of his voice. I loved working for him, and I genuinely wish he hadn't sold his practice. But then again, if he hadn't, I'd never have met Amara.

"Hi, Dr. Johnson. How's retirement treating you?"

He laughs, and my own smile turns genuine. "It's boring. I had a whole list of things I've always wanted to do, yet somehow I miss working. I miss the patients, the clinic. I miss being a doctor.

Never thought I'd say it, but it's true. Retirement doesn't suit me at all."

"You'll get used to it," I tell him. He worked long hours right until he sold the clinic, so I can imagine that it's hard to adjust. It is for me. Being home every day, watching Amara go to school to teach classes and work on her PhD project... it's hard.

"Enough about me, though. How did things go with you? Where do you work now? I've been meaning to follow up with you, but everything got so busy during the handover of the clinic that I kept putting it off. I'm sorry."

I glance at the photo of my father and me, a sense of loss washing over me. I wonder what he'd tell me today. Would he have any wise advice for me?

"It wasn't easy to find something, but eventually I got a call from Astor College and they offered me a job thanks to the recommendation you gave them. I've been meaning to thank you for that, but life ended up becoming a complete whirlwind shortly after. Unfortunately, that job didn't end up working out."

"Astor college?" he repeats, his tone confused. "A recommendation from me? Why would I ever recommend you to a school?"

I pause, startled. "The campus clinic. Didn't you send them my résumé?"

Dr. Johnson falls silent. "No. I think I'd remember. I was so busy finalizing the sale of the clinic that I didn't even think to do that. I had no idea you were struggling to find something."

I frown, confused. They clearly told me they got a recommendation from Dr. Johnson. I remember it clearly. I remember sitting on the sofa in despair, and I remember the hope that phone call gave me.

"I see," I murmur, feeling like I'm missing something. I suppress the feeling and force myself to focus on the matter at hand. "I'd love a recommendation, though. I worked for the college clinic for a while, but it didn't work out, and I'm struggling to find something new."

"Noah," Dr. Johnson says, his voice soft. "Please tell me you didn't get into trouble with Harold Astor."

I sigh. "You've heard of him, huh?"

"I heard of him utilizing his network to blacklist a young doctor. I didn't think... I never once considered that it could be you. He's promised financial ruin to anyone that dares to hire you. Why is he going after you with a vengeance? What could you possibly have done to upset a man this powerful?"

I run a hand through my hair, my gaze trailing toward the kitchen door, where I can hear Amara messing around with the ancient pans Aria bought so many years ago. "I fell in love with his granddaughter."

Dr. Johnson chuckles, and I smile reluctantly. "Yeah, that'll do it," he says. "I'll ask around, but I don't think anyone is going to risk their clinic. The Astors have large stakes in so many industries that it's almost impossible to escape them. Harold Astor isn't a man you want to cross... but then you know that better than anyone."

I lean back against the wall, my eyes drifting over the countless photos on the walls. "Yeah, I know. Thank you for trying, Dr. Johnson."

"Anytime, Noah. You'll be fine. I know you will be."

I inhale deeply as he ends the call, suddenly feeling hopeless. He was my very last lead, and I guess part of me had been holding off on contacting him because I didn't want him to feel bad about firing me so early on in my career. He's a good man, and I don't want him worrying about me.

I try my best to cheer myself up as I walk toward the kitchen, not wanting Amara to suspect just how deeply worried I am. I don't want her to be affected by my misery. I don't want her to regret being with me. For as long as I can be, I want to be the man she fell in love, instead of the person I'm becoming.

I walk in to find Amara staring at her phone, a torn expression on her face. I walk up to her, and she jumps when she notices me.

She turns around, stirring the pasta she's making in a rush, as though she'd forgotten all about it.

I walk up to her and pause behind her, my arms wrapping around her as her back hits my chest. I hold her like that, my chin on her shoulder and her body pressed to mine. My lips brush over her neck and I press a lingering kiss to her skin, enjoying the way a shiver runs down her spine. The way her body responds to mine will never cease to fascinate me.

"Your dad?" I ask.

She freezes and nods, the movement almost imperceptible. She still refuses to speak to her dad, but he hasn't given up on her. Every time he texts her, I see her expression soften just a little. She pretends she doesn't care, but her eyes betray her.

"Call him, baby. Go see him." I let my eyes fall closed and press another kiss to her neck. "I was standing in the hallway just now, wishing I could speak to my dad one last time, wishing I could ask for his advice, wishing I could hear him tell me that everything is going to be okay. But I can't, Amara. He'll never text me again. He'll never ask to see me again. I won't ever hear from him again. You can still see yours."

A tear drops down her cheek, and I kiss it away gently. "Do you think I should?" she whispers. "It's complicated, Noah... he isn't a good man, but I don't know... he's my *dad*. I was angry at the start, but now that I've had some time to let it all sink in, I realize that a part of me does want to see him. I have so many questions, and only he can answer them."

I turn her around so she's facing me, her eyes on mine. I lean in and brush her hair out of her face, tucking it behind her ear. "Do you want to talk about it, baby? I'm here if you do."

She shakes her head. "It's a lot, and I... I don't think... I guess what I'm trying to say is that I should probably talk to him before I talk to anyone else. All I know about my past is what my mother told me, and I guess I'm finally ready to hear his side of the story."

I nod. I can't help but wonder what her father did. Not even Maddie knows, and I couldn't find out anything online. There's no mention of Amara's father anywhere. No photos, no old articles, nothing. From the sounds of it, he cheated and left them, but I can't be sure.

"That's good, baby. Get both sides of the story and then decide whether you want him in your life. Don't judge him based on the words of others. Besides, it's been years, right? He might not even be the same person anymore. I'd give the world to see my father just one more time. Speak to him and then decide."

She looks into my eyes, and I can tell she's searching for something. Hope. Reassurance. Maybe both. Whatever it is, she seems to find it, because she smiles at me in that way that makes her light up, and for just a few moments, everything is right in my world.

"I love you, Noah."

I lean in and press a lingering kiss to her forehead, pouring all my feelings into that chaste kiss. "I love you more."

And I do. She's worth everything. Every bit of hardship Harold is putting me through, every hint of fear and uncertainty. She's worth all that, and more.

Chapter Forty-Six

AMARA

I blink, trying my hardest to ignore the annoying buzzing that's slowly taking away my relaxed, dreamlike state. I turn, reaching for my phone absentmindedly, closing my eyes as I lift it to my face.

I'm tempted to ignore the call, to lock my phone and put it away, but something doesn't feel right. Deep down, I can feel that something is off. My hands tremble as I answer the call and bring my phone to my ear.

"Is this Amara Astor?"

The woman on the phone sounds calm and professional. Far too professional to be calling me in the middle of the night, and her tone just worries me further. "Speaking," I say, my voice soft, laced with fear.

"I'm calling from Regency Hospital. Your phone number was saved in Mr. Simmons' phone as his emergency contact."

She pauses, and I swallow hard. "I'm his daughter," I tell her. "What happened to my father?" I sit up, tears welling in my eyes. The sheets fall away, and Noah turns in his sleep, reaching for me.

"Your father is in critical condition, Ms. Astor. The doctor will be able to tell you more." There's hesitation in her voice, almost like she wishes she didn't have to make this call at all.

"I'll be right there."

I end the call with shaky hands, feeling sick. Months. I've been ignoring him for months, and now I might lose my chance to ever speak to him again.

"What's wrong?" Noah asks, his voice sleepy. He sits up and places his finger underneath my chin, making me face him. "What happened, Amara?"

I wrap my arms around his neck and hug him tightly, falling apart in his arms. "It's my dad," I tell him, letting my tears fall. "He's in the hospital, and I know I need to move, but I'm scared, Noah. I'm so scared." I choke back a sob as Noah tightens his arms around me, one hand tangling into my hair.

"What did the nurse say?"

"Just that he's in critical condition," I manage to tell him.

Noah nods and rubs my back. "Come on, I'll take you. You won't be alone, baby. I'll be right there with you. Whatever happens, whatever we find at the hospital, I'll be right there with you."

I nod, but I can't stop shaking. I can't control the dread I'm feeling. The regret. Noah was right all along. I had so many chances to see him, to speak to him, and I took it all for granted. I had something I can see Noah longing for every single day. I saw it in the way he idolized my grandfather, the way he looks at photos of his parents. I saw it, and I still took my own father for granted.

It's all I can think about as I rush to get dressed. Part of me doesn't even want to go to the hospital, scared of what I'll find. I'm not ready to face the possibility of not having a father at all. I've been so consumed by hate and anger, but I never realized how much of a luxury that was.

Noah is quiet as he drives me to the hospital, but the way he clutches the steering wheel tells me he's worried too. Something about the look in his eyes tells me he's lost in his own past. He won't tell me how he lost his parents, but it wouldn't surprise me if it was a little similar to what I'm experiencing now. A phone call. A visit to the hospital. I might be going through a lot tonight, but so is Noah. Despite that, he's here with me. I will myself to cling onto that feeling, the love we share. It'll carry me through anything.

"We're here," he whispers, his hand reaching for mine. Noah entwines our fingers, his grip tight. "It'll be okay, Amara. Don't think about the past, or any of the choices you've made. You're here now, and that's all that matters. Focus on the present. The past can wait."

I look into his eyes and nod. "I love you, Noah. If not for you..."

He smiles at me and leans in to press a kiss to my forehead. "If not for me, you'd still have pulled yourself together and made it here. I'm glad I got to be the one to drive you, though. Are you ready?"

I nod, and Noah presses a kiss to my forehead before stepping out of the car. My eyes follow him as he walks around and opens the door for me, holding out his hand. I take it and hold on for dear life, using him to anchor myself.

I'm trembling as we walk in, my mind replaying the last time I saw my father. I told him I didn't know if I wanted him in my life, and I regret it now.

"If he's in critical condition, he'll likely be in the ICU," Noah says, point at the signs. He leads me through the hospital, stopping at the nurse's station.

The nurse's eyes widen when she sees Noah, a smile lighting up her face. "Dr. Grant," she says, a twinkle in her eyes. Her smile transforms her tired expression and makes her look a decade younger, despite her gray hair.

He smiles back, his arm wrapping around my shoulder. "Hi Susan," he says. "It's been a while."

She nods. "You're no longer a rookie, huh? It seems like a lifetime ago that you worked here."

Noah smiles. It's the first genuine smile I've seen on his face tonight. "It was only three years ago, but it sure feels like forever ago, doesn't it?"

She nods. "What can I do for you, sweetie?"

He looks at me, a reassuring look in his eyes. "My girlfriend's father was admitted to the hospital. We'd like to see him. Can you point us the right way, please?"

She looks at me, a kind smile on her face. "What's your father's name, darling?"

I straighten, keeping the panic at bay as best as I can. "It's Peter Simmons, ma'am."

Noah tenses next to me, and I turn to look at him to find him frowning, his eyes on the wall behind Susan. "Everything okay?" I whisper. He doesn't look at me. Instead, he stares into space, lost in thought.

"Your father was transferred out of the ICU," Susan tells us, giving me his room number. "Based on what I can see here, he seems to be out of danger, but he's being monitored closely. You should be able to go see him."

I breathe a sigh of relief, feeling conflicted. "Thank you," I whisper, my hand slipping into Noah's. I turn to follow Susan's directions, but Noah stays rooted in place.

"Noah," I murmur, pulling on his hand. He looks at me, but it's almost like he's looking straight through me. I don't know what he's seeing, but the way he looks at me scares me. He's never looked at me that way before, almost like I'm a stranger.

Noah nods at me, snapping out of it. He falls into step with me as we walk toward my father's room, but I can't shake the feeling that everything is wrong. I can't escape this sense of impending doom, and my intuition is never wrong.

Chapter Forty-Seven

NOAH

Peter Simmons. She said her father's name was Peter Simmons. It can't be, right? It must be a coincidence.

I'm numb as I follow Amara to her father's room. Her hand feels foreign in mine. If she is who I think she is, then that changes everything for us. Fear claws at me, warring with the denial I'm so desperately reaching for.

Amara hesitates as we reach the hospital room, her hand trembling as she knocks on the door. There's no answer, and she looks at me. She's looking for reassurance, but all I want to do is walk away.

All I can see is those beautiful blue eyes of hers. I thought they were identical to her mother's, but I can see it now. They're identical to *his*. It's these same eyes that haunted Aria for years, the eyes that had her screaming from night terrors.

I tear my gaze away, telling myself it must all be a coincidence, but I know I'm fooling myself. There's no such thing as coincidence.

Amara opens the door, and her hand falls out of mine as she

walks in. She pauses and looks back at me, her gaze searching. I stare at her, my heart sinking. Could it be?

When Amara told me her father ruined two families, I never once suspected that one of them was *mine*. I bite down on my lip and shake my head, forcing myself to do what I urged Amara to do just minutes ago. *Stay in the present.*

I force a smile onto my face and follow her in, scared of what I'll find. For once, I want to be proven wrong.

"Dad?" Amara says. I'm right behind her, my heart racing as I come face to face with Peter Simmons. He looks at Amara, his eyes identical to hers. It's indeed her father's eyes she got. Did Aria know? When Amara and I visited, did she know? Did she recognize the eyes that haunt her?

I take in the man lying in his bed, a nurse seated next to him. Peter Simmons' wrists are bandaged and his eyes are hollow, but he's alive. He looks strong. Likely depressed, but physically healthy.

Amara bursts into tears and rushes up to him. "Daddy, what did you do?" she asks, her voice wobbly. My heart twists painfully, but I can't make myself look at her. I can't take my eyes off the man that murdered my parents, leaving my sister to find them lying in a pool of their own blood.

It's him. There's no doubt in my mind. He looks older, but it's him. When Aria told me he was released early, serving only fifteen years, I didn't react the way she did. I was numb, well aware of how the justice system lets victims like my parents down. I didn't let the anger consume me. Instead, I just focused on building a good life, being a good person.

What for?

"Noah?" Amara says, her voice soft. Peter looks at me, and his eyes widen. I see the horror in them, and it gives me a sense of gratification. I look just like my father, and it brings me a small amount of peace to know he remembers my father's face. I hope his crimes haunt him at night. I hope he sees my parents every single time he closes his eyes. I take a step closer to him, my gaze falling to his bandaged wrists. Hatred consumes me, and for a single moment I let it get the best of me. For a single moment, I allow myself to forget my oaths and wish he hadn't been saved.

"Noah?" he repeats after Amara.

My eyes snap to his, and I grit my teeth. "You keep my name out of your mouth," I warn him.

He swallows hard, and Amara whips around, her eyes wide. "Noah, what's wrong with you?" she asks, her tone high. She looks confused, and I stare at her, wondering if it's all a show.

"Did you know?" I ask her. "Did you know your father is a murderer?"

Her lips fall open, the shock in her eyes apparent. "I..."

I take a step closer to her and place my finger underneath her chin, tilting her face up, forcing her to look me in the eye. "I asked you a question, Amara. Did you know?"

She swallows hard, her eyes falling closed as she nods.

I laugh humorlessly and shake my head. I should have known. I should've known something was wrong. Nothing good ever happens to me. Certainly nothing as good as Amara. I should've known our happiness was tainted. I should've expected it.

"Did you lie next to me, knowing your father murdered my parents? Did you stare at the photos in my hallway, knowing it's your father that killed mine?"

I look at her, her long red hair, the freckles on her nose, and those eyes... those damn eyes. She looks at me in shock and shakes her head in denial. "I... Noah, no. What are you talking about? Smith. Their name was Smith. It can't be. It isn't..."

I laugh, the name sounding foreign to me, even though it used to be mine. "My sister chose the name Grant. It isn't the name she or I were born with. She chose it to escape the past, to keep people from uncovering our past, to keep from being pitied endlessly. She chose it to escape the damage your father did to us."

"I'm sorry," Peter Simmons says. "I've never had a chance to say sorry to you or to your sister. I've thought of her every day since then. Nothing I can say will ever right my wrongs, but if I could go back into the past—"

"You can't," I snap. "You can't change the past. You can't undo the crimes you committed. You might be a free man now, but you'll always be a murderer." I stare at him, hatred overcoming me. "It's too bad you failed today. You don't deserve to live. You don't deserve the blood people have donated, the resources that went into saving you. You should've paid for your crimes with your life." I take a step back and shake my head. "I'll leave now, before I finish what you started, Hippocratic oath be damned. I'll spare you today, but don't fucking appear in front of me ever again."

I turn to walk away, but I've only just made it to the hallway when Amara grabs my hand. I yank my hand away, barely even able to look at her.

"Noah, I didn't know," she says, her eyes panicked.

"I don't believe you," I tell her. "I see it now. The warnings your grandfather gave me, the guilt in your mother's eyes. I thought they were being nice, but they were trying to make amends — and what a shit job they did. And you? You're just as bad. You know what he did, yet here you are."

"Noah, he's my father. You told me... you told me to..."

"Amara, when you told me he destroyed two families, I thought he *cheated*. I didn't think he was a murderer," I shout, unable to keep my emotions in check. "I didn't think he was the man that left my sister and me *orphans*."

She bursts into tears, her eyes filled with desperation and sorrow. Part of me wants to take her in my arms, but a larger part of me knows things will never be the same between us.

"I didn't know how to tell you. I've never told anyone, Noah. You're not the only one running from your past. I was embarrassed and scared of what you'd think of me. I've wanted to tell you for so long, but I was scared that you'd look at me the way you do right now."

I shake my head. "As you should've been. Stay the fuck away from me and my sister, Amara. Stay away."

I turn and walk away, leaving her standing there, crying her heart out. The sound of her heart breaking haunts me all the way home.

Chapter Forty-Eight

Amara

"Are you okay?" Dad asks. I look up, startled. I've been sitting here with him, torn between making sure he's okay and following Noah. My thoughts are whirling, shock keeping me rooted. It can't be. Out of everyone, it can't be Noah.

I glance at my father, unsure how to even feel. I've struggled with wanting to see him for months now, and on the way here I was so sure I was making the right choice... now I'm not so sure.

"I'm fine," I tell him, feeling detached. It's almost like I'm mentally completely checked out, yet at the same time I'm fully aware of the words leaving my lips.

"How?" he asks, his voice shaky.

I shake my head. "I don't know, Dad. I didn't know. I never... I knew he lost his parents when he was young, but that's all I know. I even googled him, but there were no search results at all. I didn't know."

Dad nods, the look in his eyes mirroring mine. I force myself to pull it together, pasting a shaky smile onto my face. "How do you feel?" I ask carefully. "I can't believe..." I can't even finish the words. He tried taking his own life. After years in prison, he almost threw away his freedom.

"I have nothing to live for, Amara. It was easier being behind bars. I had a routine there. Here? The world has changed, and I can't catch up. Besides... Noah was right. I should have paid for my crimes with my life. Instead, they let me out early. I did the one thing I wanted above all: I saw you one last time. You seemed happy, and you didn't need me. I just... I didn't see the point."

I hesitate before reaching out, placing my hand over his. "I'm not," I whisper. "I'm not happy. I'm mad, and I'm hurt, but I missed you. I missed you throughout the years. Every Father's Day, prom night, graduation. I..."

Dad tightens his grip on my hand and looks away, but that does nothing to hide the tears in his eyes. My heart squeezes painfully, breaking in so many different ways.

"I need time, Dad. Despite what happened, I can't tell you that I want you in my life. The things you did... I know you paid by serving your sentence, but I..."

"I understand," he says, nodding.

"I don't think you do," I murmur. "I don't know what a relationship between us would look like, Dad. It's been so long, and I... I don't know. What I do know is that I want to have a choice. Please, will you give me that? Please don't make me mourn you before I ever get to know you."

He nods, a tear running down his cheek. I squeeze his hand, a thousand regrets running through my mind. I wish I'd pushed Noah about his parents. I wish I'd questioned my mother more when she told me to stay away. I wish I hadn't ignored my father's text messages for as long as I did. I wish I'd told Noah what my father did, so he'd have been able to figure out the secrets my family were keeping even if I never did. I wish I'd heeded my grandfather's warnings. I wish I'd let Noah walk away when he tried. I have a thousand regrets, but those change nothing. I can't undo the past. I can only face the future with as much courage as I can muster.

My thoughts are whirling all the way home. *Home.* When did I start to think of Noah's house as home? I don't even know if I'm still welcome there, or if he even wants to see me. I can't shake the feeling that I lost him the second he realized who my father was. I'm scared of what I'll face when I walk in. I have no words, no excuses. Being who I am, I don't even have the right to fight for him, for us.

He might know who my father is, but I doubt he knows the full story. I doubt he knows *I am* the reason his parents died. How could he ever love me? How could he ever be with me? And how could I ever expect it of him?

I'm trembling by the time I walk up to the front door. The house is silent as I walk in, and I pause in the hallway, my eyes roaming over all the photos in the hallway. Photos of lives cut short. Because of *me.*

My stomach churns as I walk up the stairs. I can hear Noah's footsteps, and I'm scared. I'm scared to face him. I'm scared he'll look at me like I'm a stranger. I'm not sure my heart can take it, even though I know I deserve it.

I inhale shakily, pausing in front of the closed bedroom door, trying my best to gather my courage. I swallow hard and open the door, my heart beating loudly as I take a hesitant step forward.

I can't look him in the eye. Instead, I stare at the open suitcase on his bed. It takes me a few moments to realize it isn't my clothes he's packing. It's his own.

I look up, my every fear coming true. He looks at me in disgust and shakes his head, tearing his gaze away as though he can't stand to look at me.

"Where are you going?" I whisper.

"Anywhere. Away from you. Us. This," he says, gesturing between us.

I swallow back my tears as best as I can, trying my best to stay strong. "Don't." My voice breaks, and I wrap my arms around myself. "I'll go. This is your home."

Noah laughs, the sound chilling. "No, it isn't. This is just a house. Your *father* destroyed my home."

I stare at my feet, unable to face him. "I swear to you, Noah. I didn't know. I never even suspected it."

He closes his suitcase, his movements rushed. "Do you really expect me to believe that?" His voice is rough, angry. I can't blame him, but it still hurts. Every fiber of my being is pleading for me to voice the words I'm keeping in. *Please stay. Look at me. I love you.*

Instead, I fight to keep my tears hidden, my nails digging into my arms. The pain helps me keep the tears at bay, but it doesn't soothe my aching heart.

"I want you gone," he says, his voice soft. "By the time I get back, I want you gone. I don't want a single trace of you in my house. Not a single reminder of the mistake I made."

He walks past me, his shoulder brushing against mine. I so badly want to reach out for him. I want to grab his hand and beg him to stay... but I don't have the right.

So I watch him leave.

Noah walks away, and he doesn't look back once. I hear the front door slam closed, and with it the greatest love I'll ever experience comes to an end. I know it deep down to my soul. I lost him, and I'll probably never even see him again.

I drop to my knees in the room we shared, knowing I'll never spend another night here. I'll never spend another night in his arms. My tears are hot and my throat burns from the sobs I kept at bay. I curl up on the floor, crying for all Noah and I lost, for everything we'll never have.

Chapter Forty-Nine

NOAH

I key in the passcode to Grayson's penthouse and freeze when the door opens before I finish going through his countless security measures.

Aria leans against the doorway, a worried look in her eyes. "It's three in the morning," she says. "How are you here?"

Grayson appears behind her and places a hand on her shoulder. "Come in, buddy," he says, no questions asked. I follow him in and pause in the hallway. The last time I was here, I was with Amara. I push away every thought of her, barely able to bear the pain.

Aria tips her head toward the living room, and I follow her, my steps heavy, reluctant. I have to tell her, but I know that the second I do that, everything between Amara and me is truly over.

Grayson holds up a whiskey glass, and I take it gratefully, emptying it in one go. It doesn't even remotely numb the pain, but that's only because I haven't had enough yet. I'd give anything to drown out the memories tonight. Not just of Amara, but of my parents. Of Aria refusing to speak for years, the countless times I had to sit beside her as night terrors haunted her. How do I tell my sister that I fell for the daughter of our parents' murderer? How do I explain that I brought her into their home? Where do I even begin to ask for forgiveness?

Grayson sits down next to Aria, his face expressionless, and I shake my head. He used to always be by *my* side, but tonight I'm grateful Aria has him. She'll need him to endure what I'm about to tell her.

"Aria," I say, my voice wavering. "Amara is Peter Simmons' daughter."

She looks at me, and I can't quite describe her expression. She looks resigned, wary. Aria nods, her movements slow. "I know, Noah."

I stare at her, not quite comprehending her words. "You... *know?*"

She nods. "I knew who she was the second I first heard her name. Amara... it isn't a very common name."

I look at my sister wide-eyed, my mind whirling. "You knew, and you welcomed her with open arms?"

Aria nods, her expression guarded. "She is not her father."

I rise to my feet, my anger overflowing. "What the fuck, Aria? What the fuck do you mean *she's not her father?* I fucking know that, but she's still that man's *daughter*. How could you welcome her into your home? How could you not have told me? How could you let me..."

Aria crosses her arms, her eyes flashing with anger. "Let you what? Fall in love? Be happy for once?"

"Happy?" I repeat. "How could you watch me fall in love with her without a single warning? How could you, when you knew she and I were on borrowed time?"

Aria stands up, her expression one I've never seen on her before. She looks angry, but there's also understanding and compassion in her eyes. She lacks the sadness I've come to expect to find in her eyes.

"I could, and I did, because she is *not* him. Amara doesn't deserve to be punished for crimes she didn't commit. Can you honestly look me in the eye and tell me she isn't the best thing that ever happened to you? That she didn't make you happy in a way you didn't think you could ever be?"

I fall silent, unable to refute her words. "Aria... her family... God, I can't even begin to describe what they've done. They covered up Mom and Dad's murder. There isn't a trace of news available anywhere. It happened a few years ago. All of a sudden, there were no articles about the burglary anymore. They tried to cover it up."

Aria shakes her head. "No, Noah. They didn't. *I did.*"

Grayson nods and places his hand on Aria's shoulder in silent support. He knew. My best friend knew as much as my sister did, and neither of them told me.

"Why? Why the fuck would you do that?"

Aria sighs and looks away. "I didn't want that to be the last piece of news about them. Mom and Dad have done so much, they've contributed to so many charities, and they were so well-loved. I wanted the good they did to be what people would find when they look up our parents. I was tired of the past haunting us, of everyone knowing what we'd gone through. When you and I changed our last names, I also removed every trace of that horrible day. I wanted a fresh start, and I wanted to preserve the memories of Mom and Dad that mattered most. The articles still exist, they just aren't indexed by search engines."

I still remember how ruthless the kids were at the first few schools Aria and I attended. A simple search for our names told people much more than we were willing to disclose, and I remember how hard it was, how painful it was to constantly be reminded of the way we lost our parents. It felt like it was impossible to escape the sorrow, the pitying looks. I can't blame Aria for what she did, but I can't help but feel betrayed.

"Why didn't you tell me? I don't understand."

She shakes her head. "Noah, we'd finally gotten onto our feet.

I just didn't want to explain why I felt the need to do what I did. I didn't want to bring it up."

I swallow hard, my mind instantly replaying me trying to get Aria to talk. She had it much harder than I did.

"Ari, still... the Astors, they approached me knowing who I was."

She nods. "They did, but they didn't do it to harm you, Noah. Do you remember the partial scholarship you received when you thought you'd have to drop out of school? I traced that back to Harold Astor. As you and I grew older, I started keeping tabs on Peter Simmons and his family. It took me years to realize it, because Harold was clever, and he only ever gifted us amounts that didn't raise suspicion, but eventually I saw the pattern. That man... he's been looking out for us for years. I admit, he was likely motivated by guilt, but he didn't have to do any of it at all."

"*Look out for us,*" I repeat, incredulous. "You're kidding me, right? The man fired me and made it impossible for me to find another job. His family tore ours apart, and now he's ruining my career, Aria."

She nods and looks away. "He's desperate, that's for sure. I was surprised when he offered you a job, because he's always kept his distance. I guess he truly saw potential in you, and watching from the sidelines was no longer enough. The man has monitored us and our performance for years. I guess he wanted to help but never expected you to fall for Amara. I won't pretend to know what he's thinking, but I suspect he was trying to break you two apart before either of you realized how the past connects you."

I glance at Gray, diverting my anger to him. "Are you hearing this? How the fuck is she so calm? Did you know all of this?"

He nods. "I knew, and I support Aria's decisions. She did what she had to do to protect your happiness, and I think she's right. I don't think Harold Astor is harmful, despite him firing you. He's desperate, just like Aria says, but he's not a bad man. Ari has been keeping tabs on that family for years. If there was something to worry about, she'd have intervened."

I stare at the two of them in disbelief. "How the fuck is all of this okay with you? They ruined our family and then fucking invaded our privacy, acting like we're fucking charity cases."

Aria crosses her arms and sighs. "We were, Noah. Half the time we could barely afford to put food on the table."

"Because of them!" I yell, wishing I could get through to her.

Aria just shakes her head. "No. Because of *Peter Simmons*. Stop blaming an entire family for the actions of just one man." She inhales deeply and looks away. "Noah, you know as well as I do that the weapon that killed our parents was Dad's. I've gone through the case hundreds of times. He didn't expect Mom and Dad to be home. There was a struggle, and Dad must've pulled his gun. Peter Simmons didn't even steal anything expensive. All he took was food and some of my clothes. He was trying to provide for his family."

She runs a hand through her hair and shakes her head. "I'm not trying to make any excuses, Noah... but you have to acknowledge that he paid for his crimes. He served his sentence."

"Are you fucking with me right now?" I ask her, in disbelief. "He murdered our parents, Aria. I don't give a fuck how it happened or why. Mom and Dad aren't with us today because of him."

"I get that you're angry, Noah. I get it. But that same anger will hurt you more than it will anyone else. Let it consume you if you want, but I won't stand here and support your self-destruction."

She walks past me, slamming her bedroom door closed, her calm demeanor slipping for just a second. Gray winces at the sounds and looks at me through narrowed eyes, like *I'm* the one at fault here.

"She's fucking crazy," I tell him.

He pours me another glass and nods. "Yeah, she is. But she isn't wrong. Aria kept tabs on him from the second he was released and it took her months to make peace with the situation. She might act like she's fine now, but it took her months to get where she is now. It'll take you some time, too. I do think Aria is right, though. Amara is not her father."

"What the fuck am I supposed to do, man? I can't love Amara. I can't be with her. Not her."

Gray nods and lifts his glass to his lips. "Would your mother have loved her? Forget about Amara's father for just a second and tell me... would she have loved Amara?"

I empty my glass and reach for the bottle. "If only it were that simple, Gray. Mom will never even get to know Amara, because of her father. I won't ever be able to look at her again without being reminded of who she is, of what her father took from us."

Gray nods. "So you'll rob yourself of a happy future, the way her father robbed your parents of theirs?"

I stare at him, wishing I had an answer for him.

Chapter Fifty

Amara

The sound of my suitcase's wheels echo along the marble floors. I pause when my grandfather's office door opens, but I can barely see him through the tears that cloud my vision. I stay rooted in place, shame washing over me. When I walked out of this mansion, I was so certain I'd never return. I chose Noah, never understanding why my grandfather fought so hard to keep us apart.

In the end, I did exactly what I thought I never would. I walked away, only to find myself back here the way my mother did. I swore I'd never be like her. Yet here I am.

Grandpa doesn't say a word. He just walks up to me and wraps his arms around me. "You're home, Mari," he says, and I burst into tears. He hasn't called me that since I was a child.

I nod and rest my head against his chest, my body heaving from the force of my sobs. Grandpa holds me tightly, his hand stroking my back soothingly, his chin on my head. "You'll be fine," he tells me. "You're my granddaughter. You're strong, and you're resilient. There's nothing you won't overcome."

"Grandpa," I murmur, choking on my sobs. My throat closes up, my tears falling so fast that I can hardly breathe. Grandpa just stands there, letting me soak his expensive Italian suit, not a single chastising word leaving his lips. "I'm sorry," I tell him.

He pulls away and holds me by my shoulders. I've never seen him look so hurt. I've never seen tears in his eyes before, but I see them now. "You did nothing wrong, sweetheart. Enough tears now, okay? You're home, and that's all that matters."

He wraps his arm around my shoulder and grabs my suitcase, walking me to my room as I try my best to stop crying. Grandpa sits me down on my bed and kneels in front of me, wiping at my tears with his thumbs. "I know it hurts, sweetheart. I'm sorry I didn't protect you better. When your mother brought you home, I swore that your father's actions would never affect you, and I failed you."

He cups my cheeks, and I wrap my own hands over his. "Why didn't you tell me, Grandpa?"

He pulls away and sighs. "By the time I realized what was going on between you two, you were heads over heels. I thought that maybe... you'd heal quicker if it's me breaking you two up. I thought it'd hurt less than having your heart broken over circumstances you can't control. I just thought it'd be easier if you had someone to blame."

I nod, my heart twisting painfully. In his own way, he was trying to do the right thing. He was trying to protect me. I was just too stupid to see it.

"Will you let him go?" I whisper. "Let Noah find a new job. I'll do anything, Grandpa. I'll work for the family business if you want me to... and I... I'll marry Gregory."

Grandpa looks me in the eye, his expression tense. "It's not your fault," he repeats. "You are not to blame for your father's crimes, and you don't need to make amends for them either."

"I know," I murmur. "I know, Grandpa. But if not for me defying your wishes, Noah would have astonishing opportunities. I took them from him. You were mentoring him, and I... I ruined his future. If you help him get back on track, I'll do everything you asked me to."

Grandpa inhales deeply, a frown on his face. "You really love him, huh? You'd give up your company for him?"

A tear rolls down my face, and I nod. If not for him, the company never would've existed. It's not me Grayson and Aria are investing in. It's Noah. I can't ask Aria to put her money into me, the daughter of the man that murdered her parents. I can't, and I won't.

"Get some rest, Mari. Think long and hard about what you just asked me. Marriage is for life, especially when a merger is involved. Don't tie your life to Gregory's because you feel guilty now. Your heart will heal. The pain will fade. Marriage? That'll remain."

He rises to his feet and looks back at me before closing the door behind him. I curl up on my bed and let myself fall apart. When I left and moved in with Noah, I was so sure that was it for me. I knew we'd face hardships, but never of this kind. I thought he and I could get through anything together, but we were doomed from the start.

I tense when my bedroom door opens, my mother's perfume filling the room. She sits down on my bed and places her hand on my shoulder.

"You knew," I tell her, my tone accusatory. "You knew, and you didn't tell me. You let me fall for him, knowing what would happen."

Mom sighs, her hand trembling ever so slightly. "I'd never seen you so happy before, Amara. You seemed so alive. You were thriving, and it was everything I ever could've wanted for you. I just hoped... I don't know. I knew the truth would come out eventually, but I thought you two might just be strong enough to get through it together. The way he looked at you and the way you smiled at him, Amara... I wanted to believe that you two would overcome this. I was wrong, and I'm sorry."

I laugh, the sound hollow. "You thought we'd overcome my

father murdering his? Mom, don't be ridiculous. You saw what was happening, and you ignored it because you wanted me to learn my lesson. You win. You always tell me to face reality, to count my blessings. You win, Mom. I'll fall in line. I'll be just like you: broken, an empty shell, a remnant of what I once used to be. *Just. Like. You.*"

Mom doesn't respond. She doesn't argue with me the way I expected her to, the way she always does. No. None of that. She just strokes my hair gently, refusing to give me an outlet for my pain.

Truthfully, I can't blame her. I'm not so blinded by my pain that I can't see that both my mother and grandfather tried to protect me. I just wish they'd trusted me to protect *myself*. I wish they hadn't kept me in the dark. If they'd trusted me enough to tell me what I needed to know, Noah never would've gotten hurt, and his career would still be on the right track.

But then again, I've never given them a reason to trust me, with my willfulness and naivety. That changes now. I'll never again be the reason someone I love gets hurt.

Chapter Fifty-One

NOAH

The gravel underneath my shoes is the only thing that disturbs the peace as I walk up to my parents' tombstones, my heart filled with regret.

I pause in front of their graves, inhaling shakily. It never gets easier to come here. Every time I see their tombstones, fresh agony overtakes me.

"I miss you," I whisper. I'm all alone in the graveyard, yet I can't get myself to raise my voice. My eyes fall closed, and I take a steadying breath. "I'm sorry, Mom, Dad. I... I'm so sorry."

I don't even know where to begin explaining myself. I've failed them, disappointed them.

"For a long time, I believed that you two were looking down at us, protecting us. All the little bits of luck we had, winning partial scholarships, winning food vouchers or trips, or that time Aria desperately needed a new bicycle, and the guys at my college's lost and found told me I could take the one that'd unexpectedly shown up there... I thought that was you. Turns out, it was Harold Astor. It was all him. He did it out of guilt, I guess."

I shake my head and pace on the little path in front of their graves, unsure how to explain myself, how to ask for their forgiveness.

"I accepted all those instances of what I thought was good luck, but it was charity born out of guilt. Like giving us a helping hand could ever make up for losing you." I run a hand through my hair, my eyes falling closed. "I wish that was the full extent of the sin I committed, but it wasn't."

I laugh to myself despite the pain. "I fell in love. True love. The type that you two had. It was the kind of love I didn't think existed. The stuff they show in the movies. Except... I fell in love with the one person you'd never approve of. She tells me she didn't know, and at the time I didn't believe her, but now? Now that I've calmed down and had some time to think? Yeah, she didn't know. That doesn't make it any better, but at least I can tell you that much. Neither she nor I ever set out to tarnish the memory of you."

I run a hand through my hair, unsure of what I even want to say. "I'm here today because I want to ask you for forgiveness. The girl I fell in love with is the daughter of the man that killed you. If not for her father, you'd still be here. Dad, you'd be walking Aria down the aisle. Mom, you'd have had a chance to meet Grayson and tease me about how much more you love him than you love me, because you would. You'd be so happy to have him as a son-in-law, and he'd have been so happy to have a mother like you. It's because of Amara's father that you'll never experience any of that."

My eyes roam over the marble tombstones and the flowers Aria has planted over the years, my throat closing up. I raise my head up to the sky, taking a moment to gather my thoughts, to control my emotions.

"I don't regret the time I spent with her," I whisper. "I love her, and I'll live off the memories I made with her for the rest of my life... and for that, I'm so incredibly sorry. She and I don't have a future together, and I'm sorry I fell for her at all. I can't be with her knowing who her father is. I can't have her in my life and watch her reconnect with him. I can't watch him rebuild his life after he took away yours. I'll never be able to look at her again without seeing you."

I take a step back and swallow back my tears. I haven't cried in years, but today my heart feels raw, vulnerable. "Forgive me," I whisper. "Please forgive me."

I turn and walk away, my heart clenching painfully. I've never felt this defeated before. I'm out of a job and unable to find anything, and on top of that the girl I lost everything over is the one person I'd never want to be with had I known who she was when I met her. Amara and her family cost me everything, *twice*.

"Boy." I look up to find a lady standing by a florist cart at the exit. I've seen her before... the day Grayson proposed to Aria. "Remember," she says. "Life is for the living."

She resumes trimming the ends of her flower stalks, dismissing me. I stare at her for a few seconds, her words resounding through my mind. I think of her all the way home.. Life is for the living... maybe so, but that doesn't mean the dead shouldn't be honored.

Silence greets me as I walk into the house. I went straight to the cemetery from the airport, in part because I was avoiding coming here. I stayed away for two weeks, searching for jobs remotely from Aria and Gray's house. I guess I was both hoping and fearing that I'd walk in and Amara would be here.

Of course she isn't.

I leave my suitcase in the hallway and walk in, my eyes roaming over the empty living room. There isn't a trace of Amara. The candles she bought are gone, and so are her books, her prototype sketches and her tools. It's almost like she never lived here at all.

I sigh as I walk to the sofa and sit down. I reach for the remote control, needing a distraction. For just a few moments, I want to lose myself in a life that isn't my own, a movie that'll make me feel something other than pure devastation and guilt.

I pause on the town's news channel, my eyes widening when I

recognize Amara. My heart clenches like fucking crazy. But that's nothing compared to the way it feels when the camera moves to Gregory. He's holding her hand the way I used to, the way I thought no other man ever would.

"The rumors are true," he says, a smug grin on his face. "The lovely Amara Astor has agreed to be my wife."

I rise to my feet, the remote control falling to the floor. Amara smiles, looking perfectly happy. Two weeks. I ended things with her two weeks ago, and in that time she fucking got engaged to Gregory?

I laugh to myself, reminded of what Amara once told me Gregory said to her. He told her that one day, when she's done playing around with the help, she'd go back to him. I guess he was right.

I glance at one of the photos of my parents in the living room, my heart filled with intense regret. It wasn't even real to Amara. I guess she always knew she could go back home, that Gregory would want her back. It was just me risking everything.

Chapter Fifty-Two

Noah

I pause in front of the imposing building in front of me, feeling conflicted. Seven job offers. Shortly after Amara and Gregory announced their engagement, the job offers started to come in.

I guess Harold no longer views me as a threat. He got what he wanted. Amara is marrying a man he approves of, someone vastly different to me. My stomach recoils at the thought of the two of them together. My eyes fall closed as I try to push away thoughts I can't bear. The two of them together, his hands on her body, Amara smiling at him the way she used to smile at me. I bet she'll have her dad walk her down the aisle. She'd never be able to do that if she married me. I could never take that — knowing he gets to walk her down the aisle when I know how hard it's hitting Aria that she'll miss out on that.

Not that Amara and I were ever headed toward marriage. I guess I was just someone different, someone that intrigued her. I was never going to be the man she married. I don't fit into her world. All the scheming, the secrets, the cliques, I want no part

I don't.

So why does it hurt so badly? I'm the one that asked her to leave, so why does it kill me to know she did just as I asked? I guess it's because it just adds to the betrayal. I feel guilty enough as it is, but knowing that all we had didn't mean anything to her? That she walked away without a fight, choosing to *marry* someone else within weeks of leaving me... yeah, that fucking burns.

I run a hand through my hair and take a deep breath in an attempt to ground myself — to no avail. I'm a fucking mess, but I'll have to pretend like I'm not. Like my heart isn't fucking broken, like guilt isn't eating at me.

I've let my parents down enough as it is. I shake my head and tug at the lapels of my suit jacket before walking into the building, a polite smile on my face. I freeze when my eyes land on the receptionist's desk.

"Georgia?"

She looks up, a sweet smile on her face. "Good morning, Dr. Grant. It is so good to see you again."

I walk up to her desk, unable to suppress my shock. "How are you here?"

"She isn't the only one that's here." I turn around to find Maddie leaning against the wall, her fingers brushing some imaginary dust off her uniform. She looks up at me, a grin on her face.

"You're both here," I whisper, a surge of emotion washing over me. In the time I was at the Astor clinic, the three of us became a team, and leaving them behind was harder than I thought it'd be.

They both grin at me. "Of course we are," Georgia says. "We couldn't stay there after you were fired. It wasn't fair. We said we'd quit unless they reconsidered their decision to fire you, but well..."

I shake my head. "You two should've known better. The last thing I wanted to do was drag you down with me."

Maddie shrugs. "I mean, I did warn you to stay away from her."

My mood instantly sours, and I look away. I should've listened to her. What the hell was I thinking going after Amara?

"Hey, it's okay. Look around," she says, gesturing around the office. "This place is even swankier than Astor College's clinic. Come on, I'll show you your new office. You're going to love it."

I nod and follow her the way I did on my very first day of work at the college clinic. It feels like a lifetime ago. Maddie points at the beautiful view from the tall windows in my office, and I try my hardest to act excited about it, but she sees straight through me.

"Hey, for what it's worth... she seems to have really loved you. I don't know what happened and I won't ask, but rumor has it she agreed to marry Gregory in return for her grandfather letting you off the hook."

I look up, surprised. "No," I murmur. "She didn't." Part of me wants to cling to the explanation Maddie is handing me, but I can't. I know Amara. She isn't the type of woman to give up her freedom over something that small. Freedom is what she's been fighting for all her life. I guess she was just done playing around with plebs like me.

"She gave up her company, too. She sold it outright — to Grayson Callahan."

I look up, my eyes wide. "She did *what*?" Gray never told me that. Why would he keep that from me?

She nods. "I guess it hasn't been announced yet, but that's what I heard. I'm rarely wrong, you know? I'm the queen of classified information."

Her words bring a reluctant smile to my face. "That's one hell of a way to describe a gossip."

She shrugs and walks away, looking over her shoulder as she reaches the door. "You'll be okay, right?"

I nod. "I will be, Maddie. I always am."

She nods and walks out, closing the door behind her softly. I'm absentminded as I sink into my seat. Maddie's words keep resounding in my mind. *She sold her company. She agreed to marry Gregory in return for her grandfather letting you off the hook.* It can't be.

I force the thoughts away and reach into my bag to take out the photograph of my parents that has gone with me to every single place I've ever worked at. I place it on my desk carefully, tracing a trembling finger over the edge of it.

If not for Amara's father, they'd still be here. How could I ever be with her? How could I ever ask her to live with the guilt, the knowledge that I'll never want her father in our lives?

I pull my hand away, feeling torn. I should be feeling disgust toward Amara, but all I can think about is how much I miss her. How much I regret saying what I said to her.

"Would you forgive me, Mom?" I whisper. "I need you. I need you to tell me what to do. Now, more than ever, I need you. Both of you. I'm terrified I'll regret the choice I made. I'm unsure how she even feels about me, but the thought of her marrying someone else... Dad, it kills me. But I... I can't love the daughter of the man that took you from us. She *is* the reason you died. She's the reason Aria cried herself to sleep for years, the reason she still has night terrors. If not for her, Peter Simmons never would've been in our house. How could I love her knowing what role she played in your death? How could I ever face you?"

I grab the photo, holding it so tightly that the sharp edges cut into me, but I welcome the pain. "Please," I beg. "Give me a sign. I beg of you, Mom, Dad... tell me I'm not making the worst mistake in my life by trying to do the right thing. Please. Please, give me a sign."

My eyes fall closed as I try my hardest to cling to my sanity, feeling it slip away by the second. My father would be so disappointed in me. What the fuck am I even doing? Trying to communicate with spirits? What the fuck?

I put the photograph down and try my best to focus on work, but all day I find myself waiting for a sign, against better judgment. There isn't one.

Chapter Fifty-Three

Noah

I walk into the house, feeling tired right down to my fucking soul. My heart feels empty, and all I've been able to think about is Amara. I keep trying to cling onto the anger, the pain.

The love I still feel for her overpowers it all. I'm like a fucking addict, craving something I know will destroy me. Her engagement party has been all over the local news. Apparently everyone who is anyone will be at the Astor mansion tonight. Everyone but me.

I pause in the hallway, my eyes trailing over the countless photos Aria and I hung on the walls. It's all our favorite memories. Or they used to be. I used to stand here and remember the way I felt as a child. The photos used to transport me back into a time when I was happy and loved.

I didn't even notice I'd stopped pausing in the hallway. While Amara lived here, I was always in too much of a rush to be with her... because she made me happy. She made me feel the way the memories did, but a thousand times better.

I lift my fingers to one of the frames, tracing over the edge of it. My mother is smiling back at me, and for a single moment I feel like she's here with me. "Forgive me," I whisper. "Forgive me, Mom. Please. I'm sorry, but I... I can't do it. I keep telling myself that this is the right thing to do, but how could it be when I'm this unhappy? I have to believe that you'd want me to be happy. I have to, Mom. I have to believe that you'd love her, because I think you really would. I can't. I can't do this to myself, to her. I can't let the words I spoke to her be the last thing I ever said to her. I need to see her. One more time. Even if it's just to apologize. I can't... I can't let things end like this. I just can't." I brush my fingertips over the photo, wishing to be just a little closer to her. "I hope you can forgive me. I swear, Mom. She's nothing like her father. I swear it."

I take a step back, my eyes lingering on the photo. I don't even know what I want, but I know I have to see Amara. I run a hand through my hair as I walk toward the staircase, pausing when I hear rustling. I frown and turn around, following the sound into the living room.

I don't remember opening the window, but it's wide open, the curtains flowing. It seems like the window flying open knocked over some of the trinkets Aria kept in the windowsill.

I bend down to pick up the metal box on the floor and pause, my eyes widening. I swallow hard as I sink down on the floor, kneeling in front of the ring that's catching the light from multiple angles.

It's my mother's engagement ring. I had no idea Aria kept it here. I raise my head slowly, my heart racing as I look at the window and back at the ring on the floor. I could've sworn that I hadn't opened that window in weeks.

I pick the ring up with trembling hands, and for a single moment, I'm certain I smell my mother's perfume. Daisies. She always smelled like daisies. I bite down on my lip, swallowing hard. "Mom," I whisper, unable to help myself. I don't believe in ghosts or any of that stuff, and maybe this is all a coincidence. Maybe it's wishful thinking. Maybe it's my broken heart and my fucked-up mind that are making me see what I want to see, what isn't there.

Or maybe it's a sign.

I asked for one, after all. "I would have gone after her before I found your ring, Mom," I whisper. "But I... I'm going to take this as your blessing. You'd have loved her, and she'd have loved you just as much. I fucked up, Mom... Amara never would've given up her company, she'd never give up her freedom. She traded hers for mine, and a woman like that? Mom... she'd never do that if she were anything like her father."

I rise to my feet, feeling completely shaken. Maybe I'm crazy. Maybe I'm truly making this all up, but I don't think I am. I haven't smelled my mother's perfume this strongly since I was a child, but the scent is filling the living room now, right along with the warmth she exuded.

I smile to myself as I close my fist around my mother's ring. "I fucked up," I whisper. "But I'm going to make this right."

The smell of daisies follows me as I pull out the tuxedo Charlotte gave me, and even in the car, it's right there with me. She's right there with me.

I'm smiling as I park in front of the mansion, feeling at peace for the first time in weeks. For weeks, everything has felt wrong. But now? Tonight? Tonight feels different.

I inhale deeply as I walk up to the entrance, unsure of what I'll even say when I see her. I don't know if she even wants to see me, but I do know I can't let her marry someone that isn't me.

"Stop right there, sir." I pause as two bodyguards approach me, both of them wearing matching earpieces. "Come with us."

One of them grabs my arm, his grip tight as he forces me to follow along. I'm tempted to shake him off, but that won't help me. I should've known this wouldn't be easy, but they're crazy if they think they can stop me.

I'm not surprised when they lead me straight to Harold's home office. He's leaning against his desk, a cigar between his lips. He takes a deep drag, his expression unreadable.

"What are you doing here, Noah?" His voice is calm, dangerous.

I yank my arm out of his bodyguard's grip and straighten my tux, my jaws locked. "I'm here for Amara."

He stares me down as he takes another drag of his cigar. "She moved on," he says. "She's marrying a man of her own stature."

I smile at him, emboldened by confidence that might be entirely misplaced. I don't give a fuck. I'll make a fool of myself if I need to. I'll do anything. I can live with embarrassment, but I can't live without *her*.

"No. She won't. She's marrying *me*."

Harold raises his brow. "You're wearing a suit my daughter bought for you. If I hadn't let you go, you'd still be out of a job. You're drowning in student debt, and at your current salary you make a comfortable living, but you can't maintain my grand-daughter's lifestyle. You're not good enough for her, Noah."

I nod. "I know. I might never be good enough for her, but I'll never stop trying. I'll never stop trying to make her happier than she was the day before. Can you look me in the eye and promise me that Gregory will do the same? Will he make her laugh, Harold? Will he support her dreams?"

He looks away. "You can't live off happiness, Noah. *She* can't."

I laugh and run a hand through my hair. "I'm a doctor, Harold. Sure, it's early in my career, but I make a decent living. I can take care of her just fine, and you know it."

"She loves her father. She always will. What will you do if she wants him to walk her down the aisle? What if she wants him to be part of your lives? If you have children, she'll want them to know their grandfather. What will you do? Are you going to make her feel guilty for loving her father for the rest of her life? Make her feel like she's always choosing between the two of you?"

I walk over to the sideboard in his office and brazenly pour two glasses of what I suspect is incredibly expensive bourbon. I hand him a glass, and much to my surprise, he takes it.

I raise it to my lips as I mull over his questions. He's right to ask them, to demand an answer. I empty my glass and put it down on the sideboard with more force than I intended. "Life is for the living, Harold." I get it now. I get what the florist was trying to say. I turn to look at Harold, my eyes meeting his. "I won't make my wife live in the past. And let me be clear, Harold. Amara *will be* my wife. She is not a pawn in your empire. She's my queen, and I'll be damned if I let you sacrifice her for one of your fucking mergers. She's walking out of here with me tonight, if it's the last fucking thing I do."

He smiles at me and shakes his head. It's a genuine smile, one that he attempts to hide his relief behind, but for perhaps the first time since I met him, I see through it.

"You're insane if you think you can convince my grand-daughter to even look at you. You broke her heart, and she hasn't been the same ever since. She has her mother's stubbornness. She won't give you a chance. She'll have you thrown out before you even reach her."

I grin at him. "But you won't let that happen, will you?"

He smiles at me and shakes his head. "One chance, Noah. You have one single chance."

I nod. I've never felt more sure of anything. "One chance is all I need."

Chapter Fifty-Four

AMARA

"You look beautiful," Mom whispers as she helps me put on the diamond necklace Grandpa gave me to wear tonight. My gaze roams over my reflection in the mirror, taking in the stunning emerald green dress. It accentuates my every curve, and Noah would've loved seeing me in this.

I bite down on my lip as a fresh wave of crippling heartache washes over me. I let my eyes fall closed and inhale shakily, forcing him out of my thoughts.

"Are you all right, sweetheart?"

My eyes meet Mom's in the mirror, and I force a smile onto my face. "I'm great. Wonderful."

She raises her brow and sighs. "Don't do this, Amara. If your heart isn't in it, then don't do it."

I laugh, the sound harsh. *"Be thankful and do your part,"* I tell her. "That's what you told me, isn't it? *Stop chasing foolish dreams.*" I grit my teeth, trying my best to suppress the anger, the pain, the helplessness. "You were right, mother. I was foolish. I was dumb. I'm falling in line now. I'm doing my part. What more could you possibly want? How is this still not enough?"

She grabs my shoulders and gently turns me toward her. "I was wrong. I was bitter, and I was wrong, Amara. I realized how wrong I was when I saw how happy you were. I want that for you."

I chuckle. "Yeah, and how did choosing happiness work out for you? You told me to learn from you, and I wish I had. I wish I hadn't tried to chase after my own happiness — because that doesn't exist, mother. It isn't real. Love isn't real, and it isn't worth it."

She looks me in the eye, her expression unnerving. "If love isn't real, then why are you sacrificing everything for Noah? Why are you throwing away everything you worked for? Did you think I wouldn't find out about your deal with Grandpa? Your company and an engagement in return for Noah's freedom and a guaranteed prosperous career path."

I look away, facing the mirror instead. I lean in to touch up my lipstick, trying my best to hide how badly my hands are shaking. "You're wrong," I tell her. "I was just tired of the company, the continuous struggle, the failure. Besides, Gregory is a nice guy. He'll never hurt me. I'll have a good life with him."

Mom's eyes meet mine in the mirror, her expression so tense that I can't hold her gaze. "He won't hurt you because you'll never let him close enough. He'll never have your heart. That's no way to live, Amara. I wonder... what do you see when you look in the mirror? Because when I look at you, it's not my daughter I see. Not anymore. Don't lose sight of who you are. Don't let pain jade you and guide you into making choices you can't undo."

She shakes her head and walks away, pausing to look at me when she reaches the door. I stare at her through the mirror, seeing vulnerability in her expression that's never been there before. "Don't become like me, Amara."

She walks out of the room, closing the door behind her. Her words haunt me for the rest of the night. With every person walking up to me to congratulate me, my anxiety increases, but it's too late now. Noah wants nothing to do with me, and even if he did, my grandfather won't let him near me — not without taking his future in return.

"Dance with me," Gregory says, his hand wrapping around mine. I instinctively recoil, the way I have for weeks now. It's subtle, but it doesn't escape his notice. His smile drops just a fraction, and I instantly feel guilty. He wraps his arms around me, his eyes on mine. "It might take months, or it might take years. But one day, you'll look at me the way you used to. I know that you'll never look at me the way you looked at *him*, Amara. I know that, but in time, you and I will be happy together."

"Content," I whisper. "We'll be content, the way we were before. You never loved me either, not truly. You might think you did, but I doubt you've ever actually been in love."

He twirls me around on the dance floor before pulling me back to him. The way he looks straight past me... the longing, the regret. It's an expression I know all too well. It's one I've seen in the mirror every single day since Noah walked out on us. "You have," I murmur. "You have been in love."

He snaps out of his thoughts and looks at me, smiling grimly. "Aren't you going to ask me who she is?"

I blink, realization dawning. I should care. I should at least care that the man I'm marrying loves someone else, but all I feel is relief.

"How did *he* get in?" Gregory says, his voice laced with anger. He lets go of me, and I turn around, my heart racing. There's only one man that could possibly anger Gregory tonight.

It's him.

Noah stands by the entrance, his eyes on me. He walks toward me with such confidence that the crowd instinctively parts for him. His steps are slow and sure, his eyes never leaving mine. Noah pauses in front of me, rendering me speechless for a single second before I spring into action, signaling the guards to have him escorted out of the room. Instead of obeying my silent commands, every single guard looks down at their shoes, ignoring my request.

"Amara," Noah says, his voice laced with the same pain I feel.

"No," I say, cutting him off before he has a chance to say anything else. "Leave."

He smiles. He has the gall to smile at me after showing up here uninvited, today of all days. "I will, if you come with me."

I look around, finding everyone staring at us with undisguised interest. "I'm not sure you've noticed, but this is my engagement party. You need to leave."

Noah's smile melts off his face, and he nods. "You look beautiful," he says, his eyes roaming over my body. He grits his teeth, and when his eyes move back up to mine, they're filled with jealousy and pain. I instantly want to tell him it's not what he thinks, that Gregory hasn't touched me, but I resist.

"I love you," he says, his words loud enough to elicit gasps from the people surrounding us. "There's a lot I don't know, Amara. I don't know what our future will look like. I don't know if I'll ever be able to give you the life you could have with Gregory. I don't know if I'll ever be able to look your father in the eye without thinking of mine. I don't know if I'll ever be good enough for you. There's a lot I don't know, Amara... but I know that I love you. I know that I always will. I know I'll never give up on us, and every single day for the rest of our lives, I'll prove that to you if you'll let me."

Noah sinks down to his knees, and my eyes widen when he takes a diamond engagement ring out of his suit jacket. "I've been crazy about you from the second you walked into my office, Amara. Every interaction with you since then resulted in you stealing another piece of my heart. I didn't even realize my battered heart was capable of love, but before I knew it I was so in love with you I couldn't see a life without you. I still can't, Amara. I tried, and I can tell you with full certainty that a life without you in it isn't a life worth living. And that's exactly what we should do, Amara. We should *live*."

The way he looks at me, the sincerity in his eyes... I want to believe him, but I can't. Not when I know what he went through. What my family took from him, once in the past, and then all over again recently.

"I can't promise you that it'll be easy, because I don't think it will be. It'll be hard, my love. There's a lot we'll need to overcome. The odds are stacked against us, and you and I... we have some healing to do. It won't be perfect, and at times it might not be pretty, but you and I can get through anything if we're together. Every day for the rest of my life, I'll choose you. I'll choose you over the past, the pain, the loss. I'll choose you, and I'll continue to put you and our happiness first. So please, Amara Astor, will you spend the rest of your life with me? Will you give me a chance to prove my words? Will you marry me?"

I look up, finding Grandpa standing beside us, his hand on Gregory's shoulder, as though he's holding him back. Grandpa nods at me, a sweet smile on his face.

"No," I say, my voice breaking. "No, Noah."

Chapter Fifty-Five

NOAH

No? She said *no*?

Amara walks past me and rushes toward the exit. I blink in disbelief and look up to find Harold looking at me in shock. He frowns, his confusion apparent, and I shake my head. I'm just as surprised as he is.

I jump to my feet and follow Amara out of the ballroom, catching her in the hallway that leads to the wing her family lives in.

"Amara!"

She pauses, turning toward me when I reach her. "Look at me," I tell her, my voice soft. Amara raises her head, and the tears in her eyes nearly bring me to my knees.

"You don't get to do this, Noah. You don't get to walk out on us and then show up at my engagement party acting like all that stands between us is some minor disagreement, like you and I could actually be together if we wanted to."

Her eyes reflect the helplessness she feels. Her pain matches my own.

"I know," I whisper. "I know it won't be easy, but I'm serious. I'm certain you and I can get through anything together. I admit that I was shocked and angry, and yes, my first instinct was to push you away. But Amara... you are not your father. I can't blame you for crimes you didn't commit, and I can't live in the past. I won't ask it of you either."

She laughs humorlessly, the sound at odds with the tears in her eyes. "Do you know why my father was in your house, Noah? It was because of me. It was because Aria and I are the same age, and he wanted clothes and school supplies for *me*. I'm the reason you lost your parents, Noah."

He takes a step closer to me and shakes his head. "You were just a child, Amara. You aren't to blame for your father's actions."

"I might not be my father, but I'm still my father's daughter. I nearly lost him, Noah. I knew right there and then that I was done shutting him out of my life. I want to get to know him, and there's no way you'll be able to live with that. What would our lives even look like? Would I never be able to have my father over for dinner? Will he be able to attend our wedding?"

I take a step closer to her, my hands cupping her cheeks gently. Her breath hitches and her eyes fall closed. She inhales shakily, her forehead dropping to my chest. "We can't be together," she whispers.

I smile as I wrap my arms around her, threading one hand through her hair. "I missed you," I murmur. "I missed you every single day you were gone, and I won't spend the rest of my life without you. I will not promise you that it'll be easy, Amara. It's going to take me time. At times it might fucking kill me to look your father in the eye and keep my cool. I won't make you false promises.... But I can promise you this: every single day I'll try my best. I'll be with you, here in the present. I'll work on overcoming the past, on healing instead of hiding from it. I promise that I'll never ever blame you for crimes you did not commit. I swear it. So give me a chance, Amara. Just give me a chance. Let me prove to you that you and I could be happy together."

She shakes her head. "What about your sister? She won't be able to even look at me, knowing who I am. She'll never forgive me. I can't stand between you two. I can't be the reason she won't come see you."

I smile and pull away to look at her. "Baby, Aria knew who you were long before she even met you. She knew long before I did, and she welcomed you with open arms. She welcomed you into her home. She invested in you knowing who your father is. Aria told me I was stupid for letting you go at all. I spent two weeks with her, but she was mad at me the entire time. If not for Grayson, I'm not sure she'd have let me stay at all."

I see the disbelief in her eyes, and I'm not sure what to say to convince her. She and I... the odds are stacked against us.

"What about my grandfather? Your career?"

I smile. "Do you really think I'd have gotten into the ballroom without his approval? He loves you, Amara. He just wants you to be happy."

She looks away and nods. "One chance," she whispers, and I exhale in relief. "Everything you're promising sounds great on paper, Noah... but it's going to be hard. You might decide that it's not worth it after all. It might be too hard, too painful. You might not be able to live with the guilt. I'm willing to try, Noah. But I won't marry you unless I'm sure that we'd be happy together. Marriage isn't between just the two of us, no matter how badly we want to believe it is. It's a joining of families too. I won't live the life my mother did. I won't isolate myself from my family, and I have to be sure you won't ask it of me. I love you, Noah... but sometimes love isn't enough."

I nod. "One chance is all I need," I whisper, taking a step closer to her. Amara steps back, hitting the wall behind her. I smile as I lean in, my lips hovering over hers. "I love you," I whisper.

She rises to her tiptoes, her arms wrapping around my neck as she closes the distance between us, her lips finding mine. My eyes fall closed as I lose myself in her. I fucking missed her. These lips.

Her body against mine. "You look way too fucking beautiful tonight," I whisper against her lips. "I don't like the way you danced with Gregory." I drop my forehead to hers and let my fingers trail down her arm, until I've got her hand in mine. I pull back to look at her and lift her hand, holding it up between us. "This ends now." I pull the diamond engagement ring off her ring finger and drop it to the floor, enjoying the sound it makes as it bounces on the hard marble. "Would you have married him?"

She looks at me, and the look in her eyes kills me. "I would've done anything to make sure my grandfather leaves you alone. He promised me that he'd guarantee your career progression in return for this merger."

I pull away, my heart sinking. "You and I... are we going to be okay?" When I went after her, I was so certain, but she's right. It won't be easy. Our good intentions might lead to mutual destruction.

"I don't know, Noah... but I love you. I love you, and I don't want to live a life filled with regrets. I want to try. Will *you* give *me* a chance? I'll mess up too, Noah. It won't be easy. I might not always realize when something is hurting you, when I'm being insensitive. We might not see eye to eye on matters, and we'll have so much learning to do."

I sigh and lean in to press my lips against her forehead. "I will. Of course I will. We'll give it our all. That's all we can do."

She nods and rises to her tiptoes, her lips brushing against mine. "Then take me home, Noah."

I smile and lean in, lifting her off the floor and into my arms. Amara smiles as I carry her out the Astor mansion. "Let's go home."

Chapter Fifty-Six

NOAH

My eyes drift over his scarred wrists, my anger at war with the sympathy I feel. Peter seems nervous, and he's yet to look me in the eye. Instead, he's staring at his coffee cup.

I asked to meet him at a coffee shop close to my clinic. I figured meeting at neutral grounds would be best for both of us.

"I'm in love with your daughter," I tell him. He finally looks up, a spark of hope in his otherwise defeated expression. "My love for her is greater than the pain you caused. Amara cares about you. She wants you in her life. In *our* life."

I run a hand through my hair, hesitating. "So here's what we're going to do. You're going to say what you need to, and so will I. After that, we leave the past where it belongs as best as we can. That doesn't mean we won't remember my parents. It means that we leave behind the blame and embrace the good memories. We'll remember their lives, not their deaths. My sister has shown tremendous grace in forgiving you, and I'm going to try to follow her example. She's reminded me over and over again that you served your sentence, and I'll try to remember that."

"I'm sorry," he says, a tremor in his voice. "I never intended to hurt anyone. I didn't go in armed, and I didn't expect your parents to be home. I just wanted some food for my family, some clothes, and school supplies for Amara. I'd lost my job and I couldn't even feed my family. Charlotte refused to ask her father for help, and I was desperate. It doesn't excuse anything, not even remotely... but I need you to know that it was an accident. Your parents came home suddenly, and when your father pointed that gun at me, I panicked. We fought, and I made the biggest mistake I've ever made. I see them every time I close my eyes. I will never forget your parents, Noah. I'll never stop paying for the crimes I committed. I will continue to pay in whatever way you need me to, but please don't let it affect my daughter."

He looks down at his hands, desperation written all over his face. "I won't," I promise. "I wouldn't be sitting opposite you right now if I didn't mean that. I lost my father, and Amara almost lost hers." My eyes fall to his wrists, the scars still raised months later. "I won't ever get to speak to my father again. He'll never get to meet my wife, or my children. He'll never spoil his grandchildren — but you can. You *will*. You owe it to my sister and me."

I wrap my hand around his wrist, and he stiffens. "This," I tell him, "Can never happen again. I won't have Amara live the rest of her life without a father."

I pull away and cross my arms. Peter looks away, but not in time to hide the tears in his eyes. "I proposed to her, you know?" His eyes widen, and I nod. "I proposed to her three months ago with my mother's engagement ring. Crashed her engagement party to do it."

I smile to myself, remembering the way I found the ring lying on the floor shortly after I asked for a sign. To this day, I don't know if it was mere coincidence, but I don't think it is.

"Amara said no. She's said no every single time I've proposed since then. Three times in total. It's not because she doesn't love me, nor is it because she doesn't want to spend her life with me.

It's because she loves you too. She wants you to be part of our life, of our wedding, and she thinks she can't have that. She thinks she can't have both of us. It's up to us to prove her wrong."

He nods, and for the first time since he sat down, there's some life in his eyes, a hint of determination, passion. "We both love her, and I know my parents would have too. I was once told that life is for the living, and it's true. You and I... we're here. We're lucky enough to be here, to be loved by a woman as special as Amara. She forgave you for all you did, and she puts up with all my flaws. She makes me want to be a better man, so here I am, trying to be the man she thinks I am. I won't forgive you, but I won't hold the past against you. My sister is right to say you served your sentence, and I do believe you continue to pay, that the memories continue to haunt you. I won't punish you further, not at the expense of the woman I love — but I ask for one thing in return, Peter."

He straightens in his seat and nods. "Anything."

I nod and smile. I never thought I'd sit across the man that caused my parents' death, *smiling*. Yet here I am. I don't feel the resentment I used to feel. Time doesn't heal, but it dulls the pain. My priorities have shifted. I no longer want to live in pain and misery. I don't want to live in the past. Not when it could cost me my future with the woman I love.

Chapter Fifty-Seven

Amara

"Dad?" I call as I walk into his house. I promised to have dinner with him tonight, but I'm a full hour late. My meeting with Aria and Grayson went on for far longer than I expected. They aren't here very often, and every time they visit there's so much to discuss. They've been amazing, handing me back the company I sold them without me even having to ask.

In the last three months, my life has changed in ways I could never have imagined. Noah and I moved back in together, and he's kept every promise he's made me. He's worked hard at being in the present with me. We've fought for our happiness, and we continue to fight.

He's even attended a handful of dinners with my father. He barely spoke a word, but he was there with me, and that's all I can really ask for. His relationship with my grandfather seems to slowly be getting back to what it used to be too. He refuses to go back to working for Grandpa, but my grandfather is a hard man to resist. I'm pretty sure Noah will end up caving. I hope he will.

Neither of the two admits it, but they both miss each other. Grandpa perks up when I mention Noah, and Noah is exactly the same. Before the truth came crashing down on us, those two developed a bond that I'm slightly envious of. I hope their stubbornness won't ruin that. Until they make up, I have every intention of enjoying the new supportive version of Grandpa. I guess seeing me as unhappy as I was changed him.

I've been scared, but every day Noah proves to me that I was wrong to doubt him. To doubt us. He was right to say that things aren't easy, but he did what he told me he'd do. Every single day, he's putting us first.

"Amara," Dad shouts. I follow the sound of his voice with raised eyebrows, all the way to the patio at the back of the house. I freeze when I find Noah standing in the middle of the patio, my grandfather on his left, and my father on his right. Aria and Grayson stand at the side on their left, with Leia and my mother on the opposite side.

"You... you two were with me just thirty minutes ago," I stammer, my eyes drifting from Aria to Grayson.

Grayson winks at me as he wraps his arm around a beaming Aria." Sorry for keeping you so long," she says. "We had to stall," Grayson adds, grinning.

I swallow hard, emotion overwhelming me as I turn to Noah. My father places a hand on his shoulder, and the two men look at each other, both of them smiling. The sight of the two of them together is enough to have me bursting into tears. Noah rushes up to me and grabs my shoulders, a panicked expression on his face. He cups my cheeks and wipes my tears away with his thumbs, the happiness I saw in his eyes slowly melting away.

"I'm sorry," he says. "I'm so sorry, baby. I thought... I didn't mean to put any pressure on you like this. I just wanted to show you that we have our family's support. You once told me that marriage is a joining of families too, and I just thought... God, I'm so sorry. Let me take you home, okay? We don't have to do this.

We never have to get married at all if it's not something you want. I'm sorry, Amara."

I sniff, unable to hold back my tears. "Yes," I say, my voice wavering. "Yes, Noah. I'll marry you."

He freezes and stares at me in shock. His lips tip up, into a small smile first, and then into one of those that just transforms his face.

He pulls me closer and buries his face in my neck for a second, before dropping down on one knee, his arms still wrapped around me. He rests his head against my hip, a silly smile on his face.

"You have to let me ask properly, baby," he says, his voice brimming with happiness. "I had a whole speech prepared and everything."

I laugh, my heart overflowing with happiness. He's proposed to me three times already, and every time his speech was different. It astounds me that he continues to find new things to love about me. The way he sees me... I wish I could see myself through his eyes. I've never felt this loved before.

"Amara Astor, my life was forever changed the day you walked into my clinic with your rosy cheeks and your sky-blue eyes. One look, and I was smitten. You were way out of my league, and every interaction with you since then reminded me of that. You once told me you were addicted to me, but all along it was me developing an incurable addiction. I'm hooked. I can't spend a single day without you. I can't even remember what life was like without you, but I vaguely recall it being pretty damn miserable. My world was gray until you walked in, coloring outside the lines, making me feel emotions I didn't think I was capable of. You do that to me, you know? You push my boundaries in all the best way. You taught me to live life the way it's meant to be lived. You never intended to, but with every smile, you healed my wrecked heart. You gave me purpose. Because of you, just going through the motions was no longer enough. It never will be again. Every day to come, I'm going to work on making you happy, on building a life we can both be proud of... because *that's* what I want. I want to spend the rest of my life with you. Will you marry me?"

I nod, sniffing in an attempt to keep my tears back, but it's no use. "Yes, Noah." I start to cry all over again when Noah slides the ring onto my finger. He laughs and lifts me up, twirling me around as our family cheers us on happily. He puts me down carefully, his lips finding mine. I rise to my tiptoes and kiss him with all I've got, at last feeling like I'm right where I belong — in his arms.

Noah pulls back and looks into my eyes. He smiles and bites down on his lip, and my heart skips a beat. "I love you, Dr. Grant."

He chuckles, his gaze heated. "I love you more, future Mrs. Grant."

Our family surrounds us, each of them offering their congratulations. "I'm glad you said yes," Grandpa says. "I'm not sure how much more the man could take. I was pretty sure he was going to follow your lead and cry when you did."

Dad smiles at me, his eyes filled with the same happiness I'm feeling. He shakes Noah's hand, and the two men nod at each other.

"My mother's ring looks perfect on you."

I turn around to face Aria, my eyes wide. "This is your mother's?"

She nods and takes my hand. There's a hint of nostalgia in her eyes, but happiness overshadows it. "She'd have wanted you to have it. Mom would have loved you, but since she isn't here, I'll love you twice as much. Welcome to the family, dear future sister-in-law. I knew the day we met. I knew right there and then that Noah would end up marrying you."

I glance down at the ring, feeling just a little guilty for turning Noah down before, when it's his mother's ring he proposed with. I didn't realize the significance behind the ring, but now that I do, it makes it even more special.

I look around and smile. I wasn't sure Noah and I would ever get here. I wasn't sure we could overcome our shared past, but we did — and we're not the only ones. My eyes land on Noah, and I grin at him. I can't wait to see where life will take us. I can't wait to grow further with him, to grow old with him.

I can't wait to become Mrs. Grant.

Epilogue

AMARA

I STARE AT MYSELF THROUGH THE MIRROR IN MY childhood bedroom, my heart racing as I touch up my lipstick. This entire morning has been a whirlwind of laughter, tears, and moments that I know I will always cherish. I smile as I think back to the way Mom and Leia helped me into my wedding dress, the champagne Aria brought in this morning along with a crystal hairpin that was her mother's, for me to have as my *something old*. Leia let me borrow the anklet she always wears, telling me I needed *something borrowed*, while Dad gave me a thin bracelet with hidden blue stones on the inside.

He's been so involved with our wedding, and I've loved it. He went with me to go cake tasting, and he sat through hours of me trying to pick table decorations. The wedding preparations helped us get to know each other again. It helped us form a relationship, and it helped Noah too. I don't think Noah will ever be as close to Dad as he is to Grandpa, but they're friendly, united by their mutual love for me.

I step back from the mirror when I hear a knock on my door. My room is empty now... Mom is already seated in the garden that Grandpa had transformed for me into the venue of my dreams. Aria and Leia, my two bridesmaids, should already be by the door to signal the start of the ceremony, walking down the aisle ahead of me.

We got ready together this morning, and what I thought would be a stressful morning turned out to be more than I ever could've hoped for. They made me feel so loved, and I've barely stopped smiling since I woke up.

I always thought the highlight of my wedding day would be the ceremony itself, but the happiness I feel in this moment has me doubting that. Is it possible to be even happier than I am right now?

I turn when Grandpa walks in, smiling when he stares at me in disbelief. "You look beautiful, Mari," he whispers, his eyes filling with tears.

I walk up to him and raise my hand to his face, my thumb catching a tear that escapes his eyes. My throat closes up and I shake my head. "No tears, Grandpa. I'll cry if you do."

I've never seen Grandpa cry before, but today he's emotional. He looks at me with pride and unconditional love, and I blink back my own tears.

"It's not too late to have your father walk you down the aisle," he tells me, a surprisingly nervous look in his eyes.

I grab his hand and shake my head. "No," I whisper. "It has to be you. Dad will be seated in the front row, but it's you I want walking me down the aisle. You're the one that's always been there for me, Grandpa. You were the one that always patched me up when I inevitably scraped my knees with my recklessness. You saw me off on prom night, and you took me out on every Father's Day, so I'd never miss Dad." I raise our joined hand to my cheek and smile up at him. "Because of you, I never felt the absence of my father. I'm happy to have him back in my life, but as I walk down the aisle and join my hand with Noah's, I want *you* by my side... right where you've always been."

Grandpa looks away and nods, visibly emotional, and I rise to my tiptoes to hug him. He holds me tightly, pressing a kiss on top of my head. "I'm proud of you, Amara," he whispers, tightening his grip on me before letting go.

He offers me his arm, and I take it with a smile. "Ready?" I ask him, and he shakes his head.

"I'll never be ready to let you go, Mari."

I smile and rise to my feet to press a kiss to his cheek. "You'll never lose me, Grandpa. You'll always be my hero. I love Noah with all my heart, but I loved you first."

He swallows hard, blinking back his tears, and then he nods. "I love you too, Amara." He inhales deeply and straightens his back. "Let's go, before Noah comes looking for you."

I laugh, but I genuinely wouldn't put it past Noah to come find me if I take too long. He's been anxious lately, eager to finally truly make me his. It's a feeling I understand all too well.

We pause at the edge of the aisle Grandpa had built just for me. There are white roses everywhere, and our garden looks like something right out of a fairytale. The sun is shining down on us, and the seats are filled with everyone Noah and I love.

My eyes find Noah's, and everything else fades away. He's all I can see as we walk down the aisle. Grandpa places my hand in Noah's, and the two men look at each other.

"Take care of my little girl," Grandpa murmurs, his voice breaking, and Noah nods as he tightens his grip on my hand.

"Always," he promises.

NOAH

She looks so beautiful, it's unreal. I can't believe I get to marry the woman of my dreams today. Everything about the last couple of months has been surreal. The odds were stacked against us, but we defied them and came out on top.

If there's one thing we learned, it's that happiness isn't an end goal. It's something you work toward every single day, with every choice you make. And she and I? We'll always choose each other.

Amara is all I can see as the officiant asks us to repeat our vows after him. We're surrounded by our loved ones, but for just a few moments, it's as though it's just the two of us.

I'm mesmerized as Amara smiles at me and says, "I do."

We fought so hard to make it here, and hearing her say those words, saying them to her in return... it's got me feeling like I must be dreaming.

I breathe a sigh of relief when the officiant tells me I can kiss the bride, and Amara chuckles as I wrap my hands around her waist, pulling her closer.

I kiss that smirk right off her face, and she melts into me, the way she always does. "I love you, Mrs. Grant," I whisper as I pull away to look at her.

Amara smiles, the two of us finally becoming aware of the cheering that surrounds us. "I love you more," she murmurs, pressing another lingering kiss to my lips.

Everything about this day is surreal. I've never before been this surrounded by love. Our family walks up to us to congratulate us, and Peter smiles at me.

"Thank you," he says. "Thank you for making her so happy, for putting my daughter first."

He looks pained, as though he knows I'm missing my parents today. He and I have come a long way. I doubt we'll ever grab a drink together, but we're civil, and having him in our lives no longer pains me. I can't forgive him for what happened, but I've made peace with the past, and every day I choose to prioritize my future with Amara.

I nod at him and shake his hand. "Thank you for doing the same, Peter. I know how much courage it took to show up every time she needed you throughout the last couple of months, and I'm grateful you continue to put her needs above yours." I see the pain in his eyes every time he looks at me. The guilt haunts him every time he sees me, yet he continues to show up with a smile on his face.

Harold walks up to us and places his hand on my shoulder,

and I turn toward him with a smile on my face. "She might be your wife now," he tells me, "but she'll always be my little girl."

I smile at those words. My *wife*. Finally. "I know," I tell him, an indulgent smile on my face. Today is hard for him. He tries to hide it, but he's no longer unreadable to me. "Thank you for trusting me with her heart. I won't let you down."

He nods. "I know you won't."

I glance at Amara, but she's busy talking to Aria and Leia, her eyes drifting to mine every few seconds. I hesitate before asking Harold the one question I've been unable to get off my mind.

"Would you have let her marry Gregory?"

Harold looks at me and grins. "No. Never. When Amara came back home, she needed something to keep her mind off her heartache. She offered to marry Greg in return for your freedom, and I just let her be, figuring that she needed to feel like she was in control of the situation, of your future. She felt guilty, and that engagement helped relieve some of her guilt. Gregory knew he'd never marry her. I told him I wouldn't let that happen. I couldn't, not after I saw how happy she was with you. I couldn't ask my little girl to settle for any less than that. Greg agreed to the engagement, nonetheless. Maybe he was hoping Amara would truly want to marry him someday, but it's far more likely he went through with it because he knew what effect their engagement would have on his father's stock price."

I stare at him, but there isn't a trace of a lie on his face. I think he's telling the truth.

"To be perfectly honest, Noah... I also knew news of Amara's engagement would hit you hard, and I was banking on it being enough to make you snap out of your misplaced righteousness. I knew you loved her, and I hoped that love would be your salvation. I wanted to protect Amara, but once you two discovered the truth, there was no longer any need to protect her. At that point, my priorities shifted toward ensuring her happiness — and Amara's happiness lies with you." I stare at him in surprise, and he smiles at me knowingly. "So will you forgive me?"

Harold Astor asking me for forgiveness... I never thought I'd see the day. "Yes," I tell him. "But don't even dream of interfering in our lives again."

He and I both glance at Amara. She's brimming with happiness today, and I'm going to ensure she smiles the way she does right now every single day for the rest of our lives. "I won't have to," Harold says, smiling at me with full faith in his eyes.

I look down at my feet, hesitating before I raise my head to look at him. "I'll take the job," I tell him. Harold has been offering me a seat on his board for months now, and I've continuously been declining his offers, in part because I held a grudge. I'm not proud of it, but I couldn't help myself. I hated him for letting Amara get engaged to Gregory, but it looks like my anger might have been misplaced. Things are never what they seem with Harold. I should have known. Despite his cold exterior, the man loves deeply.

"Good," he says, his eyes on Amara. "Because I don't think Amara can take the workload, and she's about to get even busier. She doesn't know it yet, but my wedding gift to her is a sizable investment in her company. She won't be able to run her company and simultaneously learn how to run the Astor holdings. Her cousin returned to the States to help you, and between the two of you, you should be able to manage the company just fine. He's a lot like Amara and he refuses to give up his day job, but he promised to help."

I look at him with raised brows. "So you'd already assumed I'd end up taking the job?"

He smirks and ignores my words, nodding at a man that approaches us instead, two miniature versions of him in tow, a boy and a girl. "Speak of the devil," he says.

Amara gasps and rushes up to him, and he lifts her up in his arms, twirling her around. "Adrian!" she yells. "I can't believe you're here."

I take a step toward them, Harold's laughter drowned out by the jealousy I feel. I don't know who this guy is, but if he doesn't get his hands off my wife, we're going to have a problem.

I exhale in relief when he puts her down, and Amara walks up to me, her eyes lit up with excitement. "Noah," she says, "meet my cousin, Adrian. He's a mathematics professor, and he'll be working at Astor college. You two are going to love each other."

So this is the elusive Adrian Astor. Amara's uncle's son. Her uncle married a British woman, and Adrian grew up in England. From what I understand, Harold has been trying to get him to move back here from England for years now. I wonder what finally convinced him.

I offer him my hand, and he shakes it absentmindedly, but his eyes aren't on me. No. They're on Leia, who is staring at him in shock. She looks from him to the children behind him, and then she pulls it together and pastes a polite smile on her face. Her smile doesn't fool me, though. She's clearly stricken. Leia walks away in a rush, and Adrian follows her. Whatever is going on between them leaves me intrigued, but my attention is swiftly stolen by my wife, who twirls Adrian's two kids around in her arms.

She looks so incredibly happy, and I'm going to do all I can to protect that happiness. Amara looks up at me, her eyes filled with love, and I smile at her. I can't believe I married the girl of my dreams. I can't believe I get to spend the rest of my life with her. There will be challenges, I'm sure... but she and I can get through anything so long as we're together.

"I love you," I tell her.

She grins at me, her niece in her arms. "I love you more, Noah."

I doubt hearing her say that will ever get old. I'll never get enough of her. She's my every dream come true, and I'm going to make sure she knows it — every day for the rest of our lives.

Don't want Amara and Noah's story to end? Download an exclusive additional epilogue: https://dl.catharinamaura.com/grant

You'll also catch some glimpses of them in *Professor Astor,* Leia and Adrian's story.

PS. If you're curious about Gray and Aria and haven't read their story yet, *Until You* is available now.

Made in the USA
Monee, IL
21 March 2024